## Her left arm

Jennie stared down at her bloody jacket and remembered the stage bandits shooting at her from the second-story room. The bullet grazing her arm. The escape. She had to get out of Fillmore—now.

Mounting a horse, she headed for the road. The steady movement of the horse beneath her and the unrelenting pain in her arm lolled Jennie into a state of semiwakefulness. Ahead of her, she could see the angry faces of the thieves she'd robbed.

Then another image rose unbidden. The handsome features she'd grown to know so well. Unlike the others, Caleb regarded her with tenderness. But too quickly his expression changed to one of pain and anger.

*He doesn't despise me now, but he will if he ever finds out what I've done.* How would she explain her gunshot wound to Caleb and her family?

"Can't I have the ranch and Caleb, too?" she asked the heavens. The rumble of distant thunder was her only reply.

## STACY HENRIE

has always had an avid appetite for history, fiction and chocolate. As a youth, she enjoyed reading historical novels, dabbling in creative writing and poetry, visiting museums, exploring ghost towns and daydreaming about life in bygone eras. While she had a goal to write and publish a book one day, she turned her attentions first to graduating with a bachelor's degree in public relations. Not long after, she switched from writing press releases and newsletters to writing inspirational historical fiction as a stay-at-home mom.

Stacy loves reading, interior decorating, romantic movies, her famous chocolate-chip cookies and, most of all, laughing with her family. She lives in central Utah with her husband and three kids, where she appreciates the chance to live out history through her characters, while enjoying all the modern conveniences of life in the 21st century.

# Lady
# Outlaw

## STACY HENRIE

Love Inspired

Recycling programs
for this product may
not exist in your area.

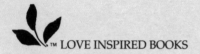

™ LOVE INSPIRED BOOKS

ISBN-13: 978-0-373-82934-7

LADY OUTLAW

**Printed in U.S.A.**

For I the Lord thy God will hold thy right hand,
saying unto thee, Fear not; I will help thee.
—*Isaiah* 41:13

To Peter
This story is as much ours as it is mine.
Thanks for never doubting.

## Acknowledgments

First, foremost and always, thank you to my family—
especially my husband who read the manuscript
about as many times as I did, who gave me the time
I needed to revise, and who never gave up on my dream,
even when I wasn't so sure myself.

Thank you to my mom and grandma
for instilling in me a love of reading, and to my dad
for passing on his interest in history and helping me
with the idea for Jennie's outlawing ways.

Thank you to my writer friends for their advice,
encouragement, suggestions and laughter—
especially Ali Cross, Elana Johnson, Jenn Wilks,
Sara Olds, Becki Clayson and Rachel Nunes.

Thank you to the ladies in book club for their interest in
my writing journey through the years. I hope this book
gives you lots to talk about—after I leave the room.

Thank you to Jessica Alvarez
for her vision and support, and to Elizabeth Mazer
who loved the story as much as I did
and was willing to give me a second chance.

A final thank-you to my Father in Heaven for
guiding my path, giving me this gift and teaching me
to trust. Thankfully we don't always get what we want
when we want it—typically the blessings are far greater
than we could imagine when we least expect it.

# Chapter One

*Utah Territory—September 1869*

"Regrettably, the answer is no, Miss Jones."

The bank president's apologetic tone might have fooled her, but Jennie caught a glint of satisfaction in Albert Dixon's gray eyes that contradicted his sympathetic words.

"I'm sure things have been more difficult on the ranch since your father's death, but you haven't made a payment on your mortgage in over a year." He cleared his throat. "That's eighteen hundred dollars you already owe us. We'll need to see five hundred of that before the end of the month, if you wish to keep your property. The full debt will be due next August—no exceptions."

Jennie gripped the handle of her purse so hard her fingers hurt. No matter the sum, she wouldn't give up the ranch. "And if I don't have the money…"

Mr. Dixon dropped a glance at the sheet of paper before him, then slid the document across the desk. Jennie read the words written in bold, black ink at the top—*Notice of Foreclosure.*

"If you can't produce the minimum amount, we'll have to terminate the loan." He shook his head and rose from his chair. "I wish there was more I could do. I'm deeply sorry."

"I'm sure you are." Jennie grabbed her small suitcase off the floor and came to her feet, eyeing him coldly. "But let me make something quite clear, Mr. Dixon. The only part of my father's cattle ranch you'll ever own is a steak dinner—and I hope it gives you a bad case of indigestion. Good day."

The bank president's round face and balding head turned a satisfying shade of red before Jennie headed for the door. She could hear him sputtering for a reply as she left the bank. She marched in the direction of the stage office, the heels of her boots stomping out a hard beat.

"I'd like to take a branding iron to that man," she muttered under her breath as she wound her way along Fillmore's storefronts.

She contemplated a number of other ways she might lower the bank president's arrogance before her fury changed to despair. As her anger ebbed so did her determined pace and finally Jennie came to a stop at the corner of the general mercantile.

Where would she find five hundred dollars to keep her ranch? She'd barely scraped together enough cash to finance her trip to Fillmore. She had no relatives to borrow money from and couldn't afford to sell any of their cattle, either. Since rustlers had cleaned them out of calves and half the herd in the spring, they had to keep every last cow in order to increase the number of cattle next year. *Besides, what good is a cattle ranch with no cows?*

A hat display in the window beside her caught Jennie's eye. *Latest Styles from the East,* a handwritten sign below the hats read. She loved hats—her father had always bought her a new one on his trips to Fillmore. The one she wore today, with a rounded brim and green braiding that accentuated her red hair, was the last one he'd purchased for her. That had been a little over a year ago, just before her twentieth birthday. On that occasion, he'd bought her a brooch, as well.

Jennie's fingers went to her throat, sliding over the simple but pretty cameo her father had said reminded him of her. She could just picture him in the store, happily chatting with the clerk as he picked out gifts to bring home. She fought back the tears that sprang to her eyes at the image.

Squaring her shoulders, she stepped toward the mercantile. She couldn't replace her father in so many ways, but at least she could look around for some small gift to bring home. The southbound stage wasn't likely to leave for another thirty minutes or so, and she needed a diversion from her depressing thoughts. Despite her limited funds, she hoped to spare one or two coins to buy Grandma Jones and Will some candy or a penny trinket instead of bringing back only bad news.

Caleb looked up at the tinkling sound of the sleigh bells hanging from the mercantile's doorknob and watched the young lady walk in. His time as a bounty hunter had honed his skills at taking the measure of a man—or woman—in a matter of moments, and it only took a glance for him to guess at the girl's story.

The clothes, neat and clean but worn, made it clear that money was tight at home. But she held her head high, coffee-brown eyes sharp and keen, a nice contrast to her red hair. He read pride and determination in her posture and expression. Times might be tough, but clearly this lady wasn't one to give up.

He'd had that kind of determination, once. After the death of his fiancée, he'd been filled with determination to find the bandits involved, and see them all brought to justice. But in the aftermath of the deadly confrontation a year ago, his determination had fled. All he wanted now was to earn enough money to start a small business of his own—something far different from the farm life he'd planned to share with Liza…and worlds away from the bounty hunting business he'd left behind too late.

He watched as the woman nodded to the store clerk, then headed toward the glass jars of brightly colored candies that sat on the long counter. He felt a moment's idle curiosity wondering what she'd choose before his attention was snagged by the two men talking at the end of the counter.

"Somebody wired the sheriff and told him the bandits were headed south," one of the men said. "He sent out nearly twenty men looking for 'em, but I think they must've slipped past."

At the word *bandits,* Caleb found himself straightening up automatically, then he forced himself to relax. He was done with bounty hunting—those bandits were someone else's responsibility now.

"When did they rob the stage?" the other asked.

"Yesterday afternoon. They met up with the coach about fifteen miles south of Nephi."

"How much money did they steal?"

"Two thousand dollars."

*Two thousand dollars?* Caleb was shocked…not just by the amount, but by the loud crash that followed the announcement. He glanced over to see that the young lady had accidentally struck one of the candy jars with her suitcase. The container had toppled off the counter and smashed on the floor, spraying glass and peppermint sticks around everyone's feet. Caleb only caught a glimpse of her hotly embarrassed blush before she dropped to her knees and began picking up the candy with trembling hands.

Shaking hands and broken glass made for a dangerous combination so Caleb crouched down beside her to help. Reaching for one of the larger pieces of glass, his fingers almost brushed against hers. When she lifted her head to look at him, he was struck by just how pretty she was, with that fiery hair and warm brown eyes. *Nothing like Liza, of course,* Caleb thought to himself, heart twisting as it always did at the memory of Liza's dark hair and sweet smile, but very pretty all the same. Especially when she blushed like that.

"You don't have to help," she murmured.

"I'd like to." He slipped the glass from underneath her fingers and placed it to the side.

"No, that's all right. I can clean up the mess myself." Apparently he'd been right about the pride and determination. But he wasn't going to let that stop him. He continued to gather up the broken shards, acting as if he hadn't heard her. When the store clerk appeared with a broom, Caleb took hold of it and swept the glass into a pile while the young lady finished collecting the candy.

"I'm so sorry," she said to the clerk as she stood. She set the peppermint sticks on the counter. "I don't have enough to pay for the damage and purchase my ticket home, but…" She reached up to her collar, her hand covering the brooch pinned there. "Maybe I could trade—"

Her fingers tightened over the piece of jewelry and Caleb could see that it hurt her to even think of giving it up. Maybe that was what prompted his next words.

"I'll pay for the candy." The hope of starting up a freighting business of his own had had Caleb saving every penny for the past year. As a result, he had plenty of cash on hand. The broken jar and candy shouldn't put him back by more than a dollar or two. He could spare that well enough. Digging around in his pocket, he extracted some cash, along with the letter he'd come into town to mail—yet another attempt to mend fences with his disapproving family. "I'd like to mail this letter, too," he said to the clerk. "So how much do I owe you?"

The girl shook her head. "I can't let you do that. I'd want to repay you, and I can't."

"I think two dollars oughta cover it," the store clerk said, seemingly in agreement with Caleb to ignore her protests.

Caleb handed over two bills along with his letter, then scooped up the candy. The clerk took the mail and money and returned to his post beside the cash register.

"You shouldn't have done that—paid for the candy, I mean." The lady frowned at Caleb as she collected her purse and suitcase. "I could have given him my brooch to make up the difference."

Certain any mention of how obviously she'd wanted to keep the brooch would just upset her, Caleb tried a different tactic. "Probably so, but I can think of a way to repay me," he said as he went to pick up another handful of peppermint sticks they'd missed near the door. When everything was gathered together, he turned to face her again.

"I can't eat all of these by myself. How about taking a few off my hands?" He offered her a fistful of candy.

The absurdity of the whole situation made her smile, just as he'd hoped. "All right," she said. "I'll take some."

She shifted her things to one arm and took the candy from him.

"I hope you enjoy them," he said, smiling back. "Always a pleasure to help a pretty girl."

For some reason, his compliment left her looking close to tears. Her reaction made him want to take her hand, ask her what was wrong. But if he tried, he was certain she'd tell him it was none of his concern. And she'd be right. Besides, now that he'd mailed his letter, it was time for him to be moving on. Tipping his hat, he gave her one more smile.

"Good day, miss," he said, then headed for the door.

Not until the stranger had disappeared did Jennie think to ask him his name. The unexpected kindness of this man almost made her forget Mr. Dixon and the debt, and she suddenly realized that she'd never even thanked him. Hurrying to the door, she tried to spot him, but he was already out of sight.

*Oh, well*, Jennie thought as she left the store. There wasn't really time to talk to him anyway. If she didn't hurry she might miss the stage that would take her home to Beaver and she certainly didn't have money to stay a second night in the boardinghouse.

She tucked the candy into her purse with her money and the four-shot, pepperbox pistol she always carried while still toting her suitcase, then she hurried to the booking office. The stagecoach stood out front, its six horses already hitched up. The man inside informed her that the driver would be along any minute.

Jennie purchased her ticket and sat outside on a nearby bench to wait. With nothing to read or do, except think over her mostly horrible morning, her mind soon filled with recollections of home. She pretended she was already riding her horse Dandy down the familiar wagon-rutted trail toward the ranch, past the corral fences and empty bunkhouse. Past the faded red barn where fourteen-year-old Will would be shoveling hay to the other pair of horses. Up to the two-story frame house with its front porch where Grandma Jones would be sitting in her rocker, mending clothes—the smell of her freshly baked bread mingling with the scent of meadow grass.

The possibility of losing everything she'd worked for and held so dear made her chest tighten. "What am I going to do?" She stared at her hands as if the gnawed fingernails and cracked knuckles held some kind of answer.

The sound of footsteps approaching brought up Jennie's chin. She watched as the stage driver made a thorough inspection of the coach before coming over to greet her.

"Afternoon, miss." He nodded, and Jennie forced a smile as she stood. He placed her suitcase on the top rack of the stage. "I hear it's just you and me today."

"Not a bad thing," she said, thinking of the crowded stagecoach she'd ridden in for two days before reaching Fillmore.

"Up you go then." He held her elbow in a gentle grip and helped her inside.

Being the only passenger, Jennie had her pick of one

of the three benches. She chose the one facing forward. She settled onto the lumpy, cracked leather next to the window and set her purse in her lap.

As the driver moved to close the small door, two gentlemen sprinted up to the stagecoach, each holding a piece of luggage. Jennie gathered they might be brothers with their matching dark hair, bushy eyebrows and brown suits.

"We got seats on this stage," the older-looking one said. He held up two stubs of paper.

From the window Jennie watched the driver inspect their tickets before nodding.

"I can place your bags on top, gentlemen."

The one with the tickets shook his head. "If it's all the same to you, we'll keep 'em with us."

The driver shot him a puzzled look, but he didn't insist they use the top rack. The men climbed into the stage and sat on the rear-facing seat. They squeezed their two bags in the narrow space beside their feet. Jennie noticed each man wore impeccable clothes, without a trace of dirt or signs of heavy wearing, and each carried a revolver in a holster beneath his jacket.

The younger and stockier brother eyed Jennie and grinned. "You traveling by yourself, little lady?"

Jennie responded with a simple nod as she slipped her hand into her purse and fingered the handle of the pistol. The young man likely didn't mean anything by his flirtatious manner, but she wanted to be prepared if things turned sour.

"Don't worry, miss," he continued. "Should we run across any Injuns or bandits…" He held open his jacket and tapped the butt of his revolver with a fat thumb. "We'll protect you."

"Shut up, Horace." The older brother drove an elbow into Horace's side. "You'll have to pardon my brother's rambling. Learned it from our ma."

With a scowl, Horace twisted in his seat to face his brother. "What you talking about, Clyde? We ain't seen Ma for eight years, so how do know what she did and didn't do? I told you, we oughta gone back home this winter, hole up before our next—"

"There he goes again." Clyde clapped a hand over Horace's mouth and smiled. "Can't help himself."

Jennie lifted her brows in amusement. The brothers' rough manners and speech didn't match their fancy clothes. What type of work did they do? Before she could ask, the stagecoach lurched forward. Jennie gripped the window ledge to keep from bouncing off her seat.

"Should've ridden those good horses we had, instead of takin' the stage." Horace righted himself and straightened his skewed hat.

"Here, have a drink," Clyde said. He pulled a silver flask from his jacket and wiggled it in the air. Horace seized the container and guzzled before wiping his mouth with the back of his hand.

*This ought to be interesting.* Jennie began chewing on her thumbnail. *They'll either drink themselves into a stupor or get fresh.* Given how her day had gone so far, she couldn't trust that they'd choose the option she'd prefer. She didn't feel like talking much—not after her long morning—but a little conversation might divert their attention from the alcohol.

"What exactly is your line of work, gentlemen?"

Horace chuckled again and glanced at Clyde. "I'd say we're in—"

"The money-making business," Clyde finished, a deadpan expression on his face.

Jennie waited for them to elaborate, but neither one did. Horace returned to his drinking, and Clyde stared out the window.

"Are you from around here?" she tried next.

Turning from the view, Clyde sized up Jennie as if trying to determine the reason for her questions. "Nope," he said after a long moment. "We're a ways from home."

"What sort of money-making business brought you to Fillmore then?"

Horace smiled. "She's a real talker, ain't she, Clyde? Not shy or silent like a lot of other girls."

"Give me that." Clyde snatched the flask from Horace. "That's enough talkin'." He gave Horace a stern look and took a long swig. Lowering the silver container from his mouth, he frowned at Jennie. "If it's all the same to you, miss, we'd prefer to do our drinking in peace and quiet."

"Suit yourself," Jennie muttered as she faced the window. Silence enveloped the inside of the stagecoach, except for the sound of the brothers passing the flask between them and gulping the liquor.

Jennie watched the sagebrush and distant hills moving past for a long time before she grew tired of the monotonous scenery. Leaning her head back against the seat, she shut her eyes. As rough as the ride could be, she preferred resting over watching two men become inebriated in front of her.

A headache began building at her temples and she tried to relax to keep it at bay. Thoughts of the bank president and her debt filled her head, but she chased them away with plans for what the ranch needed in preparation for colder weather.

A short time later, she heard loud whispering between Horace and Clyde. Curious, she pretended to still be sleeping and focused on their words.

"I told you wearing these fancy duds and takin' the stage would work," Clyde said in a slightly slurred voice.

"We sure showed 'em," Horace said, his speech thicker with intoxication than his brother's. "Slipped right past the sheriff. Bet he didn't think we'd be walkin' into town, all respectable." He snorted in obvious delight.

"Two thousand dollars, Horace! Now we can buy us some horses and land—whatever we want."

Horace murmured in agreement. "I'd like to go back to Wyoming soon and live by Ma, but I don't think she'd like knowin' we're bandits." He sighed heavily, then added in a brighter tone, "Maybe we could buy her somethin' real nice, so she ain't too mad. Whatdaya think she'd like?"

Jennie missed Clyde's response as her mind raced. *They're the bandits I heard about in the store—the ones who stole the two thousand dollars.*

Her first impulse was to jump out the door. She might not live through such a fall, but staying put could also mean death if the men realized what she'd overheard. That left her two choices: sit tight and pretend she hadn't heard a thing or try to disarm the men herself and hand them over to the stage driver.

At the pricking of her conscience, Jennie chose to act. But not just yet. Better to hold off until they were at their weakest. Perhaps all the alcohol they'd been drinking would work out in her favor in the end. She waited until their whispering turned to snores and opened her eyes. Both bandits were passed out on their respective sides of the stagecoach, mouths hanging open, their relaxed jaws bouncing with the stage's movement.

Jennie shifted her gaze from them to the luggage beside their feet. Which of the two bags held the money?

*If only I had that cash...*

She shook her head, though she couldn't rid the wish completely from her thoughts. Slowly, the innocent desire for money became an idea—a bold, dangerous idea.

If she took the money, would it really be stealing? She'd only take what she needed to pay the bank at the end of the month and buy herself time to raise more funds. The ranch would be temporarily saved, and she and her family wouldn't lose everything. The brothers had already spent some of the money—their new clothes showed that. No one would expect the full two thousand to be recovered. *It's just my informal reward for turning in these men.*

Before she changed her mind, Jennie scooted to the edge of her seat. Her heart pounded loudly in her ears and her hands grew clammy. Sliding onto the middle seat, her back to the door, she leaned over to grab hold of the suitcase next to Clyde. She hefted it onto the bench and quietly cracked it open. Desperation surged through her at finding nothing but a faded bundle of sweat-and-campfire-scented clothes inside.

Jennie placed the bag back on the floor. She had to hurry before either man woke up. She scooted down the bench to reach Horace's bag and saw that one boot rested against it. With a sigh, Jennie pivoted on the bench to face Horace straight on. She bent down and gripped the boot with both hands. She gently slid his foot toward her. The drunken Horace didn't stir.

Exhaling with relief, she lifted the bag into her lap and unfastened the clasp. Peering inside, she sucked in a quick breath. She'd never seen so much cash in one place. She could pay the ranch's debt in full with that much money.

*No,* she told herself firmly. *Only what we need to buy more time.* Grabbing two bundles and hoping it was enough, she shoved the money into her purse.

"What are you doing there?" Clyde demanded.

Startled, Jennie pushed the money bag behind her. Thankfully the pounding of the horses' hooves and the creak of the wheels muffled the sound of the bag hitting the floor.

"I…uh…needed some air," she said, motioning to the window above the coach door.

"You sick?"

"Oh, no. I'm fine." She fanned her flushed face with her purse. "Just a tad warm."

"It can be dangerous sittin' in the middle there," Clyde said in a drowsy voice as he blinked heavily.

*You have no idea.* Jennie willed herself to smile as she took several calming breaths. She set aside her purse and busied herself arranging her skirts and examining her fingernails until Clyde fell back asleep. When she was certain he was unconscious, she retrieved the money bag, closed it up and put it back beside Horace's boots. Now she needed to get those guns and hand over these men to the stage driver.

Bending forward again, Jennie peeled back part of Horace's jacket to reach his revolver. As she inched her fingers toward the barrel, she heard a snort. She jerked her head up and found Horace watching her, a puzzled expression on his face.

"You had a bee on your knee," Jennie said, thinking fast. "I moved up to swat it away." She blushed as she straightened.

Horace cocked his head to one side and lifted his eyebrows. "Oh...um...thanks."

She hoped he'd join his brother in drunken slumber, but Horace stretched and sat up instead.

"How much farther we got to the next town?" he asked.

Jennie peered out the window at the afternoon sun. "We still have several hours until we stop for the night at Cove Fort. It's a way station for travelers." *Plenty of time to get those guns, but how?*

"You ever been to Wyoming?" Horace scratched at his hairy jaw.

"No," Jennie said curtly. She needed to formulate a plan, not waste more time chatting with Horace.

"That's where me and Clyde come from. I want to get back up there someday. Our ma's still there." Horace glanced out the window and exhaled a long sigh. "Sure do miss her cookin'. And my horse, Jasper."

Jennie tried to ignore his reminiscing, but he kept on.

"Clyde made me leave Jasper behind. Probably 'cause I ride better than he does. Can shoot better, too. Pa taught me to shoot anything with a trigger."

His words prompted similar memories in Jennie's mind—times when her father had shown her how to draw a gun and shoot straight.

*That's it.*

Jennie heaved a dramatic sigh and batted her eyelashes like she remembered her girlhood friends at church doing. "I don't know the first thing about guns. Why, I wouldn't know how to go about defending myself. I wish somebody would teach me."

"I'll show you." He hurried to sit beside her on the middle bench and pulled his gun from its holster. "This here's a .44 Remington revolver."

"Is that right? Well, imagine that," she said.

"Once it's loaded, you wanna pull the hammer back." Horace lifted his thumb and pantomimed the action, then aimed the gun out his window. "You point at your target, squeeze the trigger and shoot." He shrugged and passed the revolver to Jennie. "Nothin' to it."

Jennie pointed the gun out her window, hoping he didn't see her hands shaking with nervous energy. "Seems easy enough." Setting the gun on her right side, where Horace couldn't easily reach it, she smiled coyly. "What about your brother's gun?"

"Works the same." Horace leaned across her to pull out Clyde's revolver from beneath his jacket. Clyde twitched, peering at them through half-opened eyes. "I'm borrowin' your gun for a minute," Horace explained. His brother grunted, and to Jennie's relief, his eyelids shut again.

"Clyde's gun's a Colt revolver." Horace lifted it up for her to see. "His isn't as fast-loading as mine since he can't just slip a full cylinder in."

"How do you load it? Can you teach me that?"

Horace nodded. He pushed the revolver's cylinder to the left side and pointed to the six chambers. "The bullets go in there, but you see how you wanna leave one hole empty so the gun don't fire if it's dropped?"

"May I try?" Jennie asked, swallowing back the panic

rising in her throat. If Horace gave his brother back the gun, her plan wouldn't work.

He looked from her to the gun and over to Clyde. "I s'pose." He dumped out the bullets and extended the gun toward her. "Here you go."

She took the revolver and stuck out her hand for the bullets. Horace rolled them into her palm, but as she drew her hand back, she purposely let the bullets slip from her grip to the floor. "Oh, dear. How clumsy of me."

"I'll get them." Horace knelt in the tight space and tried to capture a bullet that rolled and jumped with the stage's movement.

Clyde sat up, rubbing his jaw. "What in tarnation are you doing, Horace?"

"Pickin' these up." He finally got a hold of a bullet and held it up for Clyde to see. "We dropped 'em."

Cursing softly, Clyde leaned down to help gather the ammunition.

*Now's my chance.* Keeping an eye on the two men, Jennie tossed both revolvers out her window. Her heart crashed against her rib cage as she reached inside her purse and cocked her pistol. She slowly removed the gun. Forcing herself to breathe evenly, she aimed the pistol at Horace and Clyde.

"What were ya doing with the bullets out of the gun anyway?" Clyde barked as he shoved bullets into his pocket. Neither of them paid any attention to Jennie, which gave her enough time to steady her hands and plaster a no-nonsense expression on her face. "Where's my gun? If you ruined it, so help me, Horace…" Clyde gave a vehement shake of his head.

The back of Horace's ears reddened with anger. "I

ain't done nothin' with your gun. I was just showin' the lady here how to use one." He turned to Jennie, and his eyes went wide as saucers at the sight of the pistol in her hand. "Where'd you get that?"

"Go sit by your brother," Jennie ordered in an even tone. Out of the corner of her eye, she saw Clyde's face blanch, then turn scarlet.

"You idiot." Clyde whopped Horace on the side of the head as he scrambled onto their seat. "Looks to me like she already knows how to use a gun. What'd you tell her while I was asleep?"

Horace blinked in obvious confusion. "I…uh…told her about home. I didn't say nothin' about us robbing the stage, honest, Clyde."

Clyde lifted his hand to strike his brother again, but Jennie pointed the gun in his direction. "Leave him alone. He didn't say anything. I learned all I needed to know from your drunken whispers earlier."

"Whatya goin' do with us now?" Horace asked, frowning.

Instead of answering, Jennie pointed the pistol at the floor and fired a bullet between the men's boots. Both of them yelped and jumped aside. "That's a warning," she explained. "I shoot even better at long-range, so I wouldn't suggest making a dash for it. You'd likely break every bone in your body if you tried to jump anyway."

The stagecoach came to an abrupt stop, as Jennie had hoped, and the driver soon appeared beside the door. He had a shotgun in his hand and a look of pure annoyance on his weathered face.

Throwing open the door, he glared at Horace and Clyde. "What do you mean firing a gun while we're moving? You'll scare the horses, or the lady here." He glanced over at Jennie, and seeing her pistol, his eyes widened.

"Forgive me. That shot was meant to alert you." Jennie smiled apologetically. "I overheard these men talking. I believe they're the bandits who robbed that stage yesterday."

"Well, I'll be." The driver scratched at his head beneath his hat, his gaze flitting from Jennie to the brothers and back again. "And the money?"

Swallowing the twinge of guilt that rose inside her, Jennie pointed her gun at the bag by Horace. "I believe it's in there."

The driver leaned into the stage and proceeded to grab the black bag, but Clyde snatched the other side of the handle and refused to let go. "You can't have it," he argued. "We worked and planned for months to get this cash."

"Let go, young man, or you'll be eatin' bullets." The stage driver trained the shotgun on Clyde. The two locked gazes before Clyde finally released his grip on the bag. The driver passed his shotgun to Jennie. "Hold this on 'em for a minute, miss, while I grab me some rope."

Jennie nodded and took the shotgun in hand. Shifting the pistol in Clyde's direction, she pointed the driver's gun at the sullen-looking Horace.

As soon as the driver disappeared from view, Clyde glowered at her. "You won't get away with this, missy," he hissed. "If you think I'm going to rot in jail and lose two thousand dollars 'cause some female has a hankering to be brave, you don't know me."

"Perhaps you ought to have considered that possibility before you robbed the stage," Jennie said, edging her pistol closer to him.

The stage driver returned and tied the men's hands and feet together. With Jennie holding both guns on them, neither one made an attempt to struggle.

"You might want to ride up with me, miss," the driver said when he'd finished.

"I believe I will." She handed him back his gun, but kept hers in her grip. The driver climbed out, and after gathering her purse, Jennie hurried to follow.

"We're goin' to find you," Clyde shouted as she descended the steps. "You're gonna wish you hadn't done this. Horace and I will—"

The stage driver slammed the door against Clyde's protests and led Jennie by the elbow to the front of the stage. "Don't pay him no mind, miss. You've done a brave thing. Nothing to be ashamed of." He helped her up onto the seat. "Afraid we'll have to turn back though, so we can turn those two rascals over to the law in Fillmore."

Jennie nodded in agreement as she tucked her pistol into her bag alongside the cash.

The stage driver joined her on the seat and gathered the reins. He turned the stagecoach around, heading north again. Jennie did her best to ignore Clyde's occasional shouts from below. She concentrated instead on the thrill she felt as she imagined marching into the bank tomorrow and slapping the five hundred dollars on Mr. Dixon's desk. Let him wonder how she came up with it so fast. At least the ranch would be safe from his greedy hands, for now.

## Chapter Two

*Seven months later*

Caleb let his horse Saul pick its own way along the faint trail through the sagebrush while he sat in the saddle, finishing his cold supper of dry bread and jerky. He didn't have time to stop to eat if he was going to find lodging and a warm meal in Beaver by sundown.

He brushed the bits of bread from his chaps, and almost of its own accord, his hand rose to pat the pouch hidden beneath his shirt. Three hundred dollars sat inside—three hundred dollars his parents couldn't complain hadn't been earned through honest labor. Not that any amount of honest work would reconcile them to the fact that he wasn't coming home to the Salt Lake Valley. They hadn't liked it when he'd left, and they certainly hadn't been pleased when he'd become a bounty hunter. But the real divide had come when he'd stopped bounty hunting…and still refused to come home.

Didn't they understand how hard it was for him to think of returning to the place where he'd hoped to build a life with Liza? He'd settle down soon, but it would be someplace new—somewhere he could have a fresh start. And with God's help, he'd be ready for that soon. One more job, maybe two, and Caleb would have enough money to outfit his own freight business.

"We'll come back," he murmured to Saul as he gazed from beneath his hat at the juniper-covered hills and the distant mountain peaks. He'd come to love this rugged country. "Next time, though, it'll be with a wagon full of goods and a strong pair of horses." Saul's ears flicked back and the horse gave a long whinny. Caleb chuckled. "My apologies. But you wouldn't want to pull a loaded wag—"

The sound of a large animal crashing through the underbrush silenced Caleb's words. Reining Saul in, he twisted in the saddle, trying to discern which direction the noise came from. He gripped the butt of one of the revolvers in his holster. Neither gun was loaded, but Caleb figured whoever was headed his way wouldn't know that.

A moment later, a horse and rider burst from the trees a dozen yards up the trail. "Look out," a female voice yelled as the pair raced toward Caleb.

*A woman? Out here?* Caleb released his grip on the gun and wordlessly jerked his horse out of the way.

"You should leave," the woman added, thundering past him. Her dress flapped in the wind, revealing men's trousers under the skirt. Long red hair spilled out from beneath her cowboy hat.

Caleb peered after the retreating figure. Where would she be going in such a rush and why would she tell him to leave? Shaking his head in bewilderment, he faced forward again. Only this time he heard the faint but unmistakable sound of several horses riding hard in his direction. Someone was coming down the trail after the woman.

Out of instinct, Caleb scanned the area for a place of defense against those coming his way. To his right, on a small rise above the trail, a patch of trees provided both cover and a lookout position. He wouldn't take action—not yet, anyway. This wasn't his fight. He didn't know the circumstances and he didn't want to run the risk of being killed, or worse, having to kill a man—again. Still, from the sounds of it, there were several men coming after that woman. He'd stay out of the conflict for now, but if they appeared ready to hurt her, he'd be on hand to intervene.

He watched the woman rider until she disappeared behind a clump of trees and underbrush. She didn't reappear. If she stayed hidden, she might be all right. Maybe nothing would come of this after all.

Caleb guided Saul up the incline, behind the juniper trees, then he dropped from the saddle. He tied Saul's reins to a thick branch before lowering himself to his knees. He removed his bullet pouch just as five men rode into sight.

The riders' clothes were tattered and dirty, and each of them sported scruffy beards or mustaches beneath their dusty cowboy hats. All five had guns and wore the same hardened expressions he'd seen on the four stage robbers he'd hunted down, including the last one whose face was on the wanted poster he kept in his saddle bag.

The tallest of the five stopped within yards of the woman's hiding place and fired his rifle into the air. "Fun's over, missy," he sneered. "We know you're here, and we want what's ours."

Caleb quickly loaded one of his revolvers and crept

closer to the hill's edge, making certain to stay hidden behind the trees. Would the woman keep silent or make a stand? Either way, Caleb didn't plan on letting her be caught or shot by these ruffians.

"I'd watch it if I were you, Bart. You're surrounded," the woman called back. To her credit, Caleb didn't detect an ounce of fear in her voice. "I've got the sheriff with me and his posse's waiting down the trail for you."

Caleb scanned the nearby mountainside, but he saw no movement, no reinforcements. She had to be lying. A heavy silence followed her brave words. In the stillness, Caleb heard the distant trill of a bird. He tightened his grip on his gun, fully expecting a volley of shots in response to her bluff. But the quiet stretched on for nearly a minute.

"You're lying," Bart finally shouted back. "And you'll soon find out what we do with lying, thieving..."

Time to act. "Howdy, boys," Caleb hollered from behind the trees. All five men whipped their heads in his direction, disbelief radiating from more than one face. "Nice to see y'all are friends. Makes sharing a jail cell more enjoyable."

"It's the sheriff," a baby-faced fellow cried. "Let's split."

"Hold on. I still say she's bluffin' about him bringin' a whole posse," Bart said, scratching his motley beard. His narrowed gaze jumped from the hill, to the clump of trees beside the trail and back in Caleb's direction.

Before anyone could make a move, the woman fired a round of shots that hit the ground near one of the bandits. The man let out a loud yelp and jerked his horse away. Caleb aimed at a patch of sagebrush near another of the riders, hoping to spook the horse into bolting.

The riders attempted to return fire, but the bullets whizzing past them drove them into a tighter group on the exposed trail. Caleb could see the horses—and the riders—getting more agitated by the minute. Before long, one of them turned his horse and galloped away toward Caleb. Caleb let him ride past.

Another hurried after him. "We're outnumbered, Bart," the man screamed over his shoulder.

Bart fired once more before pointing his horse in the direction the other two had charged. "Let's go!" He threw an ugly look toward the trees, then up the hill as he retreated, the last two bandits behind him.

Caleb waited another minute to ensure they didn't double back. When the trail remained empty in either direction, he replaced his gun in its holster and untied Saul's reins.

The woman still hadn't emerged from the trees yet. Anxious to know if she'd fared well through the gunfight, Caleb led Saul down the incline and across the trail. Skirting the copse of trees, he entered the shelter they formed and found himself staring down the barrel of the woman's pistol.

"Whoa—don't shoot." He dropped the reins and lifted both hands in the air. Saul whinnied softly beside him.

"You're the one who pretended to be the sheriff." To his relief, she lowered her gun. "I thought I told you to leave."

"Are you all right? Why were those men chasing you? Have they…" He rubbed the back of his suddenly warm neck. "Have they laid their hands on you in any way?"

Her cheeks flushed. "No. Oh, no. They knew I had some money with me—that's all." She pushed up her hat, revealing amused brown eyes—not the green he'd expected. "I'd say they got the worst of it."

He'd only ever seen one other girl with red hair and coffee-colored eyes, in a mercantile in Fillmore when he'd done some work up there last fall. He suspected that young lady, though, wouldn't go around fighting in shoot-outs or wearing men's trousers under her skirt.

"By the way, thanks for the help." She stuck her pistol into the holster tied around her skirt and reached for her horse's reins.

"What were you doing out on the trail by yourself?"

Her chin lifted a notch. "No one could be spared to come with me, and besides, I can handle myself just fine."

"Apparently, but what would you have done if I hadn't come along?"

"I would have figured something out," she said as she climbed into her saddle. "I usually do."

Caleb swung onto Saul's back. "Going up against a group of armed thugs is a regular pastime of yours?"

"Hardly." One corner of her mouth lifted in a half smile. "What about you? You play sheriff for hapless females on a regular basis?"

It was Caleb's turn to smile. "Not hapless in your case. But it is always a pleasure helping a pretty girl. Wouldn't mind that as a regular job."

Instead of blushing, a peculiar expression passed over the woman's face. She stared hard at him a moment before she visibly relaxed again. "Are you looking for work?"

"You hiring?"

"Maybe. What can you do?"

"Farming, freighting, a little carpentry." He purposely

left bounty hunting off his list. That part of his life had ended abruptly a year and a half ago, and Caleb wanted to keep it that way.

She nudged her horse forward, in line with Saul. "Do you know anything about cattle ranching?"

"Can't say that I do." The question brought a twinge of disappointment. He'd never fancied himself living the life of a cowhand—a little too close to farming for his tastes. "The only cows I've handled in the past are ones that needed milking."

Her brow furrowed as she shook her head. "You don't milk these cows. What we need is some extra help on our ranch. It's only me, my grandmother and my younger brother. I've been doing most of the work myself for the past twenty months."

She set her hat on the saddle horn and rearranged her hair into a bun. "You could help with branding and looking after the few cattle we have. There are other chores around the ranch that need another set of hands. I can't pay you a lot—maybe twenty dollars a month." She stuck her hat back on and finally regarded him again. "I might be able to give you a little more when we sell the cows in the fall."

Twenty dollars wasn't much, especially when he'd heard of cowhands making closer to forty dollars in a month. Surely he could find another job—one where he could earn more money in less time.

Caleb fiddled with Saul's reins, ready to refuse her. But the words grew cold on his tongue. He hadn't missed the desperate tone behind her offer. Clearly she needed his help. He could work for a lower wage if it wasn't for long, couldn't he?

"I might consider working for you," he answered at

last, "except I don't usually accept jobs from nameless employers."

A trace of a smile showed on her lips and then disappeared as quickly. "My name is Jennie. Jennie Jones."

"Miss Jones." Caleb pulled down the brim of his hat in greeting as if they'd met on the street and not in the middle of the desert—after a shoot-out. "Pleased to meet you. I'm Caleb Johnson."

"Will you accept the job then, Mr. Johnson?"

As had become his habit since he'd quit bounty hunting, Caleb searched inside himself for some inkling, some impression from God, that this course wasn't the one for him. None came.

Smiling, he waved her forward. "Lead the way, Miss Jones."

Through the blue twilight smearing the western sky, Jennie spotted the familiar outline of the corral fence. *Home.* "That's the ranch," she said, her first words during the long trip. Caleb had been equally as quiet.

She peered sideways at him, wondering why she hadn't recognized him before. His earlier comment about helping pretty girls had sparked her memory. The man from the general store who'd come to her aid last fall had said something similar and he, too, had deep blue eyes.

After nearly an hour riding beside him, Jennie was certain the two men were one and the same. He didn't seem to remember her, though, to her relief and slight disappointment. She wasn't the same woman she'd been that day when he had paid for the candy they'd shared.

*What I am doing?* she asked herself for the hundredth time. She never should have pressed him into working for her. What if he said something to the family about

Bart and his gang? What would he do if he knew this was her third time robbing stage bandits?

"Something wrong?"

Jennie jumped in the saddle, causing her horse Dandy to dance to the side. "No. Why?"

"'Cause you've been chewing that thumbnail of yours for the last five miles, and I'm wondering if there's any of it left."

Jerking her hand from her lips, Jennie stared at her thumb. All of her nails were worn from constant work, but the one on her thumb resembled the jagged edge of a saw blade. This fingernail always worked its way between her teeth when she was nervous or had a lot on her mind.

"I'm fine," she said, shrugging off his keen observation. She pretended to focus on the road ahead, though she knew every rut and bump from memory.

Her thoughts soon returned to the man beside her. Surely she could get along without help a little longer— she'd been doing things alone ever since her father had died. And having a stranger around the place might interfere with her plans to save the ranch.

Yanking back on Dandy's reins, she twisted around to face Caleb. He tweaked an eyebrow at her sudden movement, but he pulled his horse to a stop, as well.

"If you don't want to take this job, I'll understand. We can split company right here." Thankfully she couldn't see his face very well in the fading light. "I appreciate all you did for me today, but like you said, you don't know much about cattle ranching."

"Am I being let go?"

Jennie blinked in surprise. Was he teasing her? Her jaw tightened, and she drew herself up. "I didn't mean that. But you and I both know there are other better-paying jobs. You can stay the night with us, and then in the morning—"

"I'd like to at least have the job a full day, Miss Jones, before you decide anything."

She frowned at his amused tone. It was a risk to employ him after what he'd seen on the trail, and yet, she wanted him around. He was the first person in a long time to offer help without ulterior motive—first in the mercantile, then again today.

"All right." She rubbed the reins between her fingers. "You can try the job for six weeks. I'll pay you for your work then. If we're both not satisfied, you're free to move on."

"Fair enough."

They moved their horses forward a few steps before Jennie felt compelled to stop again. "I would appreciate it if you didn't say anything about the shoot-out with those men. I wouldn't want to worry my grandmother." For more reasons than one.

"I've found it's better sometimes to leave well enough alone," he said, his face turned toward something in the distance. "No need to drag the details into the light."

"Thank you." His compassion brought her a twinge of guilt when stacked against the truth, but Jennie easily pushed it aside.

She led him up the road, past the bunkhouse, to the barn where they both dismounted. The doors stood ajar, and through the opening, the soft glow of a lantern spilled out. Will had obviously anticipated her arrival.

With a grateful sigh, she pushed open the barn doors and guided Dandy into his stall. She gave him an affectionate pat on the rump as she closed the pen door. "You can put your horse in that last stall," she told Caleb.

The other two ranch horses, Chief and Nellie, whinnied at the new company.

"Would you mind unsaddling them both?" Jennie removed the full saddlebag and flung it over her shoulder.

"You don't waste time putting your hired help to work, do you?"

"I need to take care of something," she said, ignoring his teasing. "There's hay in the stalls and the currycombs are over there." She waved a hand at the crude table littered with brushes. "I'll meet you back here to take you up to the house and introduce you."

Caleb tipped his hat. "Will do."

Jennie left the barn. She headed at an angle toward the house, then doubled back in the direction of the empty bunkhouse. She tried to force thoughts of hiring Caleb from her mind. There was one more task she needed to do, and she'd need all her wits about her. She'd been successful today in getting more money to save the ranch.

Now she had to pay the price.

# Chapter Three

Jennie approached the bunkhouse from the back, pausing in the shadows. She set down the saddlebag and called in a low voice, "Nathan?"

The only sound was the chirp of crickets, but Jennie knew better. Brandishing her pistol, she managed one step forward before an arm wrapped itself tightly around her waist.

"Evening, love." Nathan's deep voice murmured in her ear. "Glad to see you're still in one piece."

The scent of alcohol and cigar smoke that typically accompanied him made Jennie wrinkle her nose. She pushed the barrel of her gun into his side. "Let go."

Nathan laughed, but he released her. "Were Bart and his gang where I said they'd be?"

"Yes. Everything went exactly as we planned." She decided not to mention Caleb's help. Though in her mind, the deal she had with Nathan Blaine was strictly business, she knew he wouldn't be pleased to hear about a new man in her life.

She stuck her gun back in place and knelt beside the saddlebag. Opening it, she rummaged through the supplies and drew out two thick wads of cash. She stood and handed him his money. She hated parting with half of the four hundred dollars she'd taken, but Nathan's help was worth every cent. His ability to mingle discreetly with outlaws had provided Jennie with the information she needed to accomplish her second and third robberies.

Nathan ran his thumb through the money and slipped it into a knapsack on his shoulder. "I knew you had pluck," he said, leaning too close, "the moment you walked into the saloon with your chin all stuck out and your eyes all determined."

Jennie cringed at the memory of standing in the noisy, suffocating saloon, searching the crowd of leering men for someone to help her. "Is that why you agreed to work with me?" she said in a teasing tone even as she took a deliberate step back, putting needed space between them.

"Maybe, maybe not." He grabbed her hand and placed it against his chest. Jennie squirmed, but Nathan wouldn't let go. Even in the dark, she could sense his ogling gaze. "Why not give up tryin' to save your ranch and come make some real money with me? With your beauty and the way you handle a gun, we could take on banks or trains. We'd live like royalty."

Pulling her hand free, Jennie stared past him at the barn and house. The moonlight shone down on the peeling paint of both buildings and the corral fence with holes large enough for a calf to squeeze through. There were other problems she couldn't see, but they were as apparent and real as the tattered ranch around her—the looming deadline from the bank and the two or three sets of bandits she'd still need to take from in order to meet it.

*But I would never stoop to become a bandit myself.*

"No, Nathan," she said, shaking her head. She wouldn't quit. She needed this land, and it needed her. "I'm going to make this place what it used to be."

He shrugged, but his disappointment hung in the air between them. "So long, love."

Jennie watched him swagger away before picking up her saddlebag. She slipped into the bunkhouse and knelt in the corner opposite the door. Pulling up the loose board, she placed her two hundred dollars inside the small space. She'd keep it hidden here until she could travel to Fillmore and give some of it to the horrid Mr. Dixon.

After replacing the board, Jennie stood and brushed off her skirt. A thin layer of dust typically covered the unused bunkhouse. It served as another reminder of the failing condition of the ranch. Even before her father had died, they'd been forced to let go of their three ranch hands. With so few cows, she and Will had managed to keep up, but the new group of calves meant more work now.

Thankfully the money she'd relieved Bart of would pay for Caleb's help and hopefully keep the ranch going a little longer. Maybe Bart and his thugs would even see the futility of robbing innocent people. At least she only took money from crooks and used it for far better purposes than drinking or gambling or immoral company. *Once my debt is paid in full, I'll be done with all of this.*

Leaving the bunkhouse, she walked quickly to the barn. She wanted to see her family, introduce them to Caleb and climb beneath clean sheets.

The barn doors were shut, though Jennie was certain she'd left them open when she went to meet Nathan. Shrugging off her forgetfulness, she entered the barn.

The building stood dark. Jennie hurried back outside and scanned the yard. Where had Caleb gone? She glanced at the house. A light in the kitchen threw shadows against the curtains—three shadows.

"The nerve of that man!" she muttered as she marched toward the porch. Why had he gone to the house without her? What would he tell her family about fighting Bart and his thugs? She quickened her steps as anger rose inside her. Hiring Mr. Johnson might prove to be a bigger disaster than she'd imagined.

"Did you get enough to eat?" Jennie's grandmother, Grandma Jones as she'd introduced herself, asked from across the table.

Caleb finished up his last bite of rabbit stew and patted his stomach. "Yes, ma'am. Best meal I've had in months. Better than any boardinghouse, for sure."

He hadn't meant to come inside without Jennie, but the moment his boots had hit the porch steps, her brother and grandmother had come to the door. He'd hurried to explain his presence, choosing to voice just the basic facts, as Jennie had requested. He and Jennie had met outside of town, and she'd hired him when he had mentioned needing a job. Jennie's grandmother had welcomed him with a warm smile and invited him right in for supper.

"You could learn a thing or two about manners from Mr. Johnson, Will," she said to the boy seated on Caleb's right.

Will rolled his eyes as Grandma Jones took Caleb's plate to the sideboard. The boy and his grandmother looked alike with the same green eyes and brown hair, though hers was streaked with gray.

The front door slammed shut, and a moment later, Jennie appeared in the kitchen doorway, a frantic look in her eye and a smear of dust across one cheek.

"There you are, Jennie." Grandma Jones walked over and wiped away the dust on Jennie's face with her apron. "I stalled supper as long as I could, but you know Will— always hungry."

Her brother paused long enough over his second helping of stew to smile at his sister.

"Would you like supper?" Grandma Jones asked Jennie.

"Yes, please." Jennie scowled at Caleb as her grandmother crossed to the stove to fix up a plate. "I thought we were coming in together, so I could properly introduce you."

Caleb didn't miss the tense quality to her voice. *She thinks I told them about the ruffians chasing after her.* He gave a quick shake of his head, trying to communicate that he hadn't broken his word, but she didn't seem to notice.

"No need for such formality." Grandma Jones smiled at Caleb over her shoulder. "We heard somebody outside and found this handsome, half-starved young man standing there." She set Jennie's supper on the table and sat down. "Did you have a good trip into town?"

Jennie nodded before frowning at Caleb. "I've hired Mr. Johnson to help us around the ranch."

"I told them why I was here," Caleb said, matching her level look with one of his own.

"You did?" Jennie sank into an empty chair, glancing at each of them in turn. The delicate muscles in her jaw tightened.

"What a blessing you two ran into each other," her

grandmother said. "It'll be nice to have an extra pair of hands around here, what with all the new calves."

The tight lines in Jennie's face relaxed and she shot Caleb a grateful smile. "It will, won't it?"

"You a cowboy?" Will asked him.

"No. But I'm a fast learner."

Grandma Jones stood and lifted Will's empty plate. "Take the lamp from the parlor, Will, and show Mr. Johnson to your father's old room."

"I couldn't intrude like that," Caleb said. "I don't mind sleeping in the barn or the bunkhouse—"

"Nonsense." Grandma Jones waved away his protests. "As long as you're working here, you're welcome to the room. It's a bit dusty, but it's a far cry better than the bunkhouse or barn. And if there's anything else you need, Mr. Johnson, just holler. Breakfast is at dawn."

"Thank you. And please, call me Caleb." Smiling at her, he rose from his chair and gathered up his things from where he'd set them in the corner. "Good night to you both."

"Thank you," Jennie mouthed to him when Grandma Jones moved to the sink. Caleb doffed his hat to her, glad she knew he'd kept his word.

He met Will in the hallway and followed him up the stairs. At the first landing, Will opened a door on their left and stepped inside.

"This is Pa's old room." He set the lamp on the dresser near the door.

Caleb surveyed the small but tidy room. After sleeping in barns, out in the open, or in crowded boarding-houses for almost three years, the thought of having his own water basin and a real bed all to himself made him feel like a king. Perhaps the accommodations and the family's kindness would outweigh the low pay.

"Looks comfortable," Caleb said, dropping his pack onto the bed's faded patchwork quilt. "How long's it been since you had hired help?"

Will leaned his long body against the door frame. "Before our pa died. The only man that's come around recently just talks to Jennie."

"She hire him to help, too?"

The boy shook his head. "I thought that's what she was doing, but she's never introduced him or invited him up to the house. He seems a bit rough, though, you know?" He lifted one shoulder. "I haven't asked. I'm just glad you look a bit more…respectable."

"I appreciate that." Caleb placed his few belongings in the dresser.

Sounded to him like Jennie had a beau. Seemed like everyone his age did, though Caleb didn't mind so much. He wasn't sure if he'd ever care that deeply about a person again. Maybe his only chance for love and marriage had died when Liza did.

"I'm glad you took the job, even if you are a tenderfoot." Will grinned. "Jennie's been running things pretty much by herself since Pa passed. I try and help, but we need more than the two of us to make this place good again."

"Mind my asking what happened to your father?"

"No." Will put his hands in his pockets and stared at the floor. "Some Indians were rustling our cattle and Pa went after them. He was shot in the stomach with an arrow. He died before the doctor could get here."

"I'm sorry." Caleb hated how trite the expression

sounded, conveying so little of the sympathy he felt at the family's loss.

Will lifted his head and offered another shrug. "It's all right. I just don't think Pa meant for Jennie to do so much by herself. That's why I'm glad you'll be helpin' us, Mr. Johnson. I mean, Caleb. Good night."

"Night, Will."

The boy left the room, shutting the door behind him. Caleb wandered over to the window and pulled back the thin curtains. Shadowed hills merged into mountains in the distance. He let the curtains drop back into place and removed his money pouch from his shirt. He set it on the dresser as he prepared for bed.

Before climbing beneath the covers, Caleb knelt on the hardwood floor. He thanked God for the new job, even with the low wages. Clearly he was needed here. "Help me be an instrument for good with this family," he prayed. "And grant me patience as I work toward my plans." He ended his prayer and slipped his pouch under the mattress before he got into bed.

Every dollar he earned put him one step closer to starting his freight business. One step closer to that new life he'd planned for, free from all reminders of his past. Compared to that, a few months being a cowhand was a small price to pay.

# Chapter Four

Jennie scooped up a bite of stew, suddenly starved. She savored the taste of the rabbit meat and potatoes and smiled.

"He seems like a real gentleman." Grandma Jones sat down beside her. "Not to mention a face that could melt a girl's heart."

Jennie choked on the piece of potato in her mouth and hurried to wash it down with some water. "Grandma!"

Her grandmother chuckled, bringing her wrinkled hands to rest beneath her chin. "I still know a handsome man when I see one. Reminds me a bit of your grandfather. Quick to smile, a bit forthright. Your father didn't inherit his personality. He was more serious—a thinker, like you." She released a soft sigh, and Jennie wondered if she was thinking of all the people she'd lost in sixty-five years of life—her parents and sisters, a husband, two sons and a daughter-in-law. "Did you get the supplies we needed?" she asked, abruptly changing the subject.

Jennie pointed her spoon at her saddlebag by the door. She'd made sure to purchase the nails, leather straps and thread they needed in Beaver before encountering the bandits.

Her grandmother murmured approval. "I've got one other question and I don't want you gettin' all angry. How are you going to pay Mr. Johnson?"

"I have enough," Jennie said, trying to keep the defensiveness she felt out of her voice. "I only promised to pay him twenty dollars a month."

"And we have twenty dollars after buying all our supplies?" Grandma Jones raised her eyebrows.

"I sold some things." It wasn't a complete lie. Jennie had sold a number of the family's belongings last year to buy them a little more time on the ranch.

"Your mother's things, you mean?"

Jennie pushed her remaining stew around her plate. "Why does it matter? She isn't coming back for them."

Her grandmother's hand closed over hers, and the familiar warmth brought the sting of tears to Jennie's eyes. "You may not remember those first few years after we moved south to Parowan. Your mama and papa worked so hard to make a living there. Then she lost the baby." Grandma Jones increased the pressure on her hand until Jennie looked up. "I think her will just gave out after we moved to the ranch. Maybe she didn't feel like she could start all over. Maybe she was scared. I don't know. What I do know is she didn't love you and Will any less when she left."

Jennie gently removed her hand and set it in her lap. "Does that make it right then?" She hated how her voice wobbled with emotion. "To leave us to fend for ourselves?"

"Perhaps she thought we were more capable of adapting than she ever was." Grandma Jones stood and came around the side of the table to kiss the top of Jennie's head. "I think if she were here now, she'd tell you how well you've done under the circumstances, Jennie girl. I'm real proud of the way you and Will have turned out. But I'm even more proud of you for asking Mr. Johnson to help. Asking others for help was something your mother never quite learned to do."

A wave of shame ran through her as Jennie thought of the money hidden in the bunkhouse. She might have swallowed her pride enough to hire Caleb, but she hadn't bothered to include anyone else in solving the ranch's financial troubles.

Her grandmother and Will knew the ranch might go under, but Jennie had kept the seriousness of the situation and the bank deadline a secret. What else could she do? Telling them the truth would only worry them. And besides, she had the situation under control. She'd spent too many days working under the hot sun and too many nights dreaming of what the ranch could be to give up now.

"I'll see to the lamp," she said.

Grandma Jones patted her shoulder. "Good night, Jennie girl."

Jennie listened to her grandmother's footsteps shuffle down the hall. She remained in her chair, thinking back over the events of the day. She wasn't sure how long she'd sat there before she took the lamp and went upstairs to her bedroom, but the house echoed with silence.

She changed into her nightclothes, but instead of climbing into bed, she knelt beside the large trunk against the windowsill. She lifted the lid, breathing in the smell of cedar. It evoked happy memories of bringing out the thick quilts for winter and wrapping up in them to listen to her mother read.

Reaching inside Jennie lifted out two envelopes. The first had never been opened, addressed to her from her mother, Olivia Wilson Jones. From the second, she removed the telegram that had come two years before her father's death. She stared at the black, unemotional type, her chest constricting at the recollection. She could still picture the way her father's face had crumpled into tears when he'd read the few words.

OLIVIA DEAD STOP CONSUMPTION CITED AS CAUSE STOP

No other details from her mother's sister. No condolences for a grieving husband and children. Nothing.

Jennie felt moisture on her face and realized she'd started to cry. Rubbing away the tears with the back of one hand, she returned both envelopes to the trunk.

Twice she'd survived the heartache and pain of her mother leaving: first from the ranch and then in death. *I made it through then, and I can do it again. I won't give up like she did.*

After closing the trunk, Jennie extinguished the lamp and slipped into bed. Grandma Jones's words from earlier repeated in her mind: *I'm even more proud of you for asking Mr. Johnson to help. Asking others for help was something your mother never quite learned to do.*

"But I don't really need to ask others for help," she whispered into the dark. "Not really. Not when I can handle things myself."

Most of the time, she refused assistance, especially from those she loved. In that, perhaps she and her mother weren't so different after all. But her mother hadn't been able to handle things here. Jennie could. And *would*. With that resolution in mind, Jennie turned onto her side and tried to sleep.

Leaving the stuffiness of the barn, Caleb shut the double doors and breathed in the cool evening air. His first day on the ranch had mirrored those of his youth on his father's farm. He'd repaired the roofs on the house and barn and mended a hole in the loft. Jennie had told him at supper they would go round up the calves from off their range in two days. The delay before dealing with the herd suited Caleb just fine. Though he hadn't taken to farming, even with his own parcel of land, he preferred those familiar tasks over wrangling cattle.

A series of gunshots to his left made him spin around and reach for his holster out of habit before remembering he'd stowed his guns in his room. Then he saw Will, shooting at cans along the fence line.

Taking off his hat, Caleb wiped at the sweat on his forehead with his shirtsleeve and strode toward the boy. Four cans sat in a row on the top rail of the fence. The scene provoked memories of countless evenings spent shooting targets with his uncle.

"How many did you hit?" Caleb asked.

Will frowned. "None."

"Let's see."

The boy reloaded his revolver and aimed. He fired all six rounds at the cans, but every shot missed its mark.

"I can't even shoot one." Will growled in disgust and started for the house.

"Hold up, Will." Caleb motioned him back. "Try it

again, but this time remember to relax. If you're too stiff, you're going to jerk and that throws your aim off."

With a sigh, Will stalked over to him. He reloaded his gun and lifted his arm.

"You relaxed?"

"I guess so."

Caleb studied the boy's stance. "Let your shoulders drop a little more." Will obeyed. "Now make sure you bury your first sight in the second one when you aim."

Will stared down the barrel of the gun and adjusted the height of his arm.

"All right," Caleb said with a nod. "Take a nice even breath, and when you feel ready, go ahead."

Will fired the revolver and a can flew into the air. "I got one." He grinned at Caleb over his shoulder before shooting again. This time the bullet flew wild. "What'd I do wrong that time?"

Caleb chuckled. "You just gotta practice relaxing and getting your sights lined up. Then you'll be able to hit all four cans in seconds. May I?" He extended his hand toward Will's gun.

"Sure." The boy placed the gun in Caleb's grasp. "You wanna try all four?"

"You bet. I've got to show you how's it done."

Will slipped between the fence posts to retrieve the can he'd hit. He set it up beside the others and returned to Caleb's side.

Caleb aimed the gun at the first can, his eyes narrowing. His mind cleared and instinct replaced thoughts. He squeezed the trigger and shot the first can from the post with a satisfying crack of metal on metal. He dropped the second and third cans just as quickly.

He paused for a split second to readjust his aim and

squeezed the trigger, but the last can shot up into the air before he could hit it. His bullet sailed over the empty fence post. Turning his head, he saw Jennie lower her pistol to her side, a pleased smile on her face.

"Thought I needed some help?" he teased.

"No. I thought I'd join in the fun." She walked over to them.

"Caleb was helping me," Will said. "I even hit a can off myself."

"That's great, Will." Jennie glanced from him to Caleb. "Where'd you learn to shoot like that?" He liked the note of admiration he heard in her question.

"My uncle was a sheriff up north. Whenever he came to visit, he'd take me out back and make me target practice until we couldn't see the cans in the dark." Caleb passed the revolver back to Will. "Keep at it, Will, and you'll be a crack shot like your sister."

Will beamed and hurried back to the fence to set up the cans again. Caleb started for the house. Jennie fell into step beside him.

"Thanks…for teaching him," she said, her voice low.

Caleb turned to see Will taking aim. "Mind my asking why *you* haven't taught him?"

"I guess I didn't see the need. He's not quite fifteen."

"Every young man wants to learn to shoot." He allowed her to go ahead of him up the porch steps. "He'd probably prove to be a real good cowhand, too, if given the chance."

Jennie clenched her jaw. He'd made a mistake telling her what to do.

"Not that I want him taking over my job, mind you," Caleb quickly added with a smile.

Her face relaxed as she stepped through the front door. "You know anything about roping?"

"Sure. I roped stumps as a child. Even caught the family dog a time or two."

Jennie laughed as she shut the door behind them. Caleb liked the singsong inflection. He hadn't made a pretty girl laugh in a long time.

"I meant, have you ever roped something moving?" she asked.

"You should've seen how that dog ran."

She shook her head, her brown eyes still bright with amusement. "Have you used a lasso before?"

"Not exactly," he said, "but I can assure you, Miss Jones, I can handle any job you throw at me." Compared to bounty hunting, cattle ranching looked as simple as babysitting a bunch of cows.

Her eyebrows lifted. "Well, then. Let's see how well you do tomorrow. You can practice with a lasso and a sawhorse."

"Sounds easy enough."

The next morning he opened his door to find a bright bandanna, a lasso and a newer pair of boots waiting for him on the landing. Slipping back inside his room, he tied the bandanna around his neck and replaced his old shoes with the new ones. With a slight twist of apprehension in his gut at his boasting the night before, he swung the lasso over his shoulder and headed downstairs for breakfast.

The aroma of fried eggs and biscuits greeted him as he stepped into the kitchen. He joined the family at the table, hanging his hat and the lasso on the corner of his chair. "Smells delicious," he said. He ladled food onto his empty plate and began to eat.

"Have another." Grandma Jones pushed the platter of biscuits toward him. "It's going to be a long day."

Caleb heard the snickers and caught the meaningful glance that passed between Jennie and Will. "What's so funny?" he asked.

"Look, Will," Jennie said from behind her cup. "It's our very own mail-order cowboy."

"What's that?" Caleb stabbed another bite of eggs.

"A cowboy with all the right getup," Will volunteered, "but no experience."

Caleb wagged his fork at the boy. "I've got experience, boy. It just ain't in cow handling."

"Well, that will change in the next few days." Jennie stood and cleared away her dishes. Instead of a dress, she wore a billowy blouse and breeches. Caleb had never met a woman who liked wearing men's pants—his mother and sisters had always worn skirts or dresses, even to work around the farm.

"All right, you two." Grandma Jones frowned at her grandchildren but she couldn't keep it up for long. The twinkle in her eyes betrayed how much she enjoyed their bantering. "Go easy on him this week."

"Don't worry, Mrs. Jones." Caleb leaned back on his chair and crossed his arms, regarding Jennie. "I'm always game for a challenge."

After breakfast, lasso over his shoulder, he trailed Jennie outside, trying his best to appear unaffected by his new responsibilities. The apprehension in his stomach grew and he wished he'd declined his third biscuit.

Jennie easily vaulted the corral fence, dropping to her feet on the other side, and Caleb followed suit. She went to the sawhorse sitting on one side of the corral and dragged it into the center.

"Let me see your lasso," she said. He handed her the rope. "It's really quite simple. The trick is to keep your wrist relaxed as you swing and then extend your arm toward the sawhorse as you release."

She held the coils of rope in one hand as she spun the looped end over her head with the other. In one fluid motion, her wrist dropped and she thrust the lasso forward. The loop sailed through the air and around the neck of the sawhorse. She jerked the rope tight.

"Any questions?"

Caleb's jaw went slack with surprise. She made cattle roping appear as easy as walking. Embarrassed to ask her to repeat the lightning-speed lesson, he cleared his throat. "If I do have questions?"

"I'm going to start work on the fence down by the bunkhouse. You can find me there."

Caleb watched her walk away, her long braid swishing against her back, then he straightened his shoulders and marched over to the sawhorse. "I've tracked down wanted criminals before, how hard can this be?" he muttered as he unhooked the lasso.

He backed up a few feet, swung the end of the lasso like Jennie had, and released. The rope flew through the air and landed in the dirt, a good six feet from the sawhorse. His second and third throws landed closer, but the only thing hitting the "cow" square on was the dust.

Several more attempts had him working up a sweat—but with nothing to show for it. Blowing out his breath, Caleb admitted he'd met his match with cattle ranching. But he'd made a promise to Jennie to work this job for six weeks, and he intended to keep his word. Somehow, he needed to figure this out. And right now, it looked as if the only way was to admit he couldn't do this one on his own and ask for help.

He'd paid a heavy price in the past for his pride and vanity, and he wouldn't do it again. Climbing over the fence, he headed in Jennie's direction, hoping she wouldn't gloat too much.

# Chapter Five

Jennie pushed down on the post in her hands and secured it into the hole she'd dug. Stepping back, she scrutinized her work. Another rail, and the fence would be nearly as good as new.

Hearing footsteps, she turned to see Caleb approaching. "Have you mastered it already?" she called to him.

"I came to ask for another lesson," he said, stopping a few feet from where she stood.

Jennie stared at him for a moment before deciding she could spare a few minutes. "One more," she finally said, wiping her grimy hands on her breeches.

"Show me what you're doing," she said when they arrived back at the corral.

Caleb demonstrated tossing the lasso, but he missed the sawhorse by a foot.

"You need to rotate your wrist a little more as you're spinning the rope, and make sure the loop is open to the sawhorse before you release." She picked up his rope and swung it over her head, feeling the motion, anticipating the release. At the right moment, she dropped her arm and sent the loop around the sawhorse. "Did you see that?"

Caleb's brow furrowed, but he dipped his head in answer.

"Here, we'll try one together." Jennie moved behind him and helped him position the coils correctly in his left hand. Stepping to his side, she placed her hand over his right wrist and let her other hand rest at the center of his back.

"Start to swing the loop," she directed, her hand moving with his. His gaze darted to hers, and she laughed. "Don't look at me, cowboy. Keep watching your target. On the range, that calf is going to move fast. You have to train your eye to follow the cow's moving feet." She waited for him to relax his wrist, then continued her instructions. "Using the forward momentum, when you're ready, drop your wrist in line with your shoulder and let go."

After a few more swings, Caleb lowered his wrist and released the lasso. Jennie watched with held breath as the rope flew through the air and circled the neck of the sawhorse.

"Wahoo!" Caleb threw his hat into the air.

"You're not done," Jennie said with a laugh. "You have to pull the rope tight or he'll get away from you."

He returned to her side and together they yanked back on the rope. Peering up at him, Jennie realized how close they stood, close enough to feel his warm breath against her cheek and smell the musky scent of his shaving cream. She tried to step away, but her hands were still holding the rope beneath his. Her heart began thudding loudly in her ears.

"Thanks for the help," he said with a grin.

Jennie managed a nod. She'd never met someone like Caleb Johnson—someone kind and good-looking

and irritating all at the same time. She hadn't social-
ized with any young men in years—not since the family
had stopped attending Sunday services. Occasionally on
trips into town, she'd run across some boy she recognized from her time at church or school, but she'd been
too embarrassed to strike up a conversation. She felt
like an outsider, mostly because of her mother. Maybe
that's why she hadn't found it hard to talk to Nathan that
first time. Here was someone else on the cusp of society.

*Nathan.* Thoughts of him brought her traitorous pulse
to almost normal speed.

Jerking her hands free, Jennie stumbled backward. "I
think you have it," she said, her words still coming out
shaky. She forced a cleansing breath. "Keep practicing
until you can do it with ease. Then come help me with
the fence." Without waiting for his response, she spun
on her heel and hurried across the corral.

She couldn't like him—she wouldn't. Her focus had
to remain on doing what she must to save her home. No
charming, would-be cowboy was worth losing her ranch.

Muscles strained, Caleb held tight to the squirming
calf while Jennie applied the branding iron near the animal's rump. The smell of burnt hair filled Caleb's nos-
trils, and sweat ran down his back from working close
to the fire. It didn't help that the day was unusually
warm for mid-April. His clothes were now damp, dirty
and speckled with blood. He wished he'd worn his old
boots for this messy work, instead of the newer ones
he'd been given yesterday.

*It's all for the freight business,* he told himself. If he
could survive the next few months, he'd never have to
look at another cow rump again.

The calf bellowed and twisted in protest as Jennie put down the iron and took up her knife to cut a small notch in the animal's right ear.

"All right," she said, using the back of her hand to brush hair from her glistening forehead. "He's done."

Caleb untied the rope from the calf's feet and released it. He jumped out of the way as the animal scrambled through the brush in search of its mother. "How many have we done?"

Jennie blew out a long breath and plopped down in the dirt. "Twenty calves in all. We had twice that many last spring. It took me and Will three days to round them all up and brand them. We've lost quite a few since then."

"What happened?"

"A few died over the winter, but mostly it's been rustlers."

"You mean the Indians that shot your pa?" She looked up sharply at his words, so he quickly added, "Will told me what happened."

She nodded. "They took some, yes. But I think one of the other landowners around here might be stealing from us, too."

Caleb's eyebrows shot up. "Why would you think that?"

"The Indians might want a few head of cattle here and there, but since they don't have the setup to handle anything more, there's no cause for them to take very many. But the other landholders…they could add my calves to their stock with no problems at all, and have the bonus of driving us out at the same time. There are plenty of folks who think I can't handle this ranch on my own. I think someone's trying to prove it."

Her voice was strong and steady, but Caleb could see

how tired she looked, how the responsibility for running and protecting the ranch wore away at her. A surge of protectiveness filled him and he promised himself that, for as long as he worked on the ranch, he'd help lift some of that load. But that brought up another question. Would his wages take away from the family's ability to survive? Could they support another mouth to feed? "Can you afford to pay me?"

He realized she'd misunderstood the motivation behind his question when her cheeks flamed red.

"That's not what I—"

"I said I would," she interjected. "It's going to take another set of hands to make this place what I want, what my father wanted." She climbed to her feet and threw him a haughty look. "I can afford to pay you when our agreement is up. Just as I promised. And I'll pay you for every month you stay after that."

"Then I'm not a mail-order cowboy anymore?" he teased, hoping to defuse her anger.

She scowled at him, but only for another few seconds, before she laughed. "I'll admit you've done well."

Will approached them carrying a calf, its ankles tied. "I think she's the last one."

"Caleb and I'll finish up," she said. "Why don't you go get some drinking water from the creek?"

Nodding, Will transferred the calf into Caleb's arms and headed off into the brush with one of the buckets.

As Caleb wrestled to keep the calf still, Jennie crouched beside the fire and pulled out the white-hot branding iron. When they were finished, Caleb let the calf go and stood to stretch his sore back. "You're good with that iron."

"I should be." She dropped the branding iron into a

nearby bucket. The hot metal sizzled against the water inside. "My mother hated this part of ranching, but I found it fascinating. I was always getting in the way during branding season until my father finally agreed to teach me what to do. I've been branding cattle since I was twelve."

"Where's your mother now?"

Jennie eyed him with suspicion. "Why do you want to know?"

Caleb shrugged, unsure why the simple question had struck a wrong chord in her. "Just wondered, since she's not around."

Frowning, Jennie picked up a cloth and wiped off her knife. "My mother passed away two years before my father did. She wasn't living with us, though. She went to live with her sister when I was thirteen and Will was six."

The casualness of her words didn't disguise the pain Caleb heard behind them. He sat down on the ground and stretched out his legs, thinking of how to redeem himself. He hadn't meant to dredge up hurtful memories. Sometimes they were best left buried in the past.

"I'm sorry."

She stared off into the distance, the knife and cloth motionless in her hands. "You didn't know."

"That must've been tough."

"The next few years were difficult." She finished cleaning her knife and set it aside. "This is the point when you tell me it was all for the best. She couldn't care for us. She was obviously ill in mind and body. We were better off without her."

"Why would I say that?"

"Because that's what people said after she left." Jennie sat on the bare ground and wrapped her arms around her knees like a frightened child. Her vulnerability made Caleb want to put his arm along her stiff shoulders, but he didn't. She was his boss, after all.

"Maybe that's why my father stopped going to church," she said. "He couldn't stand people's feigned sympathy." Her eyes, dark with anguish, met his. "I couldn't stand it, either."

The urge to comfort her grew stronger, so he busied himself with opening the saddlebag that held their supper things. He unloaded the jerky, bread and dried fruit that Grandma Jones had packed for them. They'd stay tonight on the open range and return to the ranch tomorrow, once they'd doctored the few cows that needed it.

"I felt like that before," he finally said.

"What?" She spun her head around and blinked at him as if she'd forgotten his presence.

"There was a time I felt alone and angry, and couldn't stand it when people tried to sympathize."

"Why?"

Caleb took a long breath, steeling himself against the rush of memories. "It was right after my fiancée, Liza, died."

"Your fiancée?" Jennie brought her hand to her mouth. "What happened?"

"She...um...came down this way on the stage to visit her aunt, about a month before our wedding." He regarded a group of trees in the distance, embarrassed to see the pity he imagined he'd find on Jennie's face. It had been more than a year since he'd last recounted the story, but the pain felt as fresh as ever as the words spilled from him. "There was...an accident with the stage, and she was killed instantly."

"I'm so sorry." She set her hand on his sleeve for a moment. "That must have been devastating."

"We attended the same church congregation with our families. I tried going a few times after Liza's death, but I couldn't take the pity I saw reflected in everyone's eyes, how they'd stop their whispered conversations when I came close. I quit going to any kind of church for a long time." He tore his gaze from the landscape back to hers, hoping to make his next point understood. "About a year ago, after making peace with God, I finally realized those people who knew Liza weren't being cruel or unkind on purpose. The real reason I'd quit going to church back then had nothing to with them, and everything to do with me."

With a shake of her head, Jennie scrambled to her feet. "You make it sound so easy, but it's not. You don't know what they said about my mother, the horrible rumors that they spread. Not that the truth was much better. Do you know she only wrote me once in those five years before we got the telegram about her death? Once."

Caleb couldn't fault her entirely for her reaction; he'd been stubborn about giving up his past hurts, too. "What'd your mother say in her letter?"

"I don't know." Her cheeks flushed red. "I never read it." She stalked away from him, calling over her shoulder, "I'm going to see what's keeping Will."

Breaking off a chunk of bread from the loaf at his side, Caleb opted to appease his growling stomach while he waited for Jennie and Will to return. He ripped off a smaller piece of bread and popped it into his mouth. He didn't regret telling Jennie about Liza, despite the sadness it still stirred inside him. Rather than pitying him, she'd shown sympathy. At least before she'd gotten mad and left.

Caleb ate another bite of bread as he thought over what Jennie had told him. He was honored she would share as much as she had about her own past, but it concerned him, too. He'd grown comfortable with only having to be responsible for himself, and he didn't like the idea of having people dependent on him again. It left too much potential for disappointment, and loss. Life was a whole lot simpler on his own.

# Chapter Six

*Caleb crept through the grayish mist of the nightmare, the voices of the two stage robbers arguing somewhere unseen ahead of him. He felt none of the anticipation he had that fateful day a year and a half ago when he'd discovered the final two members of the gang who'd robbed Liza's stage were together again. In the dream he felt only dread at what he knew was coming.*

*He moved toward the cabin and peered through the dirty window. The two men hunkered around the small fire, their weapons neglected on the nearby table. Brandishing his revolvers Caleb slipped silently to the door. He paused, the hatred he felt for these men thrumming as hard as his heartbeat. Lifting his boot, he kicked in the door and rushed inside.*

*"You're both under arrest!"*

*One of the men scrambled up and tossed his chair at Caleb. Caleb leaped out of the way but the split-second distraction allowed the man to lunge through the back window with a horrific crash of glass. Caleb fired a shot, hitting the man in the foot, but he still escaped.*

"Get down on the floor," Caleb barked at the other bandit.

"Blaine," he screamed as he lowered himself to his knees and put his hands in the air. "You gutless coward, get back here!"

Keeping one gun trained on the man, Caleb stuck the other in his holster and reached for his rope. He approached the bandit. "Don't worry about your partner. I'll find him, too."

The man scowled, then hung his head.

Caleb tossed the loop in his rope over the man's head and waist, but just as he prepared to tighten it, the bandit leaped up, slashing at the air with a knife. The rope fell to the floor.

"Put the knife down," Caleb shouted as he jumped back to avoid the blade. "I don't want to take you in to the sheriff dead."

"I ain't going no other way."

The man rushed him, his arm cocked. Caleb backed up and felt the wall hit his shoulders. He was cornered. He dropped to his knees as the man came at him, hoping to throw the bandit off balance, but Caleb found himself wrestled to the floor.

Caleb tried to work his gun free from the man's weight, but his arms were quickly growing tired from keeping the knife at bay. The blade inched nearer to his skin.

The bandit grinned, releasing foul breath into Caleb's sweaty face. "So long, sonny," he hissed.

Caleb put all his remaining strength into wrenching his arm loose. He angled his gun against the man's shirt and squeezed the trigger. The bandit's eyes flew *open wide in shock before he crumpled onto Caleb's chest, dead.*

*At this point the dream whisked Caleb away from the horror of the cabin to the sheriff's crowded office.*

*"It was self-defense, Mr. Johnson," the sheriff said. "No judge would convict you otherwise."*

*"Self-defense," Caleb repeated, if only to convince himself. "Self-defense."*

"Caleb? Caleb, wake up."

Grabbing his guns, Caleb jerked upright in his bedroll. In the moonlight he saw Jennie crouched next to him.

"It's all right," she said, drawing her coat tighter around herself. "I think you were having a dream. You kept muttering something."

"I—I'm sorry to wake you." He rubbed at his eyes to clear the sleep from them.

Her shoulders rose and fell. "I couldn't really sleep. I wanted to…" She ducked her head, her next words directed at the dirt. "I wanted to apologize for my… behavior earlier. I don't like talking about my mother leaving, but it wasn't right to lash out at you, either."

"Apology accepted." He steeled himself against the questions she would likely ask about his dream, but to his relief, she moved back to her makeshift bed. Caleb glanced at Will. The boy snored softly from his cocoon of blankets. At least he hadn't awakened him. "You going back to sleep?"

Jennie slipped into her bedroll, but she shook her head. "You?"

"Not yet." He needed to occupy his mind with some-thing else, instead of the haunting images of his nightmare. Sometimes he'd had it twice in the same night. "You mind if I stoke the fire? It sure is chilly."

"Go ahead." Wrapping her arms around her blanketed knees, Jennie rested her chin on her legs as Caleb built the fire into a small but steady flame. "So does your family live around here?"

Caleb poked at the fire with a stick. "No. My folks live on a farm up north, in the Salt Lake Valley."

"What are you doing down here then?"

"Earning money. I want to have my own freight business."

She shifted closer to the fire. "Weren't there any jobs up north?"

"There were." He stared into the dancing flames. "I couldn't stay up there, though. Not with Liza gone."

"Were your parents sad to see you go?"

"Sad, yes, but more disappointed."

He sensed Jennie watching him. "Surely they understood your grief?"

"In a way." He let his stick grow black at the end and then pulled it out of the heat. "But I don't think they knew what to do about me. I quit farming the piece of land they'd given me—me and Liza. I quit going to church, like I told you. The memories of her were everywhere, and one day, I couldn't stand it anymore." A shadow of that desperation filled him and he clenched his jaw against it. "I went and told them I was leaving. Told them I knew I made a lousy farmer and I wanted to do something else with my life."

"Do they like the idea of you having your own freight business?"

"I think Pa's disappointed that I didn't stick with farming, but really I don't know if they care what I do as long as I'm working hard at something and helping others. What they really want is for me to come home. But that's not going to happen. It's time for me to make my own way."

Jennie bobbed her head in agreement. "I can relate to that—deciding to make your own way and not wanting others to step in. That's why I didn't want you paying for the candy I ruined in the mercantile seven months ago."

*The candy?* He studied her, her red hair brighter in the firelight, her brown eyes peering back at him. "You were the woman in the store?"

"I didn't want to feel beholden to you."

"I guess that's one way to look at it. But I'd say we're just about even, since you gave me a job. That was definitely worth the money to pay for the candy. And to see you smile."

She tucked her chin back down, but not before Caleb caught that same soft smile he'd seen in the store lifting her mouth for a moment.

"What were you doing up in Fillmore?" he asked.

"Meeting with the bank president about our loan." Her next question came quickly as if she couldn't change the subject fast enough. "When was the last time you saw your parents?"

"Three years ago, but I try to write every few weeks."

"It isn't the same, though, is it?"

"No." A feeling of loneliness swept over him. He hadn't realized until he had entered the close-knit circle of Jennie's family how much he missed his parents and siblings.

"I hope you get that freight business."

He cleared his throat to rid it of emotion. "Thanks.

It's a lot more exciting than farming. You get to travel, meet new people."

"Sometimes a life like that isn't so adventurous."

"What do you mean?"

"Nothing." Jennie released her hold around her knees. "I think I'm ready to sleep now. Good night, Caleb."

She stuck out her hand and Caleb shook it. He liked Jennie's firm but feminine grip. "Good night, Miss Jones. It was a pleasure talking with you."

Her cheeks colored, but he guessed it was from facing the fire. "You can call me Jennie."

"Jennie," he repeated. He banked the fire and moved back to his own bedroll. Tucking his arms behind his head, he shut his eyes and exhaled a long breath. His nightmare didn't come again. This time he dreamed of a girl in a green dress with a pretty smile and a pile of candy around her knees.

After a morning of doctoring the cattle that needed it, Jennie couldn't stand the smell of smoke and sweat in her hair any longer. She left Caleb and Will napping and walked to the creek to wash her hair, armed with soap, a cup, a blanket and her gun.

She removed her dusty boots and socks and dipped her feet into the water. The cool wetness on her bare toes brought a quick intake of breath, then a sigh of contentment.

When was the last time she'd taken a break in the middle of the week? She had Caleb to thank for that. For a farmer-freighter, he handled the cattle rather well, and she had to admit she was glad to have him around.

She had enjoyed talking with him the night before. Maybe too much. She didn't need him distracting her from her goal to save the ranch. Which meant she needed to keep their friendship professional—like Nathan's. But Nathan didn't cause butterflies in her stomach when he teased her or when he smiled, and she didn't care one whit what Nathan thought of her appearance.

"Is that why I'm doing this?" she murmured, glancing down at her washing things. To impress Caleb? She shook her head. "I just want to feel clean." Though she couldn't help recalling the few times he'd called her pretty.

Picking up the cup and soap, she hurried to wash her hair so the three of them could ride back to the ranch.

She shivered as she doused her head with the cold water and began scrubbing the dripping locks. If only she could wash away her silly romantic thoughts as easily.

Caleb yawned and sat up to stretch his arms. His muscles felt less sore today, evidence he was growing more used to his job as a cowboy.

"Where's your sister?" he called over to Will.

The boy jumped as though he'd been prodded with a pitchfork. "I...uh...don't know." He stuck the book he'd been reading behind his back. "Maybe she went to the creek."

"You reading somethin' interesting?"

Without answering, Will picked up his hat and rolled it between his hands.

"Care if I have a look?" Caleb asked, as he stood and approached Will.

Will studied him a moment before reaching for the book. He plunked it into Caleb's outstretched hand. Caleb cocked an eyebrow when he saw it was the Bible.

"Is there a reason you're hiding it?"

"Maybe."

Caleb feigned a thoughtful nod as he handed back the book. "I guess you never know when those non-believer cows might demand you hand it over or they'll rough you up."

A smile replaced the frown on Will's face, then faded just as quickly. "I'm not worried about the cows." Setting the Bible on the grass, he ripped up a blade and twisted it between his fingers. "It's just that Jennie doesn't take too kindly to anything that smacks of religion."

"And that's the problem?"

Will nodded. "She won't go to church 'cause of stuff people said about our ma after she left us, but I'd like to go. Not just for the preaching, either." He broke the piece of grass in two and tossed them both aside. "I had to quit going to school after Pa died. So it'd be nice to be around people my own age again."

"I think that's real commendable," Caleb said, taking a seat on the ground. He admired Will's honest heart. "I don't know if I appreciated going when I was younger. Now, though, I realize how much I need it. It helps me be a better person." He studied Will's lowered head. "Maybe if you told Jennie it would help you meet new friends and be a better brother, she might let you go."

"Or she might just be mad at me for wanting the day off."

Caleb chuckled. "I don't think your sister's as hard-hearted as that. Tell you what. I was going to ask her for some time off this Sunday to go to church myself. Why don't you come with me?"

"Really?" Will grinned, then he coughed and a look

of nonchalance replaced his excited one. "I mean, that would be nice. If you don't mind."

"Not at all."

"So you'll ask for both of us?"

"Wait. What?" How'd the boy rope him into that arrangement?

"She's likely to tell me no but not you."

Caleb blew out his breath. He didn't want to ruffle Jennie's feathers by sticking his nose places it didn't belong. He needed this job. But Will looked so hopeful.

"All right," Caleb said, rising again to his feet. "I'll go talk to her, but you owe me some lousy ranch task in exchange."

"Deal."

Caleb put on his hat. "Where can I find her?"

"Since Dandy's still tethered here, she didn't go for a ride. I'd try the creek first." Will pointed southeast.

Caleb headed in that direction. He made his way around some scrub trees and found the creek, a greenish brown flow of water. He couldn't see Jennie, but he heard her soft humming from farther upstream.

He trudged along the bank, following the sound of her tune, before he caught a glimpse of her. She stood bent over, a cup in her hand. She appeared to be rinsing soap from her hair. The red color resembled wet copper, but it was the peaceful expression on her face that made him pause. No worry sharpened her face; no stubbornness tightened her full lips.

*She really is beautiful, when she lets herself relax.*

Clearing his throat, he circled a bush blocking his path and stepped into the open. He might as well have fired one of his guns. Jennie jumped, her hair spraying water in all directions, and drew her pistol from its holster near her feet.

"Oh, it's you." She lowered the gun aimed at his chest. "Did Will tell you where to find me?"

"He said you might be here," Caleb said, walking to the water's edge.

Jennie stuck the pistol back in the holster and wrung out her hair. Rivulets ran into the dirt at their feet. "I'm almost done."

"I think you could use a second rinse." He wiped at some suds above her left ear.

Her face turned pink. "Oh, right." She bent and picked up her cup and filled it with water from the creek. After flipping her hair over again, she resumed rinsing, but she still missed half the soap.

Caleb chuckled. "Here, let me."

He held out his hand for the cup. Twisting her head, Jennie peered at him, uncertainty written on her face.

"I have four sisters," he explained. "I observed many hair-washings growing up."

She bit her lip, but she finally passed him the cup.

Caleb scooped some water and poured it over her hair, making sure to cover her ear. She sucked in a sharp breath. *From the cold water, no doubt*, he thought, as the chilly liquid ran over his hand. When he finished rinsing the suds, he set down the cup and squeezed the excess water from her hair.

"There you go." He stepped back. Jennie straightened, visibly shivering now. The sunlight shining against her wet hair and face enhanced her beauty even more. He lifted her blanket off the ground and wrapped it around her shoulders. Their hands met for a second as she grasped the ends of the rough material.

"Thank you—for washing my hair."

"Just consider it one of my ranching duties."

She gave a soft laugh. "Good at roping, cattle branding and washing hair? You're very versatile."

He meant to tease her back, but he got caught up staring into her eyes. He noticed for the first time the tiny green specks among the rich brown color. Of its own volition his gaze wandered down to her mouth. What would it be like to kiss a girl again, to feel the feminine softness of those lips?

The sudden noise of someone pushing through the undergrowth shattered his thoughts. His neck and face went hot, and Caleb hurried to turn away from Jennie. Thank goodness she hadn't known his thoughts. He could hardly believe them himself. He hadn't given any girl a second thought romantically since Liza. Surely he wasn't ready to care for anyone in that way again.

"Can I go? What did she say?" Will asked as he approached.

Jennie frowned at Caleb. "Go where?"

"To church." Will joined them beside the creek, glancing from one to the other. "Caleb said I could go with him, but I told him to ask you first."

"I see." Her knuckles whitened where they gripped the blanket and she glared at Caleb. "This was your idea?"

Caleb forced calmness into his voice. "I meant to ask you before Sunday if it would be all right if I went. I offered to take Will when I saw him reading the Bible just now."

"Why didn't you mention this to me?" Jennie turned her glare past him to direct it at her brother.

Will shuffled his feet and stared down at the dirt. "I knew you wouldn't like it. But I want to go with Caleb."

The crease on Jennie's brow deepened. "You want to go back, despite the horrible things people said about us and about Ma?"

Will lifted his chin. "Maybe those people aren't there anymore. Even if they are, that was a long time ago, Jennie." He shot a look at Caleb who nodded his agreement. The boy definitely had the makings of a mature young man.

Jennie exhaled a heavy sigh, her eyes focused on something in the distance before she drew herself up. "I suppose if that's how you feel, you're welcome to go on Sunday—both of you." She yanked the blanket off her shoulders and quickly gathered up her things. "You'll need to hurry back, no socializing for long afterward."

"Sure thing," Will said.

"Why don't you come with us?" Caleb offered. "Your grandmother could come, too."

Jennie was shaking her head before he even finished. "I'm not coming. More than one person judged our family and our mother with no real knowledge of the situation."

Caleb tried to swallow back the retort that popped into his head, but he couldn't. "Kind of like you're judging them now?" he asked in a low voice.

The air between them went deathly still. Jennie gaped at him for a moment before her face flushed with fury. "I told you he could go. I don't wish to discuss my church attendance or the absence of it any further, especially with you." She marched off through the trees, slashing at branches with her free hand and muttering under her breath.

Will blew out a sigh. "Sorry she got mad. Just like I said."

"I thought that went rather well," Caleb said with a smirk. "At least she's allowing us both to go. We can still ask your grandmother if she wants to join us."

"I bet she'd like that." Will's expression brightened. "I'll ask her first thing when we get back." He headed away from the creek.

Caleb followed at a slower pace. He wasn't thrilled about the ride back to the ranch. *So much for not ruffling feathers.* He'd even entertained the thought of kissing her a few moments ago.

Shaking his head at his folly, he reminded himself that he knew better than to allow another woman into his life right now. He hadn't completely let go of his feelings for Liza yet, and then there was the guilt he still had over his bounty-hunting days. He'd done things he wasn't proud of, things he'd done to avenge someone he loved.

No, love and courting were out of the question. They only made a man do foolish things.

# Chapter Seven

Jennie watched from her bedroom window as Caleb drove the wagon away from the ranch Sunday morning. Her grandmother sat next to him on the seat and Will lounged in the back. Even from a distance, Jennie sensed their enthusiasm.

Dropping the curtains into place, she turned abruptly from the sight and folded her arms tight against her body.

*It's all* his *fault,* she thought, her thumbnail meeting her mouth. If Caleb hadn't showed up to "save" her from the stage bandits, if she hadn't foolishly hired him, everything would be the same. She wouldn't be so edgy and self-conscious all the time, and the family certainly wouldn't be trotting off to church.

*He wouldn't have been staring at my lips yesterday, either.* Try as she might the memory of Caleb rinsing her hair and watching her mouth, even for a moment, made her pulse speed up in a way that had nothing to do with her anger.

With everyone gone, she left her bedroom and tromped loudly down the stairs, her footsteps echoing in the empty house. Her irritation cooled a little when she found the plate of breakfast food Grandma Jones had set on the back of the stove for her.

Jennie ate slowly, trying to decide how to occupy the next several hours. There were numerous ranch chores to be done, but there was no rush. The family usually rested for a bit on Sunday anyway and she didn't see the need to change that habit now.

She washed her few dishes, grabbed a book from the parlor and went out on the porch to read in the sunshine. Though early still, the air already felt pleasant.

A single chapter took her much longer than it should have as her mind skipped back and forth from the story to what people at church might say about seeing her family come to services again for the first time in years. Finally Jennie tossed the book onto the rocker and walked to the barn. She could at least ride out to check on the cattle.

She had the saddle on Dandy and was cinching the straps tighter beneath the horse's belly when the barn door creaked. With quick fingers, Jennie reached for the pistol tucked into the waist of her breeches. Maybe the family had changed their minds about going to church, but she wasn't taking any chances.

"Going somewhere, love?"

Nathan stood at the barn entrance, his own horse crowding the doorway behind him.

"As a matter of fact I am," she said, frowning. She put away her gun, placed her foot in the stirrup and climbed into the saddle.

"Where to?" Nathan swung onto his horse and they fell in step beside her as she and Dandy rode from the barn.

"I'm off to see my cows." She smiled when Nathan

gave a disdainful snort. "You're back sooner than I expected."

He nudged his horse close to hers and took her hand, rubbing it against the dark bristles of his face. "Missed me that much, huh?"

Jennie cringed at his touch and firmly removed her hand from his grip. She urged her horse into a trot, but Nathan kept pace.

"So why are you here?" she asked, hoping it wasn't just to make passes at her.

"Heard about a job last night. They'll be robbing the northbound stage a week from Friday."

"That soon?" Her second and third robberies had been several months apart. "How much?"

Nathan grinned, revealing his tobacco-stained teeth. "They think they'll collect five hundred greenbacks."

"I'll do it." As the words escaped her lips, Jennie clutched the reins harder between her fingers. Excitement, and a small dose of fear, coursed through her at the thought of besting another group of armed men.

"There's a problem, though." Nathan's expression changed from one of enthusiasm to soberness. "They know about you."

Jennie whirled around in the saddle. "How?"

"Seems you really made Bart mad last week. He got good and drunk the other night and spilled the story to all his friends about a redheaded spitfire who stole his stage money. They'll be watchin' for you."

"Should I pass up the job then?" She desperately needed the money, but she didn't want to wind up dead, either.

Nathan shook his head. "You'll be fine. Just be careful. It's two men and this is their first time robbing a stage."

"Thank you for the information, Nathan." She read the silent question in his eyes and knew that he still wanted her to run away with him. He liked her ability with a gun and the adept way she handled bandits—that's why he wanted her to leave with him. But he didn't know the real Jennie Jones, the person she was inside. That girl was much more than what he saw—much more than what desperation had driven her to become. She had to be.

"Always a pleasure, Jennie 'Spitfire' Jones." He pulled his horse up short, and Jennie did the same. "I'll be off—unless you got somethin' else in mind for us to do besides stare at your pitiful cattle." He winked at her.

"No," she said with an emphatic shake of her head. She still held to her morals when it came to some things.

"Of course not. You may be an outlaw, but you're a prudish one at that." He laughed and wheeled his horse around. "They'll attack the stage about ten miles south of Cove Fort. Then they'll hole up for the rest of the day in a cave, just west of there. You can overtake them while they're hiding out, but you'll have a good, long ride ahead of you. Make sure you get there in enough time to steal the money before they split at dusk."

Jennie waved as he galloped away and renewed her course. Her thoughts soon returned to Nathan calling her an outlaw. She didn't think of herself in those terms. She certainly wasn't a criminal like these thugs she came up against.

A niggling doubt struggled to free itself, but Jennie quickly silenced it by reviewing the week's tasks: finish mending the fences, repair the chicken coop and decide what seeds they would plant in the garden.

Before long she located the bulk of the herd, resting in the shade of some juniper trees. She whistled loudly so they wouldn't be spooked and rode in a circle around the cattle. She observed each cow, checking for any sign of sickness or injury. They appeared to be in good health, besides being a bit skinnier than their cows in the past. She turned Dandy north and began a lazy search for the rest of the cattle.

After a mile or two, she realized she hadn't run across a single cow since leaving the main group, and she didn't remember seeing any calves back at the junipers, either. She headed east for a ways, then turned south again, pausing in confusion. Surely all the mother cows wouldn't have wandered off together.

She returned to the herd for a count. Thirty of the cows were missing, along with all the newborn calves. Which could only mean one thing. Someone had rustled her cows—again.

Jennie yanked Dandy to a stop, causing the horse to pull against the bit. The thieves couldn't be far away—the calves would slow them down and they'd want to stick near the prairie grass so the cows could feed. She scrutinized the ground, searching for any sign of the rustlers. She nudged her horse in one direction and then another. At last she saw what she'd hoped to, a few hundred yards to the west: patches of trampled grass.

She spurred Dandy forward to follow the tracks until reason caught up with her anger and she pulled back on the reins. Without knowing how many rustlers there were, she wouldn't know if she needed help or not. Even if she could overtake them and get the cows back, she would have a hard time driving the cattle back to the ranch alone. Yet the prospect of waiting until the others returned from church, allowing the thieves time to move the cattle farther away, made her groan with impatience. *If I went and got Caleb at the church, though...*

If she hurried, she could make it to the church in less than an hour. Then she and Caleb could fetch his horse and any supplies from the house and head back to the range without waiting for Will and Grandma Jones to come in the wagon.

Jennie pointed Dandy toward town. "Yaw," she cried, prodding the horse with her heels. Bending low across Dandy's back, she urged him into a full gallop.

Jennie found the churchyard empty, except for the waiting horses and wagons. The meeting wasn't over yet. She slid to the ground and tied Dandy to the nearby hitching post. She ascended the few steps and gripped the door handle, her heart pumping harder with more than fear about losing her cattle.

The memories of the last time she'd been to the little church washed over her and for a moment she couldn't move. All the things people had said about her mother whirled through her mind. Then she lifted her chin. She was only here to get Caleb and save her cattle.

Swallowing back her fear, she pulled open the door an inch. The murmur of a man's voice floated out from the church's main room. Though she meant to slip in quietly, inconspicuously, a sudden gust of wind jerked the door from Jennie's grasp and sent it crashing against the outside wall. Every person in the room spun around to stare at her.

Jennie nearly bolted back down the steps, but the

thought of losing her cows kept her rooted to the spot. She searched the faces of the crowd until she located the surprised but pleased ones of Grandma Jones, Will and Caleb.

"Caleb," she whispered, motioning for him to come to the door.

He furrowed his brow and tipped his head at the pastor who'd managed to keep to his sermon in spite of Jennie's interruption.

"Caleb," she tried again a little louder. But he'd turned forward again.

Someone to her left shushed her, bringing a blush to Jennie's cheeks. Humiliated but determined, she half crept down the aisle and wormed her way into the family's pew next to Caleb.

"If you were going for a big entrance, that was it," he said in a low voice. "I'm glad you changed your mind about coming."

"Do I look dressed for Sunday services?" She glared down at her trousers, then back up at Caleb. "You need to leave with me. Now."

Another person behind them said, "Shh." Jennie gripped the arm of the pew to keep from spinning around and glowering. The room felt too hot, the crowd too close.

"Someone's stolen my cows," she hissed into his ear. "I think we can catch them if we go now."

His eyebrows shot up. "We?" he said out of the corner of his mouth. "Why don't you get the sheriff?"

That was the last thing she wanted. Her association with stage thugs compelled her to stay far away from any lawman. "Not enough time," she whispered back. "We have to hurry. You can ride Dandy back with me."

Caleb exhaled loudly through his nose. "You sure you know what you're doing?"

"Yes." She held her breath. If he didn't help her, she wasn't sure what she would do.

"All right."

"Tell Will and Grandma Jones there's a problem with the herd. We can explain later. I don't want to worry them too much now."

Without waiting for him to follow through, Jennie rushed from the pew and toward the door. She couldn't leave fast enough—both for her cows and for herself. Outside she gulped in air.

She finished untying Dandy as Caleb emerged from the building. "What did they say?"

"Your grandmother said not to let you do anything impulsive." He walked over, concern evident on his face. "If she thinks I can stop you, then she doesn't know you well at all, does she? Are you sure you don't want to go get the sheriff and his men or maybe one of your neighbors here?"

Jennie gave an emphatic shake of her head. "I told you there isn't time. The tracks they left are still fairly fresh. I think we can catch up to the rustlers if we hurry. Now are you comin' or not, cowboy?"

Caleb frowned, but swung up into the saddle. "I didn't leave a perfectly good meeting just to chat." He leaned down and helped her climb onto Dandy's back.

Reluctantly, she wrapped her arms around Caleb's waist as he nudged Dandy into a full gallop and headed for home.

Jennie tried to distract herself from Caleb's nearness, from the knowledge of her hands encircling his strong back, by talking. But it sounded like nervous chatter, even to her ears.

"We'll ride to the house first. And then…then we need to get your horse and your guns. Probably something to eat. I found the cattle's tracks but didn't follow where they led completely."

"We'll find them," he reassured. "In the meantime, since you want my help, can I assume you've forgiven me for draggin' your family to church?"

Jennie's cheeks flamed. Thankfully he couldn't see her face. "I'm sorry." This was starting to become a pattern. "I guess I was…" She let her voice trail into silence as she tried to pinpoint why she'd been so angry with him about taking the family to church.

"Afraid?"

"Maybe." Was she really afraid of returning to church? Or was it something else, something deeper?

"What do you want to do once we find the rustlers?" Caleb asked, gratefully changing the subject.

Jennie resisted the urge to bite her thumbnail, knowing Caleb would only tease her if she did. She hadn't really formulated a plan. "We'll figure that out when we know how many there are."

"From what I saw the other week on the trail, fewer than six shouldn't be a problem."

She smiled at his back. "Are you saying I could have handled those men without your gallant assistance?"

To her surprise he didn't laugh. "We've got to figure out exactly how we're going to proceed once we track down these rustlers. We don't know who we're dealing with here, and things could go south mighty fast."

"All right. I'll think of something."

They rode on in silence as Jennie's thoughts raced

ahead to where the rustlers might be and how to go about stealing back her own cows. Hopefully with a little luck she and Caleb would be able to bring all of the cattle— and themselves—home safe and sound.

# Chapter Eight

After collecting his revolvers from his room, Caleb saddled up Saul and met Jennie beside the corral. A lumpy saddlebag, probably holding food and lassos, straddled Dandy's back.

"You ready?" Jennie asked as she swung back up into her saddle.

Though apprehension had begun to unwind itself inside his stomach, Caleb nodded and climbed onto Saul. He reminded himself he wasn't operating in his old job as a bounty hunter, tracking down someone associated with Liza's death. He was simply going to help Jennie rescue her cattle. Without those cows he wouldn't have a job.

He kept Saul at a gallop, in step with Dandy, slowing his horse only when Jennie did hers. Before long, Caleb recognized the spot where they'd done the branding. Jennie signaled for him to stop.

"Those are the tracks the cows and calves made when they separated them from the herd." She pointed to a wobbly line of crushed grass that led west. "With all those new calves to slow them down, they can't be more than a few miles away. They'll have to stay near the prairie grass, too."

Caleb rode beside her as they followed the trail, but the tracks disappeared soon after in a thick patch of sagebrush.

"That can't be the end of the trail," Jennie said with a groan.

"We'll find them. Why don't you head that way?" He pointed due north. "I'll go this way."

Caleb led Saul to the right. Every few feet he stopped his horse and scrutinized the ground for signs the cows had passed this way. Soon he found what he wanted— several new hoofprints in a patch of sand among the brush. A little farther on he discovered some fresh cow dung.

"Jennie!" He stood in the stirrups and waved her over with his hat.

"Did you find something?"

"Here's their trail. The rustlers took them west, this way."

Jennie glanced from the ground to Caleb, respect evident in her eyes. "I didn't know you were a tracker."

"My uncle taught me more than just how to shoot a gun."

When the trail faded a second time, Jennie waited for him to find it again before they continued on. Caleb appreciated her trust in his skills, and for the first time since coming to the ranch, he felt useful, competent. Perhaps the abilities he'd honed as a bounty hunter could be put to good use and not just as triggers for memories he'd sooner forget.

They came to a small stream, and Jennie stopped him. Still in their saddles, they watered the horses and ate some of the jerky and bread she had brought along in her saddlebag. The setting sun changed the sky overhead to a dark blue and stole the warmth of the day.

Caleb paused and slipped on the coat he'd brought along when he caught the smell of smoke. "Can you smell that?"

Jennie drew Dandy to a stop and sniffed the air. "It's got to be a campfire. We must be close."

"If we are then we're also more likely to be seen, too," he cautioned.

Twisting in his saddle, Caleb surveyed the surrounding country. The scent of smoke came strongest toward his left, probably on the other side of the steep incline just ahead of them. Several patches of junipers stood nearby, and to the south, Caleb thought he spied a ravine.

"Let's tie the horses in those trees over there," he said, pointing, "then we'll move on foot up that ravine to see if we can get a better view of who we're dealing with."

"I was thinking the same thing." Jennie nudged Dandy toward the trees.

"I think that's a first."

She shook her head, a smile tugging at her lips. "Things are never dull with you around, are they, Caleb Johnson?"

"I could say the same for you, Jennie Jones."

Once the horses had been tied up, Caleb led Jennie toward the ravine. To his relief, she didn't put up a fuss about following. If she had, he might have refused to help her. He wasn't about to let her lead the way right through trouble's door, not if he could help it.

At the edge of the bank, he peered down. A trickle of water ran between the rocks and bushes scattered along the bottom.

"I'll go first," he offered, jumping down and landing with a soft thud beside the stream. He turned back to assist Jennie, but she maneuvered the jump on her own. With an amused shake of his head, he watched her brush the dust from her trousers and fix her skewed hat.

With Jennie close behind him, Caleb stepped as softly as he could up the ravine. He figured they'd come about a hundred yards when he smelled the smoke even stronger. This time it was mingled with the scent of stewing meat. Caleb's stomach grumbled in response. Their cold supper hadn't been enough to fully satisfy his hunger.

Putting a finger to his lips, he motioned for Jennie to stop. "They've got to be right above us," he whispered. "We need to be able to see."

He pointed at a large rock that jutted out above the stream. Scaling the rock, he turned and offered his hand to Jennie. To his surprise, she accepted this time. He pulled her up beside him and lifted his head above the bank.

Three cowboys sat around the fire, their backs to the ravine. Beyond them to the north, the cattle milled about in the bushes. Caleb studied the cattle and the men. How would he and Jennie get her cows back without anybody getting killed?

"I know what we can do," Jennie whispered.

He indicated she should jump down from the rock, and he followed after her. In hushed tones, Jennie outlined her strategy for stealing back her cows. When she finished, she stepped back, her eyes bright with expectation.

Caleb regarded her with a frown. "Most of your plan hangs on my theatrical abilities?"

"You did so well playing the part of the sheriff when we met on the trail."

"That was different. We weren't trying to rustle fifty head of cattle then." He blew out his breath. He didn't like her idea, but he'd failed to come up with an acceptable one himself. Anything they did would be dangerous, but Jennie didn't have a ranch without those cows. "All right. I'll do it."

"Good. Let's go back for the horses, then you can ride into their camp."

Caleb forced a nod.

This time he allowed Jennie to take the lead as they hiked back up the streambed to the place where they'd entered the ravine. Using his hand as a cradle, he hoisted Jennie up and over the bank. Once she gained her footing, she turned and pulled on his arm with surprising strength, until Caleb managed to get himself out. When they returned to the horses, Jennie transferred the saddlebag to Saul.

"Are your revolvers loaded?" she asked as she readied her pistol.

"I've got them," he said, dodging her question. He tapped the butt of one of the guns beneath his coat.

"So they're already loaded?"

He frowned at her bent head. "No, they aren't."

Jennie shot him an impatient look. "How are you supposed to protect yourself riding around with unloaded guns? You'd better load them quick."

"I wasn't planning on it."

"What?" She returned her pistol to its place at the waistband of her breeches. "These men are likely armed—"

"I'm aware of that, Jennie." The words came out

harsher than he'd meant. "I don't usually keep them loaded," he added in a lower voice.

An expression of bewilderment settled onto her face. "Why ever not? You know how to handle a gun. I saw you."

"I have my reasons."

"And I have mine—for wanting you to load them. You're no good to me dead."

He growled, ready to argue with her—he wasn't likely to be the one who ended up dead in a gunfight against the rustlers—but he thought better of it. He could tell from her mulish expression that she wouldn't let him walk away without a loaded weapon. "If I load one, will that satisfy you?"

Her brow creased with irritation, but she nodded.

Caleb removed the bullets he'd brought along and hurried to load one of the revolvers before stowing it in his holster. He slipped the rest of the bullets into his coat pocket.

"You know the plan, right?" Jennie walked over to him.

"I divert their attention," he said, untying Saul's reins, "while you lead the cattle away. Then I catch up with you as soon as I can."

"I'll move fast."

"Right." The plan sounded easy enough, but carrying it out would likely prove to be much trickier. Caleb swallowed hard, hoping to push back the dread rising into his throat. He turned around to mount his horse, but Jennie stopped him with a hand to his arm.

"Wait."

He faced her again, raising his eyebrows in question. "Did you change your mind?" Part of him wished she would.

"No..." She still gripped his sleeve. "If you don't want to do this, I'll go on alone."

He forced a laugh. "You can't do this by yourself. You need those cows, and as your cowhand, so do I. That means it's my job to help. Let's just say assisting a pretty girl is becoming a weakness—"

Without warning, she went up on tiptoe and pressed her lips to his.

Too stunned to think, Caleb didn't draw away. Her kiss felt warm and wonderful. Then Liza's face appeared in his mind's eye, and he realized what he was doing. He'd sworn off love and courting. It only meant loss and pain and doing crazy things, like kissing his employer.

He stepped back. Jennie peered up at him, her face more vulnerable and open than he'd seen yet. But what was she doing?

"Jennie. I..."

She silenced him with a finger to his mouth. "Don't say anything. Not now. We need to get going."

He climbed into the saddle and cleared his throat. "I'll be watching for you," he said, more to the tree near her than to her face.

"Be careful," she said, grabbing Dandy's reins.

"I will."

Caleb pointed Saul toward the hill. He twisted around to see Jennie watching him from atop her horse. He felt the memory of her kiss, but he clenched his jaw to squash it. He could think more about it later. Right now he had to concentrate before he ended up doing something else foolish. He had a job to do.

He waved to her, hoping to inspire her with confidence he didn't quite feel, and she returned the gesture. As he guided Saul between the hill and the ravine, he let out a long breath that became a whispered prayer. *Please keep her safe, God. Help us be successful.*

The knot of nerves in his stomach didn't go away, but he felt a little better. Keeping his face pointed straight ahead, he braced himself for the moment when he would arrive at the thieves' camp.

Jennie watched him disappear behind the hill, half relieved after her blunder, half fearful for his life. Would Caleb be safe? What had she been thinking to kiss him? She hadn't, not clearly anyway. One remark about her being pretty and a moment of staring too long at those blue eyes and the arch in his lips, and she'd been lost.

She gripped Dandy's reins tighter, her cheeks hot. At least she'd managed to feign indifference when he'd stepped away. Inside, though, she felt her heart drop to her boots. She'd never kissed a man on the lips before. Had Caleb thought it a weak kiss? Could he tell it was her first? Or was there some other reason he'd looked almost frightened afterward? Jennie thought of what he'd said about his fiancée. What had she been like? Was she pretty? Did he mourn her death as much as the sadness behind his words implied?

*Enough,* she scolded herself. Caleb was riding into danger to help her and protect the ranch. She didn't want to imagine what she'd tell his parents if something happened to him. What would *she* do if he didn't make it back? What would her life be like without him in it? The thought left her feeling lonely, something she hadn't felt in a long time. Caleb wasn't just a good hired hand—he was the first friend she'd had in years.

Lowering her chin, hardly aware of the gesture, she shut her eyes and offered a quick prayer for his safety. The words felt awkward, even in her mind, but her fear eased a little as she finished. Wheeling Dandy around, she headed in the opposite direction. It was time to get her cattle back.

# Chapter Nine

Quicker than he wanted, Caleb rounded the hill, placing him twenty yards from the thieves' campsite. He approached slowly, leisurely, but all three men jumped to their feet at the sound of his horse.

"Howdy, fellows," he called, lifting his arm in greeting.

They eyed him with plain suspicion, their hands already on the guns at their waists. One cowboy stood much shorter than the rest, but the other two—one skinny and one with a drooping mustache—regarded him as though he were the leader.

"Evening." He tipped his hat in Caleb's direction.

"Mind if I join you at your fire?" Caleb asked.

The short cowboy flicked his gaze to the others and nodded. "Sure thing. Have a seat."

Caleb dropped to the ground. He pulled a hobble from his saddlebag and put it on Saul's legs, purposely keeping his horse away from the others. He strode over to the three men, carrying the saddlebag with him. They'd resumed their seats.

"Care for some stew?" The short cowboy waved to a pot hung over the fire.

"Much obliged," Caleb said, though the smell wasn't as tantalizing as it had been before.

He sat in the dirt and accepted the full tin cup and a spoon. "You from around here?" he asked as he took a bite of food. Despite his earlier hunger, he wasn't sure how much he could stomach right now.

"We work not too far away," the leader said. "You?"

Caleb shook his head. "Naw. I'm from up north. I'm down here looking for a job."

Their tense postures relaxed, dispelling the strain in the air, though Caleb felt as edgy as ever.

"You might be able to get work with Marshall King," the skinny one said. "We work for him."

Caleb made a note of their employer's name for Jennie. "Maybe I'll do that. You roundin' up the calves for spring branding?" He was glad he'd learned a thing or two in the past week, enough to pass as a real cowboy.

The three exchanged a meaningful glance. "Just pickin' up the strays," the short one said toward the fire. His light tone sounded forced.

In the ensuing silence, Caleb watched the cattle milling about among the brush. He couldn't see Jennie yet, but she'd be coming soon. He had to get these men talking, distracted. "Name's Johnson, by the way."

"I'm Gunner," the short cowboy said. "That's Haws." He pointed at the skinny fellow. "The other fellow is Smith." The man with the mustache lifted a hand.

A movement out of the corner of his eye caught Caleb's attention, and he turned toward it. In the soft light of the evening, he could see the cattle starting to lumber through the brush. It was his signal.

"So," Caleb said, louder than he intended. He cleared

his tight throat before continuing. "What's it like working for King?"

Haws shrugged. "Not bad. He pays better than anywhere else in these parts."

"How much?" Caleb feigned interest in Haws's lengthy answer. He only had another minute or two before the three noticed the moving cattle.

His mind raced for a way to distract the cowhands without having to shoot anyone, if he could help it. Caleb leaned forward, his elbows on his knees, and the heaviness in his right pocket reminded him of the bullets he'd stuck inside. They gave him an idea. He slipped one hand into his pocket and scooped up the bullets.

"Mind if I have a little more stew?" he asked as he stood.

Gunner took his cup, and while he filled it from the pot near the fire, Caleb edged closer and let the bullets slip from his hand into the flames.

Accepting the cup from Gunner, he took a few steps backward as if to sit back down, his muscles tensed.

Gunner glanced in the direction of the cattle and jumped to his feet. "Where'd the—"

Before he could finish his question, the bullets exploded in a terrific boom. The three cowhands tripped over themselves to get away from the fire and flying ash. Not waiting a second, Caleb dove at Smith. He wrestled the man's revolver from its holster and pointed it at the stunned cowhands.

"Sorry I can't stick around, boys," he said, enjoying the perplexity on their faces. Jennie's plan was going better than he'd expected. "Appreciate the supper, but I think I'll just be takin' back these here cattle. 'Cause I know they don't belong to you. Now drop your guns."

Gunner and Haws obeyed, setting their guns in the dirt. Caleb kept the gun in his grip aimed at them as he walked over and knelt to collect the others. As he reached down to grab one of the guns, someone plowed into him from behind.

"Go get the cattle," Smith said from above him.

Caleb scrambled to get up off the ground, but Smith landed a punch to his lower jaw that knocked him back down. From the corner of his eye, he saw Haws and Gunner scoop up their guns and sprint toward their horses.

For one awful moment he froze—images from his nightmare flooding his thoughts and making his heart leap in fear. He couldn't—wouldn't—use his gun that way again.

*But what about Jennie?*

The possibility of the other two rustlers, who were armed again, reaching her first fueled Caleb's numb body with new energy. Pretending to be hurt, he waited for Smith to come at him again. When the cowhand approached, Caleb kicked out with his boot, connecting with the man's leg.

Smith cursed and stumbled backward, giving Caleb time to come to his feet. He lunged at Smith and planted a hard fist into the cowboy's belly. Groaning, Smith twisted away, but not before throwing a wild punch that connected with Caleb's right cheek.

Ignoring the taste of blood and the momentary ringing in his head, Caleb pounded a blow at the man's jaw. Smith fell back into the dirt, moaning loudly.

Caleb grabbed Smith's gun from where he'd dropped it and ran to Saul. He threw off the horse's hobble and mounted.

"Yaw," he hollered, driving his heels into Saul's flanks.

When he rounded the hill, he saw the cattle running hard a quarter of a mile away. He couldn't spot Jennie, but the other two cowboys were racing to head off the herd.

Urging Saul faster, Caleb headed for Haws. The sound of pounding hooves matched his heartbeat as he drew closer.

*Where's Jennie?* Concern pulsed through him. Then he spied her to the left of the cattle, doing her best to turn the stampeding group in the direction of the ranch.

Caleb drew alongside Haws. The gap between them was less than thirty feet when the cowboy suddenly turned and fired his gun. Caleb bent in the saddle to avoid a direct hit from the shot, but a wave of pain and fire still pierced his right ear. He reached up and found to his relief that the bullet had only grazed the skin, tearing off a small piece of flesh.

He pushed his horse back toward the herd, leaning low in the saddle. It was time to put his gun skills to work. He aimed Smith's gun at Haws's hand and pulled the trigger. A second later, the cowboy screamed and dropped his own gun to the ground.

With two of the three thieves down, Caleb yanked his horse in the direction he'd last seen Gunner. The cows along the left side of the herd charged in closer to the others at his approach.

A quick glance at the front of the herd told him Jennie was still there, riding unharmed. Over his shoulder, he saw Gunner had given up the fight and was racing back toward the cowhands' camp. Haws, his injured arm cradled to his chest, rode hard behind him.

A surge of victory pushed Caleb up in the stirrups with a whoop. "We did it!" he yelled, with all the voice he could muster over the racket of pounding cattle hooves. He removed his hat and waved it in the air, hoping Jennie understood the signal.

He kept waving until Jennie saw him. Even from far away, he thought he saw a smile on her face as she lifted off her own hat and swung it in the air in answer.

Sitting once more, Caleb replaced his hat and stuck his newly acquired gun in the slot on his saddle. *Now to get these cows off the range.*

He and Jennie drove the cattle through the dimming light. When they reached the other half of the herd, they joined the two groups together and guided them toward the ranch.

Caleb's face and ear throbbed and his legs and back felt stiff from being in the saddle so long. He didn't let the complaints linger, though. He felt too exhilarated at their success. Perhaps cattle ranching wasn't so boring after all.

At last he spied the dark outline of the fence in the distance. As they drew closer, Jennie charged ahead and opened the corral. She helped him steer the cows inside, then she secured the gate.

"We'll give them something to eat in the morning," Jennie said in a weary voice as they dismounted and led their horses to the barn. "They should be fine for one night."

He followed her into the barn and put Saul away. The light of the moon coming through the open doors allowed enough light to see by. Caleb pulled off the saddle and gave Saul a quick brush over.

"Do you need a hand?" he asked when he finished.

Jennie shook her head, running a currycomb once more over Dandy's flanks. "I'm done for tonight."

Tossing the brush onto the table with the others, she joined him near the doors. A soft gasp escaped her lips as she took in the sight of his face. "What happened? You're covered in blood." She lifted her hand as if to touch him, but she clearly thought better of it.

A strange twinge of disappointment flared inside him and then disappeared. "One of the cowboys grazed my ear with his shot," Caleb answered. "I'm just glad he didn't take the whole thing off."

"I heard the gunfire, but I couldn't tell who was firing at whom. When I saw you waving your silly hat, I knew you were all right." A faint smile lifted her mouth. "Let's get you patched up inside."

She closed the barn doors and fell into step beside him as he started for the house. He shot a glance at her and saw her quickly look away. Now that the excitement of rustling back her cattle had faded, Caleb felt awkwardness between them.

"About that…um…" He coughed, suddenly unsure how to proceed.

"You mean the kiss?" Jennie stopped walking and turned to face him, her arms folded.

Caleb ran a hand over his stubbled chin. "Yes, that. If I've been too casual in my teasing…"

"If you're worried about your job, you shouldn't. I won't…do that again." She stared down at her boots and shrugged. "I don't know what I was thinking. I suppose I was just caught up in the moment and the possibility of something happening to either of us."

"Jennie."

He touched her sleeve, but he wished he hadn't done

it when the gesture made her peer up at him. Even the dim light couldn't erase the hurt he saw reflected in those dark eyes. He wanted to say something to take the pain away...but then the front door flew open and the moment was lost.

Jennie looked up as Will came out onto the porch. "We thought we heard you," he said. "What happened?"

Jennie seized the opportunity to distance herself from Caleb and hurried toward her brother. "We're fine, Will. The cattle are fine, too."

Grandma Jones appeared in the doorway. "We've been sick with worry."

Caleb trailed the family into the kitchen, and Jennie heard Grandma Jones and Will gasp at the sight of the blood trickling down his neck and into the collar of his shirt.

"Oh, my! You're bleeding. What happened?" Grandma Jones asked Caleb, fussing around the kitchen for medical supplies.

"We went after the cattle, Grandma." Jennie sank into a chair. "Someone stole them."

"What?" Will exclaimed.

"For goodness' sake. And you went after them yourselves?" Grandma Jones stopped midway through cleaning Caleb's injury with a damp cloth. "Good thing I didn't know. Why didn't you go for the sheriff?"

Jennie placed her elbows on the table and massaged at her forehead. Her head ached and she felt weighed down with weariness. "There wasn't time. I tracked their trail before I came to the church. I figured if Caleb and I hurried, we could find the cattle."

Will flipped around a chair and sat down, his arms resting against the back. "How'd you get 'em?"

"Caleb pretended to be traveling in the area." She looked over at Caleb, careful to guard her expression. "While he distracted the three cowhands, I drove off the cattle."

Grandma Jones shook her gray head in disbelief. "No one was hurt?"

"Just Caleb's ear," Jennie said. Perhaps God had heard her awkward prayer for his safety, after all. "He didn't duck quite fast enough to dodge a bullet."

All three turned toward him.

"I'll be all right." Their attention brought a flush to his neck. "I just need some sleep."

Grandma Jones clucked her tongue. "You need a good deal more than that. The alcohol may sting some, but it'll help." Jennie's grandmother dabbed the liquid onto her rag and pressed it to his ear. Once she seemed certain the wound wouldn't get infected, Grandma Jones bandaged his ear with quick fingers and stood back.

"You're all done." She smiled.

Caleb gingerly touched the bandage. "Thank you." He climbed to his feet, then paused, seeming to remember something. "By the way, I found out who those cowhands were working for."

"Who?" Jennie questioned.

"A Mr. King."

Anger was Jennie's first reaction—one that was shared by Will, if the way he slapped his fist against his chair was any indication. Grandma Jones just looked shocked.

"You know him?" Caleb asked.

Grandma Jones nodded. "He's practically our neighbor."

"I should have known it was him," Jennie said, her voice strained from trying to hold in the fury she felt. "Whenever we see him in town, he's always asking how things are now that Pa's gone. He might even be the one who stole our calves last spring." At the time, she'd thought he was just another rancher who thought she couldn't handle it—couldn't run things now that her father was gone. Now she wondered if he was the one arranging things so that she *couldn't* hold them together, sabotaging her deliberately to make her fail, no matter how hard she tried.

"Now, Jennie." Her grandmother shook her head. "We don't know that for certain. Besides, Mr. King was here just the other day asking to talk to you about sharing water. Why would he come over if he planned to steal our cattle?"

"I don't know, but I still don't trust him."

"We ought to go to the sheriff," Caleb suggested. "Have the man arrested, or at least questioned, for cattle rustling."

"No," she said, more adamantly than she intended. All three of them stared in surprise at her. Involving the law would only make things worse, Jennie was sure of that. "I don't think that's wise." She made her voice more even. "We only have the word of his cowhands, since King wasn't actually a part of the theft. It would be our story against theirs." She scraped back her chair and stood. "And for that matter, they could have been lying. They said they worked for Mr. King, but they didn't have any proof, did they?"

"We shouldn't let him off." Will scowled.

Caleb nodded. "I agree with Will."

"Either course has its repercussions," Grandma Jones interjected. "By not going to the law, we're running the risk that it could happen again, which means we'll have to keep a better watch on the cattle. But accusing the man of something as serious as cattle rustling would definitely stir up trouble."

"Mr. King's a powerful man. If we accuse him without any proof, he could make this difficult for us. And we've got difficulties enough already. No real harm was done," Jennie added. "Well, except to Caleb."

"Thanks," Caleb muttered. He didn't seem pleased, but at least he didn't try to change her mind.

"I think we should be grateful we found the cattle," Jennie said, "and leave it at that."

"I agree with Jennie. The cows are back and we don't want to go ruffling feathers." Grandma Jones moved about the kitchen, putting away the supplies she'd used to mend Caleb's ear. "Now it's time for this old woman to turn in."

She ushered Caleb and the others from the kitchen and up the stairs. Jennie let out a sigh of relief that the day was nearly over. It was one of the most frightening, exhilarating and, ultimately, disheartening days she'd ever known. She would be very glad to put it behind her. But she tensed when she saw that Caleb had paused outside his room.

Was he going to make her talk about what had happened between them after all?

Caleb knew he couldn't go to sleep until he'd at least tried to make things right with Jennie. He hated the idea that he'd hurt her, however unintentionally. He hadn't been the one to instigate their kiss, but he hadn't refused her at first, either. Little wonder she felt hurt and confused by his behavior after their return. How could he make this right?

"Jennie?" he said as she passed by him.

She stopped, her attention on the floorboards. Grandma Jones threw them a questioning look and then disappeared into her room. Will continued on up the stairs to his room in the attic.

"Jennie, I didn't mean to—"

"Please, Caleb." Her voice wavered until she lifted her chin. The steeliness had returned to her eyes. "It was my mistake. I appreciate all your help, I really do. I'll be fine. Good night."

She crossed the landing and went into her room. Caleb stared at the shut door. He thought less of Liza the more time he spent with Jennie and he'd come to prize her friendship. It was nice talking to a woman again, making her smile. But that didn't mean he was ready for a more serious relationship. He couldn't risk caring that much for someone else. Not yet. Jennie would be fine, just like she'd told him. But somehow he still felt like he'd made the wrong move.

# Chapter Ten

Jennie tucked bean seeds into the small holes in the dirt Caleb had made with his stick. Pushing up her hat, she watched him working farther down the garden row. They'd both been quieter since rustling back her cattle, twelve days ago, less teasing, fewer smiles.

*If only I hadn't kissed him out on the range,* she told herself yet again. She had talked herself through the different reasons he'd spurned her. She was after all his employer, and he was still grieving the loss of his fiancée. Yet his rejection stung just the same.

Her poor grandmother had interpreted the awkwardness between Jennie and Caleb as something different—a sign they felt something more for each other but were too shy to act on it. The woman had been making not-so-subtle attempts to matchmake by having Jennie and Caleb work alone—like planting the garden. Will could have helped, but Grandma Jones had insisted he give her a hand in making a new batch of soap, a task he loathed.

If only life were different. She bent and pressed another seed into the ground with a sigh. If she had met Caleb at church, if she didn't have the bank debt looming over her, maybe then they might have made something more of their friendship.

Thoughts of the debt reminded Jennie of the stage robbery tomorrow. She'd nearly forgotten about it in all the excitement of rustling back her cattle. She needed to contrive a way to get to town. Sitting back on her heels, she stared unseeing across the garden.

"Something wrong?"

Startled from her thoughts, Jennie glanced up. Caleb watched her closely, one elbow resting on the top of his stick.

"No." She lowered her chin and placed the seeds into the next hole. "Just thinking."

"About?" he prodded. Out of the corner of her eye, Jennie saw him return to his job, stamping his stick into the soft dirt.

"I think I'm going to town tomorrow." She did her best to keep her voice nonchalant, even bored. "We need more seeds, and perhaps I'll see about finding something new to wear...to church."

The words were out before she could stop them, but did she really want to go again? Her grandmother and Will had shared with her how kind everyone had been, and their acceptance back into the congregation had stirred wants inside Jennie—a longing to be a part of something normal and inclusive.

Caleb's face brightened into a genuine smile—the first she'd seen in days. "You'll come with us on Sunday?"

"Not this week, but soon," she hedged. Her stomach still twisted at the thought of being inside the building for more than a few minutes. Not even a new hair ribbon or comb would cure that.

"You still worried about what people will think?"

"They weren't exactly welcoming the other week."

"No one knew what was going on with your cattle—they were just trying to listen." Caleb set down his stick and removed his hat to wipe his brow with his sleeve. "What do you say to taking a rest? A short one?" he added, a teasing glint to his blue eyes.

Jennie nodded, grateful to see him acting more like he had his first week at the ranch. She missed having him around as a friend, not just hired help. She followed him to the shade beside the barn where they sat with their backs against the weathered wood. Jennie took off her hat and used it to fan her flushed cheeks. The coolness of the shadows brought relief from the hot sun.

Caleb fiddled with his hat brim. "What do you think people are gonna say if you come with us some Sunday?"

"You don't beat around the bush, do you?"

"Don't usually see a reason to." He smiled, but the reaction was short. "It might help to share what's on your mind."

Setting her hat beside her, she stared at the hills in the distance. Would it help to share her burden or would reopening the wound be too much to bear?

"It isn't what they'll say now, but what they said right after my mother left." She swallowed hard, hoping to dislodge the lump sprouting in her throat. "Looking back I realize she was unhappy. There were days I'd find her on the porch, staring at nothing. I took over more of her responsibilities, like caring for Will and helping my father. But nothing seemed to make her happier."

Jennie sniffed back the tears that stung in her eyes, afraid they might spill over anyway. "One day, I went out on the porch and she wasn't alone. A neighbor and his wife were waiting in front of the house in their wagon. My mother's suitcase was sitting on the steps beside her."

A traitorous drop of moisture slid down her cheek. Caleb lifted his hand and wiped the tear away with his thumb.

"What happened next?" he asked.

Jennie exhaled a long breath. "She apologized half a dozen times, kissed us all goodbye and left. Later we found a note that said she'd gone to her sister's back East." She studied a smudge of dirt on her trousers. "None of us really understood why she left, especially Will. Grandma Jones kept telling us that she wasn't well and maybe she'd come back once she got better. But she never did.

"After the shock wore off a little, we went to church again. I wanted to see my friends, return to something normal. But someone had already spread nasty rumors." She cringed as the ugly insinuations leaped to her mind. The passing of eight years hadn't dulled the memory one bit. "My friends told me they'd heard my mother had some secret lover and my father had been cruel to her. Apparently everyone believed that those were her reasons for leaving."

"And you believed them?" The question held only curiosity, not accusation.

"Not at first."

Jennie tightened her hands into fists. She dug her nails into the flesh of her palms to keep her emotions from boiling over into greater resentment, or worse, more tears.

"I never questioned my father's love for her—you could see it in his eyes whenever she came into the room.

And yet, after a while I started to wonder if she really had a secret life. I even asked my father about it." She shook her head, tasting the regret in her mouth. "I can't imagine what pain my question caused him, but his response shocked me even more. 'I wish that were the reason, Jennie girl. That would be easier to swallow than the truth.' But he never told me what the truth was."

Slowly she uncurled her fists and peered down at the tiny marks from her nails. They were raw and tinged with blood but so small when compared to the marks left on her heart.

"Over time I forced myself to believe the nasty lies about her." Her voice rose in pitch as the pain washed over her anew. "It made things easier, gave me the anger I needed to survive. If I believed what they'd said, then I didn't have to face what I suspected was the truth."

"Which is?"

"That she left because of me." Jennie choked on a sob. "Maybe I didn't help her enough or maybe I helped her too much. Either way, I must have made it hard for her to…to…love me." Turning her face, she swiped at her tears with the back of her hand, but they were coming too fast. A strong arm wrapped around her shoulders, drawing her to him, and she buried her face in Caleb's shirt as she wept.

When she had no more tears, she lifted her head. Her eyes were dry, but her cheeks were warm with embarrassment. She scooted away from Caleb's protective arm. "That's why I haven't been back to church and why I worry about going again." She'd never told anyone the truth about her mother before.

"I'm sorry, Jennie. I can't imagine going through something like that at a young age." Caleb set his hat on his raised knee, his brow furrowed. "I do have to disagree with one thing, though."

Unsure she'd heard him right, she gaped in shock. "I'm not asking if you agreed. You wanted to know what I was worried about, and I told you."

Jennie scrambled to her feet, but he grasped her arm and pulled her gently back down beside him. "Hold on. Hear me out. I only meant to say I think you're wrong about being hard to love."

She struggled against his grip, but his hand stayed firm. "How would you know?"

"Because your grandmother cares about you and your brother cares about you..." Had his face gone a bit red? "And well...I care about you, too."

He released her arm and locked gazes with her, freeing butterflies in her middle, despite the somber topic. "Your mother's leaving likely had nothing to do with you. You were just a child, Jennie. Don't let her mistakes dictate who you are or what you do."

"Maybe you're right."

"About time you admitted that out loud." He stood and offered her his hand. She allowed him to help her up. "You're strong and caring. Don't let anyone make you think otherwise."

"Thank you...Caleb."

With a nod, he put on his hat. "Back to work."

She walked beside him to the garden and resumed planting the seeds they had on hand, but she couldn't help shooting glances at Caleb as he worked.

Could he feel a bit more than friendship for her, something more than obligation as her cowhand, even after rejecting her kiss? Deep down she hoped so, though her practical self argued with her heart. His friendship, how-

ever comforting and exciting, wouldn't save her ranch
or clear her debt. Only she could do that.

Jennie encountered little opposition about making the
trip to Beaver alone. She had assigned enough tasks to
Caleb and Will to keep them busy and Grandma Jones
had begged off coming, saying she wanted to start sew-
ing a new skirt.

She arrived in town with enough time to buy the
seeds they needed before starting on her long ride to
the bandits' hideout. Turning onto Main Street, Jennie
slowed Dandy to a casual gait as she observed the activ-
ity on the street. Shopkeepers swept their front stoops,
men called greetings to one another from the wagons and
horses shuffling past, women hung laundry on bushes or
lines and young children played about their feet.

She guided Dandy toward the general store and dismounted. Before she could tie up her horse, Jennie's
neck prickled with the unsettling sensation she was
being watched—intently. She peered over her shoulder at a group of women bustling down the street, but
they seemed to be ignoring her. Thankfully she'd worn
a dress instead of her breeches to be less conspicuous.

Turning in the opposite direction, she saw a cowboy hitching his palomino pony to the post outside the
saloon. His short stature drew her attention. When he
darted a quick glance at her, Jennie looked away, embarrassed to be caught staring. Perhaps she'd given too
much weight to Nathan's warning that the bandits would
be watching for her today.

She tied Dandy to the hitching post and entered the
coolness of the mercantile. She maneuvered her way
through the assortment of home goods and tools to the

far end of the counter where seeds of all kinds were displayed.

"Can I help you, miss?" A man wearing a long white apron and wire spectacles smiled as Jennie approached.

She pointed at the seed display. "I'll take two packets each of cucumbers, carrots, beets and potatoes."

"Certainly." The storekeeper began pulling the seeds off the shelf.

Lifting the flap of her saddlebag, Jennie reached inside for her money. Her fingers grasped a folded piece of paper, and she pulled it into the light. A single word was scribbled across the front in unfamiliar handwriting: *Jennie.* It had to be from Caleb.

She set her bag on the counter, her pulse racing. What would he possibly need to say in writing that he couldn't say in person? Would he say something more about her stolen kiss? Would he confess he liked her?

She opened the paper with trembling fingers and three dollars slipped onto the counter. Picking them up, Jennie stared wide-eyed at the cash, then she read the words scrawled on the page.

This money is for you to buy a new dress for church. I don't want you to repay me. Find something you like.
Caleb

"I say, miss, are you feeling all right?"

Jennie blinked. She'd forgotten the storekeeper was even there.

"Oh, yes. I'm fine," she said. A feeling of light-headedness washed over her and she gripped the counter. "Actually, I think I could use a chair and a glass of water."

He bobbed his head and hurried around the counter to her side. Jennie held on to his arm as he led her toward the back of the store. Several chairs crowded the black stove. Jennie sank into the closest one, the money and letter still clutched in her hand.

"I'll get you some water."

Jennie nodded and shut her eyes, hoping to clear her head. *I can handle swindling armed robbers of their stolen loot and I can practically run the ranch single-handed. But I get faint over the generosity of one handsome young man.*

Releasing a mirthless laugh, she opened her eyes and read the letter a second time. Caleb's thoughtfulness and the idea of something new to wear left her stomach fluttering with anticipation.

She didn't have time to order a new dress, not if she planned to be at the bandits' hideout before they left. Then again, the money in her hand might be put to better use for the ranch. If she returned home empty-handed, though, she would have to either lie about her reasons for not buying something or divulge her financial troubles to Caleb. She didn't want to do either, fearing he would read the truth on her face.

Resting her elbows on her knees, she dropped her head into her palms and groaned. What could she do? She felt like a horse being jerked one way and then another by a lead rope.

*What if I simply pass on this job?*

Jennie sat straight up in the chair, some of the tension and light-headedness disappearing with the thought. Her loan wasn't due in full for another four months—plenty of time to get the $850 she still owed before she lost the ranch. Nathan could easily find two lucrative jobs before

August. Besides, if she was being watched, a simple trip to town for supplies and a new dress might convince the bandits she'd given up her thieving ways.

"Here you go, miss." The storekeeper handed her a cup. "You look like you're feeling better."

"I am." Jennie swallowed the cool well water. Handing back the cup, she stood. "I'll pay for those seeds now."

"Of course."

The man followed her to the main part of the store. He placed her seeds beside the cash register. Jennie lifted her neglected saddlebag and placed the money and note into one of the interior pockets. After purchasing her seeds, she left the general store.

Outside, she paused to locate a suitable dressmaker's shop along the street. To her surprise, the short cowboy she'd been staring at earlier sat in one of the rocking chairs outside the saloon, watching her. The moment their eyes locked, he yanked his hat over his eyes and appeared to be sleeping.

Was it just coincidence? Shrugging off the unsettled feeling creeping up her spine, Jennie darted into the roadway between two wagons and onto the opposite side of the street. A whitewashed sign over one of the buildings read Miss Felicity's Tailoring Shop. A tremor of girlish excitement leaped inside Jennie at the thought of something to wear besides faded dresses and men's trousers.

Inside the shop, bolts of fabric—deep blues, mint-greens and butter-yellows—spread over chairs, a table and several dress dummies. A smartly attired woman met her at the door, a tape measure hanging about her neck.

"What can I do for you, miss?" She sized up Jennie.

Jennie flushed, conscious of the patched calico she wore. She'd never ordered a dress before. "I need a new dress." She lifted her chin. "Something suitable for church and special occasions."

The woman smiled. "I think I have just the thing to go with those beautiful brown eyes of yours." She waved Jennie into a vacant chair and headed into a small room at the rear of the shop. A moment later, the seamstress returned holding a dress of rich brown draped over her arm. "I finished this last week, but the woman who wanted it changed her mind."

Reaching out, Jennie touched a corner of the silk material. The brown dress was edged in cream-colored ruffles. "It's gorgeous," she murmured, wondering if she had enough to pay for it.

"See how it forms a slight bustle in back? Very stylish." The woman spun the dress around to show Jennie. "It might be a little big for you in the waist, but I can take it in." She reverently laid the gown over a nearby dressing screen, calling over her shoulder, "Come try it on, honey, so we can see how it fits."

Jennie ducked behind the screen to change. She gladly slipped off her own dress and pulled the smooth silk over her head and shoulders. Glancing down at her figure, she could tell the woman had been right about the size. She swished the skirt like a bell.

"How does it fit?" the seamstress asked.

Jennie stepped around the screen and curtsied. "Rather well, I think."

The woman laughed. "Ah, you've fallen in love with it." She adjusted the seams at Jennie's waist and arms and fastened some pins into the proper places. "I'll take a little in here…and here. Then it ought to fit like a glove. You can come for it this afternoon."

"How much will it cost?" Jennie held her breath, her fingers toying with one of the cream cuffs.

The dressmaker pursed her lips in thought. "With the adjustments I'd say $2.75."

Jennie exhaled, her shoulders drooping slightly. She'd hoped for a new hat, too. Running a hand over the dress, she knew she'd never find anything so lovely.

"I'll take it."

She stepped behind the screen and changed back into her drab gown. This time she didn't care quite so much about the state of her appearance. She would have a beautiful dress before the day was over.

She handed the dress to the woman with a promise to return. Once outside, Jennie surveyed the other shops. She was rarely in town long enough to study the options. Down the way stood the saloon where the cowboy in the chair still appeared to be napping.

Relieved, Jennie decided to cross the street so she wouldn't have to walk past him. She hurried at her usual pace until she remembered she had the whole day to wander. When she spotted a millinery shop, she stopped and lingered in front of the window. She thought of Caleb's words: *Find something you like.* And that something was a new hat for her dress. With a little money left over after buying the seeds, she hoped she might find a nice, simple one for less than a dollar.

Determined, she walked into the shop and viewed the stunning creations bursting with flowers and feathers. She breathed in the smell of straw and new cloth. Tears came to her eyes at the memory of the stylish hats her father had purchased for her. How many times had he come into a shop like this, excited to find a millinery treasure for her?

One of several customers, Jennie had time to browse uninterrupted among the shop's wares. A green velvet hat captivated her interest, and she reached out to stroke the luxurious fabric. Upon seeing the price card, she forced herself to peruse the modest straw bonnets. When she discovered she couldn't afford any of them either, she headed to the box of leftover trimmings.

Jennie rifled through the contents and found a long piece of gold ribbon and three tiny brown flowers. She could use them to make over one of her old bonnets into something new and no one need know differently.

She took the trimmings to the counter.

"Twenty-five cents," the young female clerk said.

She waited while the girl wrapped her purchases in brown paper. Tucking the package under her arm, Jennie left the shop. Her stomach rumbled with hunger. She'd brought along jerky and bread for her trip, but the nearby hotel advertised fresh pie.

With her remaining coins from the mercantile, she purchased a glass of milk and a slice of pie for twenty cents. Jennie gobbled up the sweet treat as she watched the passersby through the window.

She hadn't been sitting long when the cowboy from the saloon strolled past the window. Jennie thought nothing of it until he turned and saw her through the glass. He stopped and his eyes widened with recognition at the same moment hers did. From the brief glance she'd had of the men who rustled her cattle and Caleb's description of them later, she knew this man was the short cowhand who worked for Mr. King.

Jennie jumped up from her chair, prepared to go outside and confront him, but the cowboy sprinted down the street away from the hotel. Unnerved, she sat down and forced herself to finish the last few bites of her pie. This time the treat tasted less scrumptious.

Why would Mr. King's cowhand be following her? Why did her neighbor care how she spent her time? Was he waiting for her to be away from home so that he could go after her cattle again? For a moment, she considered leaving the dress behind and heading straight back to the ranch, but she forced herself to sit still. She trusted Caleb and Will to look after everything in her absence.

When she left the hotel, she searched the street for any sign of the cowboy. She couldn't see him anywhere. Hoping the whole incident had been some bizarre coincidence, she returned to the dress shop. Inside, the woman was spreading a large sheet of wrapping paper on a table.

"It will fit better now." She smiled and lifted the gown for Jennie to see.

"Thank you. Your work is amazing."

The dressmaker beamed as she wrapped up the dress and handed it to Jennie. "Do you have a beau?" she asked after Jennie paid for the gown. "He'll be dreamy-eyed for days after he sees you wearing this. See if I am right." She laughed.

"I'll count on it," Jennie said, smiling. She moved slowly back up the street toward her horse. She imagined the admiration she hoped to see on Caleb's face when she modeled the dress for him and her family. She frowned a little and reminded herself that Caleb didn't see her that way. He was kind to her, protective, even generous. But loving her was clearly something he had never even considered.

Just as she reached her horse, she remembered with

all the excitement of the new dress she'd forgotten to post the letter Caleb had given her for his family. She'd nearly given in to the temptation to open it, curious if he'd written anything about her, but she didn't feel right about prying into his personal affairs.

"I'll be right back, Dandy," she muttered, shifting the parcels in her arms to give the horse a reassuring pat on the nose. "I won't be long."

She walked back to the hotel.

"Back so soon?" the proprietress asked. "Would you like more pie?"

Jennie blushed. "No, thank you. I forgot to post a letter." She handed Caleb's letter to the woman, along with the money for postage.

"Would you like me to see if any mail has come for you?"

She nodded, though she didn't expect anything. Her grandmother occasionally received a letter, but Jennie rarely did. "It would be for Jennie or Aurelia Jones."

"One moment." The woman entered a small room off the main entryway.

As Jennie waited, she hugged the bundle in her arms to her chest. A new dress and new trimmings for a hat. Much better than dealing with foolhardy bandits. In spite of the strange encounter with the cowboy, she'd thoroughly enjoyed her outing to town and almost wished she had a reason to stay longer.

"There are two letters for you, miss." The hotel proprietress handed them to Jennie.

She thanked her, added the letters to her pile and stepped out of the hotel. When she reached Dandy's side again, she stuck the letters between her teeth as she stowed away her other purchases for the ride home.

Once her hands were free, she studied the letters. The first was for Grandma Jones. Jennie recognized the name of a long-time friend written on the back. The other was addressed to her. Curious, she turned over the envelope. The words *Albert Dixon* brought a deep frown.

*What does he want now?* She tore open the letter and drew out the paper, forcing herself to take a steadying breath. Perhaps the bank president had come to his senses and forgiven her debt—or at least extended the deadline.

Hoping for good news, Jennie unfolded the letter. To her surprise, the date at the top read only two days earlier.

Dear Miss Jones,
In light of circumstances both difficult and unforeseen for our banking establishment, I regret that I must change the date for which the total balance of your debt is required. Your debt must now be paid in full by the first of June in the year of our Lord 1870 or we will be forced to foreclose on your loan.
Regrettably,
Albert Dixon, bank president

"No, no!" Jennie crushed the letter in her fist. The new deadline gave her less than five weeks. Five weeks to come up with nearly a thousand dollars—an impossible task.

"What do I do? What do I do?" she moaned, pressing her head against the worn leather of her saddle. Panic brought the taste of bile to her throat and she clapped a hand over her mouth to keep from retching.

She'd been a fool to buy the dress and a meal in town instead of going after the bandits' stolen money. Even if another robbery came along, it wasn't likely to pay what she needed, especially after she gave Nathan his half.

*Nathan.* Whirling around, Jennie hurried in the direction of the saloon, forgetting her horse and bags for the moment. She had to get another robbery job as soon as possible.

Jennie pushed her way through the saloon doors and paused, allowing her eyes to adjust to the smoky, dim light. Though midmorning, the place still held a large crowd of patrons. Men sat at tables, drinking and playing cards, or lounged at the bar beside one of several saloon girls. The stench of alcohol and unwashed bodies made her cover her nose and reminded her all too well of the last time she'd been here, when she'd hired Nathan.

"Where is he?" Jennie hissed under her breath as she searched the room, trying to identify the faces beneath the assortment of hats. In one corner, a man and a girl with too much rouge sat close, a bottle of something between them. The girl whispered something in his ear, and the man threw back his head in uproarious laughter. Jennie recognized Nathan at once and frowned. *So he fancies whichever pretty face is in front of him.*

Ignoring the catcalls and attention she drew from the other men as she crossed the room, she strode purposely to Nathan's table, determined to speak with him. He lifted his head as she approached his table.

"Done already?" He set down his shot glass and leaned back in his chair, chuckling. "You get faster every time."

Jennie shook her head. "I didn't go. That's why I need to talk to you." She threw a pointed glance at the saloon girl who was scowling at her. "Alone," she added.

Nathan's thick eyebrows drew together in annoyance and possible anger, but he nodded. "Excuse me," he said to the girl.

He took Jennie's elbow firmly in his hand and propelled her down a narrow hallway off the saloon's main room. Releasing her arm, he regarded her with a surly expression in his dark eyes. "What's so blasted important you skipped out on a perfectly good job? I needed that money, too, Jennie. You goin' soft on me?"

"No." She stared at her hands. "It doesn't matter why I didn't go. I came to see you because…I need another job." She lifted her head, silently pleading for his help. "The bank sent me a notice—they're calling my loan due. I have five weeks, Nathan. Five weeks to come up with the rest of the money or I lose my ranch."

He cursed beneath his breath. "Those rich folks think they can run other people's lives. That's why I say forget 'em, forget the cattle and come away with me."

Jennie bit back a comment about his lady friend waiting in the saloon. "Can you find me another job? I'll take anything."

"I'll try to hunt up something new. But there might not be another robbery for weeks. The job today came sooner than I'd expected."

He fingered a lock of her hair, but instead of exciting butterflies in her middle like Caleb's touch, Jennie felt only tension. She crossed her arms and stepped back.

"You sure you want to go to all this trouble to keep that dying ranch?" he asked.

Jennie's hands tightened into fists, but she forced herself to stay calm. She needed his support. "I won't let it go without a good fight."

Nathan laughed. "Well I'll give you credit for that, love."

"I don't need credit. I need money."

"Money's not the only reason I'm risking my hide for you, you know."

Jennie feigned interest in the wall beside her. Would he refuse to help her this time if she didn't agree to run away with him? Without Nathan's help she would have to hang around the saloon again, weaseling information about upcoming stage robberies from drunk and leering men. The thought made her stomach ache. What choice did she have, though? She wouldn't go with him.

"I'm sorry, Nathan." She drew herself up. "We want different things. So if you don't wish to help me any-more—"

"Our business ain't over yet. I'm makin' too good of money with you, Jennie Jones, to quit now. At least when you follow through."

She released her held breath. "Thank you, Nathan."

He sauntered past her into the main part of the saloon, a sure sign their conversation had ended. "I'll come as soon as I've found something," he said in a low voice before he resumed his seat beside the pouting bar girl.

Without making eye contact with anyone, Jennie wove her way through the maze of tables and out the saloon. She blinked as she stepped into the street, telling herself it was the bright sunlight and not threatening tears. She walked in a daze back to Dandy.

Untying his reins, she noticed her forgotten purchases hadn't been disturbed in her absence. Somewhere inside she felt relief, but the feeling quickly disappeared beneath numbing apathy. A new dress meant nothing when she faced the reality of losing everything she'd worked

# YOUR PARTICIPATION IS REQUESTED!

Dear Reader,

Since you are a lover of historical romance fiction – we would like to get to know you!

Inside you will find a short Reader's Survey. Sharing your answers with us will help our editorial staff understand who you are and what activities you enjoy.

To thank you for your participation, we would like to send you 2 books and 2 gifts – **ABSOLUTELY FREE!**

Enjoy your gifts with our appreciation,

*Pam Powers*

**SEE INSIDE FOR READER'S SURVEY**

# YOUR READER'S SURVEY
## "THANK YOU" FREE GIFTS INCLUDE:

▶ 2 Love Inspired® Historical books
▶ 2 surprise gifts

## PLEASE FILL IN THE CIRCLES COMPLETELY TO RESPOND

**1)** What type of fiction books do you enjoy reading? (Check all that apply)
- ○ Suspense
- ○ Inspirational Fiction
- ○ Modern-day Romances
- ○ Historical Romance
- ○ Humour
- ○ Mysteries

**2)** What attracted you most to the last fiction book you purchased on impulse?
- ○ The Title
- ○ The Cover
- ○ The Author
- ○ The Story

**3)** What is usually the greatest influencer when you <u>plan</u> to buy a book?
- ○ Advertising
- ○ Referral
- ○ Book Review

**4)** How often do you access the internet?
- ○ Daily
- ○ Weekly
- ○ Monthly
- ○ Rarely or never.

**5)** How many NEW paperback fiction novels have you purchased in the past 3 months?
- ○ 0 - 2
- ○ 3 - 6
- ○ 7 or more

**YES!** I have completed the Reader's Survey. Please send me the 2 FREE books and 2 FREE gifts (gifts are worth about $10) for which I qualify. I understand that I am under no obligation to purchase any books, as explained on the back of this card.

102/302 IDL FS65

FIRST NAME                    LAST NAME

ADDRESS

APT.#          CITY

STATE/PROV.    ZIP/POSTAL CODE

## The Reader Service — Here's How It Works:

and fought for over the past seven months. She settled herself into the saddle and guided Dandy down the street toward home—and her impending fate.

## Chapter Eleven

Seated in the saddle, Caleb rolled up his shirtsleeves and gave Saul a pat. "Sure is warm today, huh, boy?"

Most of the cattle rested in patches of shade, except for one that Caleb had rounded up twice already for straying too far. He removed his hat and used it to create a breeze. Out of the corner of his eye, he spied movement and turned toward the ranch a quarter mile away. Will rode toward him.

"Is it your turn?" Caleb called.

Will stopped his horse beside Saul. "Slow morning?"

"Mostly. Watch that one, though." Caleb pointed at the wandering cow with a glare. "Old cuss has made a bolt for it twice."

Will chuckled. "You're just too slow, old man. I'm gonna take a nap." He slouched in the saddle and pulled his hat low, feigning sleep.

"Then I'll come to your funeral once your sister gets finished with you." Caleb put his hat back on and pointed Saul in the direction of the ranch. "Did she say what she wanted me to do this afternoon?"

"Nope," Will said, tipping up his hat. "She's washing clothes in the yard, if you want to ask her."

Nodding, Caleb rode back to the ranch. He was pleased Jennie had started giving Will more responsibility. The boy had a knack with the cattle and he'd be a great help to his sister once Caleb left to start his business.

After giving Saul his feed and water, Caleb went in search of Jennie to ask what task she wanted him to start on next. He found her in the yard between the house and the barn, hanging wash on the clothesline. She stood with her back to him, her red hair falling loose past her shoulders today. Not for the first time, he wondered what her hair would feel like to the touch.

"Jennie," he said as he stepped closer.

She whirled around, her hand to her throat. "Caleb, you scared me."

"Sorry."

She'd been more distracted the past week and a half, ever since her trip into town. Instead of visiting with him and her family after supper, she would excuse herself and go outside alone. He'd gone to the door once and saw her leaning against the corral fence, her chin on her hands.

"Will's watching the cattle. What would you like me to do next?"

She shook her head as if to clear her thoughts. "Did you get lunch?"

"Your grandmother packed me something to eat."

"We could use some more wood."

"Chopping wood it is then." Caleb started to walk away, but he changed his mind and turned back. "Are you all right, Jennie? Not feeling sick or anything, are you?"

"No, no." She reached for one of Will's shirts and pinned it to the line. "I'm fine, really. Just a lot on my mind. Things will be better soon, I'm sure of it."

With a nod, he left, unsure what more to say. Her words sounded positive, but he sensed the hope missing from them. Maybe her concerns were money related. He knew the ranch wasn't anywhere near thriving like it once had been. Not for the first time, he considered giving Jennie the money he'd saved so far. Then she could buy more cattle and food and hired help.

He dismissed the thought almost as quickly as it came. Jennie wouldn't accept his help. He'd been surprised she'd used the money he had given her for a new dress. No, it was better that he kept that money. He needed it for his business, for the chance to start fresh somewhere and build a life for himself.

Caleb located an ax in the barn and went to the dwindling woodpile. He placed a piece of wood on top of the nearby chopping block and swung down the ax. The log split in half and he tossed the pieces onto the pile.

Sweat soon dripped down his neck and chest, but he reveled in the hard labor, something he missed when he was just sitting on his horse watching over the cattle.

At the sound of an approaching horse, Caleb lowered his ax. Was there a problem with the herd? But it wasn't Will riding toward the ranch. The rider was taller and Caleb didn't recognize the horse.

Should he move closer to Jennie? In all the weeks he'd been here, the family had never had a visitor. Will's words from Caleb's first night at the ranch repeated in his mind: *The only man that's come around recently just talks to Jennie...he seems a bit rough, though.* Could this be the stranger Will had been talking about?

Frowning, Caleb took a defensive step toward the horse and rider. "Howdy," he said, keeping his voice light, friendly.

"Afternoon." The stranger tipped his hat at Caleb, but he nudged his horse past him.

Something about the man's black eyes and square face sparked familiarity in Caleb's memory, but he couldn't think where he would have met him. Certainly not in the saloons the stranger likely frequented.

"Is there something *we* can do for you?" Caleb called after him, annoyed at the man's presumptuous attitude.

He pulled back on the reins and twisted in the saddle to peer down at Caleb. "You are…"

"The family's hired help. And you'd be?"

"Here to carry out some business with Miss Jones." The stranger turned and resumed riding toward the house.

Fighting the urge to follow, Caleb forced himself to pick up his ax and the next piece of wood. He kept watch, though, from the corner of his eye.

The man dismounted at the house and walked toward Jennie. When she saw him, her face registered surprise and something else. Relief, delight? She led him around to the back of the house, out of sight. Caleb frowned. It wasn't his business who the stranger was or what his dealings were with Jennie, and yet, he couldn't squelch the protectiveness he felt for her and her family.

*Is she kissing him, too?* he wondered. The possibility brought a twinge of jealousy, something he hadn't felt in years. He shook his head at his foolishness. Jennie wasn't his girl. Maybe he'd been working too long in the sun.

He reached into his pocket to pull out his bandanna. His fingers brushed the slip of paper he'd used to practice writing his note to Jennie. It reminded him of another paper he'd kept in his pocket for months until he gave up bounty hunting. Now it resided in his saddle-bag up in his room. He'd memorized the wanted-poster's contents long ago—the bearded face and dark eyes, the names *Otis Nathan Blaine* or *Black-Eyed Blaine*.

Caleb stared at the corner of the house where the stranger and Jennie had disappeared. The two men had some similarities, like their dark eyes and rough appearance. Should he be worried? But no, how could they be the same person? This man was clearly someone Jennie knew, and surely she wouldn't be associating with a wanted stage thief.

Removing his bandanna, Caleb wiped his face and neck, then resumed his work. His shirtfront was wet with perspiration by the time the stranger returned to his horse and rode away.

Caleb kept chopping wood, though curiosity nearly drove him to find Jennie and ask her what was going on. He refrained, though, not wanting to get her ire up again for treading where he shouldn't. She'd been unusually quiet the past week, but he preferred that to having her fired-up angry at him.

"Would you like a drink?"

He looked up to see Jennie holding a water bucket and ladle. "That'd be nice. Thank you."

He accepted the ladle and drank the entire thing. The water felt delicious on his dry throat. He passed back the ladle and she filled it again.

"You've got quite the pile of wood already. You're faster at that than I am at the washing."

Caleb dumped the water over his head and shook it from his hair. "It helped that I didn't have a visitor," he said dropping the ladle into her bucket. He regretted the words at once, but she didn't lash back at him. Instead she blushed.

"Yes, well, that was unexpected."

He waited for her to say more, but she didn't. "Just be careful, Jennie."

"What do you mean?" Her brown eyes narrowed, and the old expression of mistrust flitted across her pink cheeks.

"Be sure he treats you right. You deserve that."

Now her face went crimson. "Not that it's any of your business, but that man is not my beau. He's helping me with a financial venture. It should pull the ranch out of its poverty, if all goes well."

Relief filled his gut at her words, despite exciting her temper again. "What is it?"

"I'd like to see if it works out before I say anything— to anyone."

Caleb respected that. "I'm glad to hear you might be able to make this place great again. It would be something to see."

"Do I detect a fondness for cattle ranching?" she asked, her question full of amusement. She hadn't bantered with him like this in days and he'd missed it.

"Not a chance. I'd rather take bounty on a bunch of smelly bandits than a branding iron to a bunch of cows."

She laughed. "What do you know about taking bounty?"

Too late Caleb realized his slip. "Thanks for the water. I ought to finish up with this wood."

"Caleb?" The merriment on her face died at once. "What do you know about taking bounty?" she repeated.

Running a hand through his damp hair, he blew out

his breath in frustration. He didn't want to recall those days. "It doesn't matter now. That job's over."

"Y-you were a bounty hunter?" She matched his steps back to the woodpile, the bucket still in hand. "You didn't tell me this when I asked about your other jobs."

Why did she sound so upset?

"I didn't see the need. I quit that job long before we met." He picked up another piece of wood and set it on the chopping block.

"How come?"

"Does it really matter?" He didn't bother hiding his frustration as he grabbed up the ax. Jennie stood rooted to her spot near his elbow, her chin lifted in stubbornness. Apparently she wasn't going anywhere. Had he really admired her tenacity earlier? "I shot someone, all right?"

"Don't you have to do that sometimes as a bounty hunter?"

"Not necessarily. A good bounty hunter should never have to kill anyone. You're just supposed to bring the crooks in." The images of that day rolled over him again and he pushed aside his piece of wood to sit on the chopping block. He stared at the ax in his grip. "I killed a man. It was ruled self-defense by the sheriff, but I stopped after that. I never want to be in that position again. That's why I keep my guns unloaded in my holster. It might seem foolish, but it's to remind me never to rob another man of his life, however ill spent. I still relive that day in my nightmares."

Jennie set down her bucket and knelt in front of him. She looked as though she might touch his arm, but she lowered her hand back to her side just as quickly.

"Is that what you were dreaming about—that night on the range?" she asked.

He nodded. Her eyes were almost on the same level as his and he found himself gazing into those dark depths. He hadn't told anyone his reason for quitting his job as a bounty hunter, not even his parents. What was it about Jennie that made him share it with her?

"You're a good man, Caleb."

He shrugged off her compliment. If he'd truly been a good man back then, he wouldn't have let hatred and vengeance rule his life so completely. The death of that bandit had brought him up short and helped him find God again, find greater peace with Liza's death.

"I'm trying—just like all of us. Going to church helps a lot."

Jennie stood and hoisted the water bucket. "In that case, maybe I'd better go with you this Sunday," she said in a rush, her eyes focused on the dirt at her feet.

His eyebrows shot up. "Really?"

She banged his leg with the bucket, sloshing water onto his boot. "Don't act so surprised or I might change my mind."

Climbing to his feet, Caleb smiled. "So you coming or not?"

"I'll go," she said, returning his smile. "I'm always up for a challenge."

He laughed at hearing his own words turned against him. Jennie walked away and Caleb placed his wood back on the block. He whistled a tune as he added to the woodpile, feeling happier than he'd been in a long time.

After dressing with care in her new brown silk, Jennie stepped out of the house Sunday morning to go to church with the family. The nerves in her stomach nearly made her bolt upstairs and hide in her room, but Caleb was sure to drag her back outside, even kicking and screaming.

She fiddled with her hands, her skirt, her fingernails the entire ride into town, her anxiety too great to make conversation with Caleb and her family. Thankfully the others seemed to understand the source of her quiet and didn't press her to talk.

Would the people at church remember her—or worse, her mother? Would they accept Jennie as readily as they'd accepted her brother and grandmother? As the church came into sight, Jennie struggled to breathe normally.

"You look real nice in your dress," Caleb said when he helped her down from the wagon. He extended his elbow to her, and after a brief hesitation, she linked her arm through his.

She kept her chin up in feigned confidence as she took a seat beside Caleb and the family in one of the middle pews. The meeting started soon after, and Jennie found her jitters returning full force. Could she make it through the entire meeting? She chewed her thumbnail as the opening hymn started. Caleb nudged her with his shoulder and pointed at her mouth. She flushed and dropped her hand to her lap, but she was still too filled with nervous energy to sing.

When it was time for the pastor to speak, Jennie sat up straight and tried to concentrate. But as he entreated the congregation to love their neighbors, she felt a flash of irritation. As if any of the people here had showed any love or concern for her family in the past few years. They'd all but forgotten the Joneses.

Turning her head, she stole glances at those across the aisle from her. Several of the families were familiar. A few stared back, suspicion plain on their faces. Most of those who met her eye, though, did so with curious but friendly expressions.

At last the pastor finished his sermon and announced the final hymn, one of her father's favorites. The throaty tones of the small organ filled the room as a middle-aged woman rose to lead the group in song. Caleb extended an open hymnal toward her, and Jennie took the other end. Their fingers touched beneath the book before they both scooted their hands to the outside edges.

This time she sang along with the rest of the congregation, enjoying Caleb's deep baritone and her grandmother's sweet soprano. The music and the singing rose in volume with each verse, and something inside Jennie responded.

A feeling of love and warmth began at her heart and spread outward, reminding her of the way she'd felt when her father would sing or play his harmonica for them at night. How she missed him and his music. If she could see him, talk to him, would he praise her efforts to save the ranch he loved or would he lament her decisions?

Tears of regret blurred the words on the page, and her throat could no longer sing out the notes. Jennie passed the hymnal to Caleb and clasped her hands together as she pushed at the worn, wood floor with the toe of her boot. She was a hypocrite, judging her neighbors for their past actions when her present ones were perhaps just as erroneous.

The pressure of Caleb's hand on top of hers caused her to look up.

"I'm glad you came," he said softly. To her disappointment, he released his gentle grip.

His words brought the blossom of hope inside her. She could still make things right—once the ranch was safe. Maybe then she could find a way to pay the rightful owners what she'd taken from the bandits.

When the song ended, the chorister took her seat and the congregation bowed their heads for prayer. Jennie wished they could sing again. She wanted to keep the warm feeling inside her a little longer.

Once the meeting ended, Jennie headed for the door, the other three following behind. She tried to push her way gently through the throng, but more than one hand reached out to stop her progress.

"Jennie Jones. It's so good to see you." Jennie recognized the young woman but couldn't remember her name. She held a baby on her hip and wore a smile.

"How you and your brother have grown," an older woman added.

"We're glad you joined your family at meeting this week."

Jennie peered into the friendly faces, too overwhelmed to speak.

"We hoped you'd come back to us."

"Who is this fine-looking young man?"

A hand closed over her elbow. "I'm Caleb Johnson. I work at the ranch."

With a smile to the crowd, Caleb guided Jennie out of the church and down the front steps. "I'm sorry if you wanted to stay. You just looked like you could use some air." Only when they reached the wagon did he let go of her arm.

He had been more solicitous the past while—first

with the money for her dress and now the way he held her arm or touched her hand. Did he regret his rejection of her kiss? Did she want him to? The more she came to know Caleb, the more she admired and cared about him. She hated to think of him leaving the ranch for good in a few months. But she also knew that a man who valued his faith as strongly as Caleb could never understand or forgive the things she'd done to hold on to the ranch. The thing she'd do again, if she could.

"Thank you, for your help back there," she said, leaning against the side of the wagon.

"Was the meeting as bad as you'd imagined?"

She shook her head as she watched Will and Grandma Jones standing in different groups talking with what appeared to be new friends. "Everyone seems happy to see us."

"You may still find one or two who insist on dredging up the past, but those are the ones you just ignore."

Jennie opened her mouth to protest. She'd told Caleb what horrible things members of the congregation had said. How could she ignore people like that? The memory that he, too, had wrestled with hurts in the past stilled her anger.

"It took courage to come today, Jennie." He reached up to brush a strand of hair back beneath her bonnet, his blue eyes dark with intensity. Jennie reminded herself to breathe. "Just remember the only person whose opinion really matters is God's. I don't doubt He cares a great deal for you."

"How can you be so sure?" The question came out demanding, unbelieving and broke the intimacy of the moment. But she was glad she'd asked it. Did God really care what happened to her and her family? God hadn't stopped her from losing her mother—twice—or her father. How could she believe that a God who allowed all that to happen wanted her to be happy?

Caleb turned around and rested his arms on the rim of the wagon bed. His answer came so softly that Jennie had to step closer to be sure she heard him. "It's like that song—I was lost and now I'm found." He gave a self-deprecating laugh. "That was me, three years ago. I was lost in grief and anger, but after killing that bandit, I woke up, so to speak. I realized God hadn't gone anywhere after Liza's death—I was the one who'd put the distance between us. When I was ready, He was waiting, ready to take my burden away if I let Him." He twisted to look at her. "He can do the same for you."

The sincerity of his declaration had the same effect as the song, bringing hope to Jennie's troubled heart. Maybe he was right. There were still too many complications to figure out such things for herself right then, but Jennie could admit the morning hadn't been as bad as she'd anticipated. For once she had made the right decision.

Now if only she could save the ranch. It was all she had left—she couldn't lose it. Not if there was any way to hold on. And when she'd done whatever needed to be done, she could only hope that God, and Caleb, would forgive her.

# Chapter Twelve

T hough supper had been over for some time, Caleb
wasn't ready to head to bed. For now, he just wanted to
sit around the table with the family and relish the end of
a very good day. The church service had been edifying,
even more so with Jennie there, and he'd enjoyed two
slices of Grandma Jones's delicious spice cake. Jennie,
Will and their grandmother didn't seem in a hurry to
leave the kitchen, either.

"I'd like to go to Fillmore—tomorrow," Jennie announced during a lull in the conversation about the
warmer weather and the cattle.

"What for?" Grandma Jones asked.

Jennie's cheeks tinged pink, though Caleb wasn't sure
why. "About finances for the ranch."

Caleb leaned forward and rested his arms on the table.
"Are you going alone?"

"We can't spare you or Will," Jennie said. "Not when
the cattle need watching during the day and rounding
up into the corral at night. I've gone up there alone before. I'll be all right."

He wanted to remind her about their encounter with

the thugs on the trail before he'd come to the ranch, but he couldn't, not in front of her family. He didn't doubt Jennie's abilities to handle herself, though he wasn't keen on the idea of her traveling alone. But what could he say? He was only their hired hand.

Grandma Jones patted Jennie's hand. "Promise me you'll be careful, Jennie girl."

"I will, Grandma." Uneasiness flitted over Jennie's face, but Caleb shook off the observation. Likely her nervousness stemmed from whatever financial meeting she had planned. "I'll be back in four days. Can you get along without me until then?"

Caleb gave a deep sigh and eyed Will. "Whatdaya think, Will? Think we'll manage for a couple days without your sister?"

The boy grinned, then feigned a frown. "I don't know. I think those cows are plottin' a revolt."

Caleb smothered a laugh with a hand to his mouth. His sarcastic wit was clearly rubbing off on Jennie's brother.

Jennie glared at them both. "Very funny, you two. Just try not to get the cows rustled again in my absence."

"I take offense at that," Caleb said, arranging his face into a deadpan expression. "I lost a piece of my ear for those lousy cows. You think I'm gonna stand by and let them get stolen again—just to lose some limb this time? I don't think so."

Grandma Jones and Will chuckled, and finally Jennie's mouth broke into a smile. "You're impossible."

"I'll take that as a compliment." Caleb tipped his head. "What I don't understand is how Will here can get those cows to stay still. I'm always having to ride after one or two that get it in their thick heads to run for the hills."

"I play my harmonica." Will unearthed the instrument from his pocket.

"Play something for us," Grandma Jones requested. "It's been ages since we've heard any music."

Will put the harmonica to his lips and began to play a jaunty tune. Caleb tapped his feet in time to the music and Grandma Jones clapped her hands. After a minute, Caleb couldn't remain seated anymore. He pushed back his chair and stood.

"Would you care to dance, Mrs. Jones?"

Smiling, Grandma Jones nodded. Caleb led her around the table in a slow polka as Will continued to play.

A few turns later, Grandma Jones begged off. Will lowered the harmonica. "I'm not as young as I used to be, but thank you for the dance, young man. Why don't you join him, Jennie? Play another, Will."

Caleb threw Jennie a questioning glance. Would she dance with him or make up an excuse so she wouldn't have to? She had been more receptive to him today, taking his arm in hers before and after church. Holding his breath, Caleb held out his hand to her.

Jennie stood, her expression unreadable, but she allowed him to pull her into dancing position. Caleb exhaled as Will started another catchy song.

"You ready?" he asked Jennie.

She gave a wordless nod and he led her in a circle around the kitchen. He liked the feel of her small waist beneath his hand and the way her hair smelled of perfumed soap.

"It seems you can dance as well as you can shoot,"

she said, turning her head to look up at him with those big, brown eyes.

Time and sound seemed to slow. Caleb peered into her face and then at her parted lips. What would it be like to kiss her, not in a moment of fear or as her hired hand, but because they both cared for the other? The thought made his heart pound as hard and fast as their feet because he knew he *did* care for her. He'd never expected to want to love again after losing Liza, but then nearly everything about Jennie took him by surprise. There was nothing he could have done to prepare himself for her or the way she made him feel. Her beauty, her loyalty, her stubborn pride and fierce determination, her wonderful family, even her annoying cows had somehow won him over. But was he truly prepared to give love another try?

Without warning, his boot caught the corner of his chair as they rounded the table again and Caleb stumbled forward. He nearly dropped Jennie, but she managed to fall against the table with a laugh.

"Guess I'm still better at shooting." He rubbed the back of his warm neck. "Thank you for the dance, ladies. I think I'll step outside for a bit."

He hurried to the door. Behind him he heard light footsteps start to follow, but they stopped when Grandma Jones whispered, "Let him go."

Caleb welcomed the baptism of cold night air on his face as he walked outside and to the corral. The notes of another song could be heard from the direction of the kitchen. Placing one foot on the bottom rung of the fence, he rested his arms against the top and stared at the milling cattle.

Unbidden, Liza's face, framed in dark hair, appeared

in his mind. She and Jennie were as different in personality as they were in coloring.

Liza had always been drawn to people and get-togethers, while Jennie had struck Caleb as quiet and reserved, at least until he'd gotten to know her. Now he knew she could be as witty and teasing as him. And that rock-hard strength—that was what he respected the most. When she put her mind to something, she wouldn't give up.

Had she given up on the idea of them together? Part of him hoped not, but the other part cringed at the thought of caring for someone so deeply again. It had been three years. Could he open his heart to the possibility of pain and loss and love a second time?

He reached into his pocket and pulled out the wanted notice he'd fished from his saddlebag the other day. It was too dark now to see the face or type, but he'd memorized every detail anyway. He stared unseeing at the paper, feeling as though he held the last surviving shadow of his past. The notice represented all the grief and hate and vengeance that had driven him to be a bounty hunter. He'd made his peace with God about his actions, and yet, he'd kept this final reminder of all he'd lost—a love, a marriage, a family.

Shutting his eyes for a moment, Caleb opened them and blew out a long breath. Something deep inside him whispered it was time. He ripped the notice in half and then half again. When all that remained were tiny scraps of paper, he left the corral and walked north, past the house and barn. In the dark, he lifted his hand and let the pieces go. The wind whipped them into the air and scattered them like bits of snow over the sagebrush. The remnants of his past were gone.

Caleb headed back to the house, one of Will's songs rising to his lips. He whistled as he strode through the yard and up the porch. Music still came from inside, which meant maybe he could get another dance with Jennie.

After the stage rolled to a stop in Fillmore, much later than Jennie had anticipated, she rushed down the steps and in the direction of the saloon. According to Nathan's information, that was where the bandits would be lying low until midnight. She pulled her short jacket tighter around her body to keep out the chill of the evening air. The drop in temperature and the dark clouds smearing the sky signaled a good storm and made it seem much later than suppertime.

With her fingers gripped tightly around her purse, her pistol inside, she pushed through the saloon doors. Her entrance went largely unnoticed in the crowded room except for the men at the closest tables who grinned lewdly at her over their mugs of beer.

Ignoring them, Jennie headed toward the bar, scanning the room in both directions as she walked. Nathan had told her to search for a tall, redheaded fellow and a dark one with a scar on his cheek. No one in the mass of cowboys and businessmen matched his descriptions, but Jennie hadn't expected to find them down here. Men who'd robbed six hundred from a stagecoach yesterday wouldn't be openly mingling with the saloon crowd.

"Excuse me," she said to the man behind the counter.

He glanced up from the shot glass he'd been cleaning with a rag. A look of surprise settled on his face. "Do you need something, miss?"

Jennie nodded. "I believe some friends of mine are

staying with you tonight." She gave the bartender the false names Nathan had provided. "Could you tell me which room they're in?"

The man lifted a bushy eyebrow, still clearly puzzled by her presence. "Up the stairs, third door." He waved a thumb at the nearby staircase.

"Thank you." Jennie made her way across the room. Instead of ascending the stairs, though, she walked toward a group of saloon girls milling about a large table where a poker game was in full swing. She stopped a few feet away to observe them, scrutinizing the faces and behavior of each girl. She needed the cleverest and the prettiest to help her.

Once she decided, she strode forward and tapped the bare shoulder of a shapely blonde. The girl spun around, the smile on her face freezing into place at the sight of Jennie.

"What do ya want?" Her painted face scrunched in annoyance.

"I need your help with a couple of men upstairs." Jennie pulled four five-dollar bills from her purse and showed the girl. "I'm willing to pay you and your friend there—" she pointed to a dark-eyed young lady loitering nearby "—twenty dollars to split between you."

"Ten dollars apiece?" the girl exclaimed.

"Shh." Jennie glanced around the room, relieved no one appeared to be listening to them.

"For ten dollars, I'd kiss the Pope."

Jennie chuckled. "Not necessary. I only need you and your friend to get these two men to leave their room and come downstairs with you without any luggage. Then I need them detained for at least half an hour. Can you do that?"

"Consider it done, sweetheart." The girl waved a hand at her friend. "Nellie. Come here." The other girl frowned and wandered over.

"We got ourselves a more profitable job," the blonde whispered to her, "that beats waitin' around for these cowboys to finish up."

Jennie led the girls to the stairs where she repeated her instructions, emphasizing the part about no luggage coming downstairs.

"Here's your money." She handed each girl two bills, which they tucked into their boots. She knew it might be foolish to give them all of the money up-front, but she was already behind schedule. "Whatever you do, don't tell them about me."

"Don't worry. Your secret's safe with us." The blonde one sniffed, her hands on her hips. "We'll have 'em down here in five minutes or you can have your money back."

Jennie smiled at her confidence. "I appreciate the help."

"Anytime," the dark-eyed girl said over her shoulder as they sauntered up the stairs.

Jennie watched them until they reached the upstairs hall, then she slipped into the shadows beside the staircase. She'd carefully constructed her plan during the tedious stage ride, and yet, she couldn't help but worry. Everything hinged on the girls' ability to get the bandits downstairs—without their money—and hold them long enough for Jennie to do her job.

With nothing to do except wait, she gnawed on her thumbnail, her stomach churning with nerves. The nervous action reminded her of all the times Caleb had noticed it and she lowered her hand to her side. She didn't want to think about Caleb now, not in the middle of a saloon about to take money from thugs.

To clear her mind, she reached into her purse for her pistol. She checked her gun again, even though she'd loaded it before leaving home.

The sound of footsteps at the top of the stairs made her press against the wall. Holding her breath, Jennie trained her gaze on the last few steps. High-pitched giggles and the murmur of male voices moved closer.

At last, she saw them. The tall redhead had his arm draped around the shoulders of the dark-eyed girl and the bearded man with the scar clasped the waist of the blonde.

"Why don't we buy you ladies a drink?" the taller one said.

As the group walked to the bar, Jennie slipped out of the shadows. She put her gun back into the purse dangling from her wrist. She forced her feet to take slow, measured steps up the stairs, so as not to draw attention. When she reached the upstairs hall, she allowed herself a long, full breath at having made it this far.

She counted the doors as she walked, stopping in front of the third one. She turned the knob and found it locked. Expecting as much, she knelt on the worn carpet and removed a hairpin from inside her hat. Like she'd learned, she stuck the makeshift key into the lock and jiggled it until she heard a soft click. She turned the handle and the door opened.

Smiling at the relative ease of it all, Jennie rose to her feet and walked into the room. The sound of snoring brought her footsteps to a halt and made her heart leap painfully in panic. Nathan had told her there would only be two robbers. Did she have the wrong room?

She leaned out the doorway and counted the doors off the main hallway. She had the right room. *But who's inside?* She hesitated, unsure whether to proceed or leave, until the memory of Mr. Dixon's notice with the ugly word *foreclosure* on top entered her mind. *I'm not giving up yet.*

Squaring her shoulders, Jennie crept back through the open door. She shut it softly behind her. The room was modestly furnished with a dresser, a wash basin, a table and chairs and a bed.

A large man lay facedown across the bed, his massive back rising with deep snores, his hand still gripping a bottle. Two more bottles and several dirty glasses sat on the table. The stench of alcohol hung in the stale air.

Jennie made a slow canvas around the room, searching for the bag of money and keeping her steps mere whispers against the floor. The man on the bed continued his drunken slumber. She found two saddlebags dumped into one corner, but neither of them held the cash.

Frowning, she set the bags back into place and surveyed her surroundings once more. Nothing appeared odd or out of place except a lumpy blanket wadded up beside the man's feet. She tiptoed forward and knelt at the foot of the bed. Lifting a corner of the blanket, she pushed her hand under the fabric. Her fingers touched something smooth and hard—a bag.

Squelching the urge to laugh, Jennie inched the bag toward her. A muffled groan made her freeze, her hand caught beneath the blanket. The bed shook as the man shifted his weight. Once more the room filled with the sound of heavy breathing.

Jennie waited another half minute before resuming

her task. At last the bag bumped softly against the foot-board. In one quick movement, she lifted the edge of the blanket and pulled the bag onto the floor. She untwisted the metal clasp and peered inside. Neat stacks of cash brought a smile to her face.

Jennie stowed her purse and gun inside the bag before taking it with her to the door. She needed to hurry; it had taken her more time than she'd intended to find the money.

With a last look at the sleeping bandit, she walked out the door and closed it. She headed down the hall, hoping to slip out the saloon's main doors unnoticed, but a short man blocked the way to the stairs. She stopped, and their eyes met.

"I know you." She pointed an accusing finger at him. "You're one of the cowboys who stole my cattle for Mr. King. You were in Beaver the other week. Have you been following me?"

She knew the answer even before his face blanched.

"Why are you here?" She took a defensive step forward, the money and the bandits momentarily forgotten in the wake of her anger.

Frowning, the cowhand hurried down the stairs, plowing into the tall redhead and the scarred dark-haired man coming up. Too late, Jennie realized her time had run out. She spun around, away from the bandits, searching for some way to escape.

"Whataya got there, missy?" one of them asked.

Jennie ignored him and sprinted toward the closest room. She prayed it wasn't locked. She grabbed the knob and pushed against the door, throwing a glance at the men coming after her.

"Hey, that's our money," the man with the scar on his face said.

"It's the little imp who's been stealing everybody's dough," the tall one replied as Jennie bolted into the room and slammed the door behind her.

Twisting the lock into place, Jennie frantically searched the empty apartment for a way to escape. There was only one choice.

She crossed to the window, listening to the sound of the men's boots smacking the floor outside the door. Soon they were pounding their fists against the wood. Shouted profanities and threats seeped into the room from the hallway.

Visibly shaking, Jennie pushed up the window and stuck out her head. Crates of empty bottles and several old barrels were scattered along the outer wall, about ten feet below. She could probably jump and survive.

Realizing the pounding had ceased, Jennie pulled back inside the room and stared at the door. Had they given up? The blast of a bullet through the door and into the nearby dresser told her otherwise. She considered firing back with her pistol, but that might end her chance for escape.

She tossed the money bag out the window and crawled through the opening. Clinging to the casing with both hands, Jennie tried to determine the best position to drop.

Another shot fired inside the room. Even if the men didn't break the door soon, they'd be racing down the stairs and around the building to get her before long. Shutting her eyes, Jennie let go.

For a brief moment, she felt the strange panic of free-falling until she crumpled to the dirt below. The impact knocked the wind from her, forcing her to lie still until she could breathe again. From above came the sound of the bandits crashing into the room.

*Come on. Get up.* Thirty feet away, Jennie spied an alley between the saloon and the next building.

She grabbed the bag and ran as hard as she could toward the alley. *Twenty more feet.*

A shout shattered the air behind her. "Don't let her get away!"

*Ten more feet.*

A gun exploded behind her.

*Five more feet.*

She stumbled on a bottle but righted herself. Then something hot and piercing bit through the side of her shoulder. Gasping at the pain, Jennie hurried into the alley and slumped to the ground. Pricks of light danced before her eyes. She reached up and gingerly touched her arm. When she let go, blood covered her fingers.

"This isn't happening," she said with a moan. She pressed a fist to her forehead, hoping to clear the haze filling her brain. She had to get out of the alley and out of Fillmore, fast.

Using a barrel as leverage, Jennie climbed to her feet. The men would expect her to exit the alley near the front of the saloon. She'd have to make her escape elsewhere.

She held the money bag with her good arm as she searched along the back side of the next building for a suitable place to hide. At last she spied the rear entrance of a livery stable.

Sucking air between clenched teeth, she reached the outer door, but it was locked. Jennie braced herself against the wall and removed another hairpin. After some fiddling, the padlock fell open on the ground.

She pushed her way inside and shut the door. She could make out the odd shapes of half a dozen carriages and buggies and heard the restless shifting of the horses in their stalls.

Jennie hauled herself into the bed of the nearest buggy. She set her bag between her feet and removed her jacket, pressing it against her wound to slow the bleeding. Her near escape and throbbing arm brought the dizzy feeling back, stronger this time. She rested her head against the cool leather seat and gratefully passed out.

# Chapter Thirteen

Jennie forced open her eyes and blinked at the strange shadows around her. Why was she lying in a buggy indoors? Confused, she sat up. Her left arm throbbed. She stared down at the bloody jacket next to her on the seat and remembrance flooded her aching head. The stage bandits shooting at her from the second-story room. The bullet grazing her arm. The escape into the livery stable.

She pressed her back against the seat, her muscles tensing as she waited for someone to materialize beside the buggy and snatch the money. No one appeared, though.

Careful to put little strain on her injured arm, she climbed out of the buggy and picked up the money bag. She had to get out of Fillmore—now.

Enough moonlight came through the high windows that she was able to locate the horse tack in one corner of the livery. Gathering what she needed, she walked down the line of horse stalls, assessing each animal. She needed a strong horse, one that could get her to Cove Fort and then to Beaver as fast as possible. Once there she'd make arrangements for returning the horse.

Jennie opted for a black thoroughbred mare about sixteen hands tall that stood alert and awake in its stall. Sliding her hand along the horse's nose, she let the animal nuzzle her to get used to her smell and presence before she entered the stall. She saddled the horse and tucked the cash, her purse and pistol into a saddlebag she'd found with the tack. After hiding the empty money bag beneath the straw in a corner of the stall, she looped the reins around her good hand. The horse whinnied softly as Jennie led her out of the livery.

Outside, she used a broken crate to hoist herself into the saddle and tied herself to the saddle horn, in case she fainted. A wave of nausea from jostling her wound made her bend over the side of the horse and retch on the ground.

Jennie drew a shaky hand over her mouth. She needed medical help and soon, but first she wanted to be as far away from Fillmore and the bandits as she could. Once she reached Cove Fort, she'd only be a day's ride from home.

She held the horse to a trot, hoping to avoid any undue attention, as they rode down the quiet street. Most of the windows still had lamps shining in them, which told Jennie that she hadn't been unconscious for too long.

A quarter mile outside of the city, she pushed the mare into a full gallop. The moon disappeared at intervals as the storm clouds moved across the evening sky. Jennie hoped the dark night and the horse's black color would keep her from becoming a target for other thugs or Indians.

The steady movement of the horse beneath her and the unrelenting pain in her arm lulled Jennie into a state of semi-wakefulness. Ahead of her, she could see the faces of the thieves she'd robbed. They watched her with hard, ugly eyes, their lips pulled back in angry sneers.

Knowing she was half dreaming, Jennie tried to force the images from her mind, but another rose unbidden. The blond hair, the firm jaw, the handsome features she'd grown to know so well. Unlike the others, Caleb regarded her with tenderness as he had two nights before while they were dancing. But too quickly his expression changed to one of pain and anger.

Jennie buried her head in the horse's mane and squeezed her eyes shut against the apparition. *He doesn't despise me now, but he will if he ever finds out what I've done.* How would she explain her gunshot wound to Caleb and her family?

"Can't I have the ranch and Caleb, too?" she asked the heavens. The rumble of distant thunder was her only reply, and yet, the answer pounded in her ears as if someone had spoken it aloud.

She couldn't hope to save the ranch this way and expect to win Caleb's affection. Sooner or later she'd have to make a choice, between this man she realized she loved and the land she'd fought—honorably or not— to save.

Moaning as much from the pain in her mind as the pain in her arm, Jennie allowed the blackness to overcome her senses again. Occasionally she startled awake when the mare slowed her step. Jennie would search for water and let the horse rest and drink, checking to make certain they were headed in the right direction, before urging the animal into a canter again and drifting back into unconsciousness.

The pictures in her dreams ran together like the images in the kaleidoscope her father had brought home years ago. Happy pictures of the family before her mother had left, meeting Caleb in the store, kissing him out on the range. Then the vision would whirl and change into the frightening imageries of her other robberies and Mr. Dixon shoving the foreclosure notice at her again and again.

She awoke, cold with sweat, when a crash of thunder rolled above. The horse responded with a nervous whinny. Rain began to fall, and a flash of lightning illuminated the landscape. In the sudden light, Jennie spotted the fort's sturdy stone walls half a mile away.

By the time Jennie reached the massive door, the rain was pummeling the ground in large, angry drops. She slid off the horse and landed in a heap in the mud. Her legs didn't want to move. She half crawled the few feet to the fort's west entrance and pounded a fist against the wood.

"Open up," she cried as loud as she could. "Please, open up."

Only the sounds of rain and thunder pulsed in her ears.

"Please," she repeated. She leaned her forehead against the door, giving in to the tears building behind her eyes.

"Who's there?" someone finally called out.

Jennie choked back a sob of relief. "My name is Jennie Jones. I was here yesterday with the northbound stage. I've been attacked and I need some help."

The door jerked opened and a man hurried out, a lantern held high in his hand. "Let's get you and your horse inside, Miss Jones."

Warm sunlight shone on her face, and the smell of fried corn cakes and ham filled her nose. She'd overslept. Jennie opened her eyes and stared in panic at the door.

Had the bandits come for her? Had Mr. King's cowhand followed her to the fort?

A knock at the door sent her heart racing. Were they here for her? She sat up, her injured arm protesting the movement, and searched the room for her gun. Then she remembered she'd put the pistol in the saddlebag.

Before she could scramble out of bed, a woman with a kind smile poked her head into the room. "You're awake."

Jennie released her held breath in relief. "Yes, come in." She recognized the woman as the fort owner's wife, Adelaide, who Jennie had seen before on her trips to and from Fillmore. The woman had bandaged Jennie's arm upon her arrival and given her a nightgown to wear. "What time is it?"

"About eleven o'clock. I'm afraid you missed breakfast, but there are some leftovers. Are you hungry?"

"A little." Jennie's stomach rumbled, making them both laugh. "Maybe more than a little."

Adelaide approached the bed and set a folded piece of calico cloth next to Jennie on the quilt. "I thought you could use a new dress to replace your other one. I believe we're about the same height."

"You don't have to do that. I'm already indebted to you."

She lifted her shoulders in a shrug. "No trouble." She leaned in as if imparting a secret. "Would it ease your mind, if you knew the dress has never been one of my favorites?"

Jennie gave a soft laugh. "That does make it easier."

"Good." She pointed at Jennie's left arm. "May I re-wrap that for you?"

"Yes. Thank you."

Adelaide gathered some supplies from the bureau and sat on the edge of the bed. Jennie pushed the nightgown over her shoulder and watched as Adelaide gently removed the bandage.

"The bleeding's stopped."

"It actually feels better this morning," Jennie said, grateful she wouldn't sustain any permanent damage, beyond a scar.

Adelaide rewrapped her arm and stood. "How did you get such a wound in the first place?"

Biting her lip, Jennie mentally scrambled for a simple explanation. "A saloon brawl."

*It's half true,* she told herself, her body stiffening as she waited for Adelaide's judgment. *What was she doing in a saloon anyway?* she could imagine this proper woman thinking. But Adelaide's green eyes shone with compassion.

"I'm sorry to hear that. The good news is the wound isn't too deep, and I think your arm will heal quickly." She smiled. "Would you like some help getting up?"

"I can manage."

Adelaide bent and patted her hand in a way that reminded Jennie of her grandmother. A sudden longing to be home brought the sting of tears to Jennie's eyes. No matter the befuddled mess she'd made of things, she wanted to see Will and Grandma Jones. And Caleb.

"Do you remember where to find the kitchen?" Adelaide asked, moving to the door.

Jennie nodded. "Um…Adelaide…has anyone come asking for me?" She bit her lip, fearful of the answer, but the woman shook her head.

"We haven't had any new travelers since you came in early this morning."

Relieved, Jennie gave her a genuine smile. She waited until Adelaide shut the door before she swung her legs over the side of the bed to get dressed. Her sore arm made putting on the borrowed long-sleeved gown more difficult than she'd anticipated. When Jennie finally had all the buttons done up and her shoes laced, her breath came quicker and her arm ached worse.

Running her fingers through her hair, Jennie stepped to the chair where her hat and saddlebag waited. She opened the bag with the money and started to recount the number of bundles when a wave of guilt washed over her. The fort owners had been more than gracious to her; they wouldn't steal her money. Why did she always feel suspicious of others?

Too weary to determine the answer, Jennie pushed the plaguing question to the back of her mind and left the room, her things in tow. She crossed the courtyard, past two girls playing with their dolls, and entered the dining room and adjoining kitchen. Adelaide looked up from stirring something in a bowl at the sideboard and smiled.

"I hope you enjoy the food and the quiet, now that all our travelers are gone."

Smiling back, Jennie slipped into the chair in front of the single place setting and began to eat. Usually the room was crowded with people, all talking and eating at once. She was relieved to not have to make conversation or answer questions, though her long sleeves hid any sign of her bandage. No one but Adelaide and her husband had to know the state in which Jennie had shown up to the fort in the wee hours of the morning.

The hot food tasted delicious, and Jennie ate every morsel. When she finished, she rose from the table and cleared her dishes.

"If anyone from Fillmore should come looking for me," Jennie said in a low voice, though no one else but Adelaide was about, "please, don't give them my name."

Adelaide stopped cooking and peered intently at Jennie. "Are you in trouble, Miss Jones? Is there something we can do for you?"

Jennie blushed at the sincere concern. "No, no. It's just…I would rather return home knowing I don't have some angry, drunken man on my heels."

Adelaide gave a decisive nod. "I think I understand. We'll not share what you wish to keep secret."

"Thank you." Jennie realized she'd been holding her breath. "For the wonderful meal, too." She took a step toward the door. "I should probably be going."

"Are you sure? You don't want to rest one more day?" Adelaide glanced purposely at Jennie's arm.

Jennie shook her head. Right now the only place she wanted to be was home.

"Very well." Adelaide wiped her hands on her apron. "Let's rummage up some food for your journey and then we'll get your horse."

With some bread and cheese tied up in a handkerchief, Jennie followed Adelaide to the stable where they found Adelaide's husband, Ira, attending to the horses.

"Morning, Miss Jones," he said cheerfully. "It's good to see you up and moving. You were a bit worse for wear this morning."

"She's ready to go, Ira," Adelaide announced.

Ira's face registered the same surprise Adelaide had shown in the kitchen, but he nodded. "I'll get your horse ready."

While he saddled up the mare, Jennie discreetly withdrew a wad of cash to pay the couple for their care.

"Here, please take this." She held out the money to Ira. "I would have been in a bad spot without your kindness. And it wasn't like I was traveling with the stagecoach this morning."

Ira shook his head and gently pushed back her hand. "We're glad we could help. We'll leave it at that."

Jennie blinked in open curiosity at him. With all the people they had coming through their fort and eating their food, surely they felt justified in accepting a little reward now and then.

As if reading her thoughts, Adelaide spoke. "That's what we were asked to do here—help folks like yourself on this lonely stretch of road. Every time we do, we find we're more than compensated by God's bounty."

"I'll help you onto your horse," Ira said, smiling.

A growing lump in her throat prevented Jennie from responding. She put one foot into the stirrups and allowed Ira to help her onto the saddle. Why was she so touched? *Probably because this place reminds me of home.*

Instead of an image of the ranch filling her mind, she pictured the scene in the kitchen the night before she'd left for Fillmore. Will playing their father's old harmonica and her and Caleb dancing. She could still recall the warmth and love she'd felt, surrounded by the people she cared for most.

Forcing her thoughts back to the present, Jennie thanked Ira and Adelaide once more. They walked her to the fort's main entrance, and Ira opened the giant doors. Jennie rode through, pointing her horse south. Twisting in the saddle, she waved goodbye to the two figures framed inside the doorway.

Jennie alternated the mare's gait from a canter to a

walk and back. If she hurried, she might reach the livery stable in Beaver before dark to collect Dandy—a day ahead of schedule.

She located a stream a few hours into her ride where she watered and rested the horse and ate her lunch. A nearby rock helped her maneuver again into the saddle without reinjuring her arm.

More than once, her mind returned to her experience at the fort and Ira and Adelaide's selfless service. Jennie might have sacrificed quite a bit—even risking her life—yesterday to save the ranch. Was all her sacrifice really worth it?

"We need it to survive," she argued out loud. The mare's ears flicked back at the break in the silence. "How would we ever make it without the ranch?"

She tried to convince herself that everything would work out for the best. Nathan could surely find her another job in the next two weeks without garnering suspicion. Then she could pay the bank and keep her home. She'd never take from another stage thief again. No one would ever have to know how she pulled her family out of their current poverty. They would be safe, provided for and happy on the land she valued so dearly.

These thoughts brought her some measure of comfort, but one nagging question remained. What was King's man doing in Fillmore? Had it merely been coincidence she saw him there, like their encounter in Beaver, or was he really following her? What did he want? Jennie hated that she didn't have the answers. Hopefully the cowhand didn't know what she'd been doing at the saloon and her confrontation with him in the hallway would deter him from coming around again.

She reached Beaver a short time after sunset and led

the mare to the livery. Taking some bills from her saddle-bag, she paid for Dandy's stay and made arrangements with the livery owner to have the mare go with the next stage to Fillmore and the livery stable there.

Exhaustion seeped from every muscle, but she still had to find Nathan at the saloon. Thankfully he was waiting outside for her. She gave him his half of the money and quickly related her experience in Fillmore, leaving out the part about being shot. If he thought she couldn't handle another job soon, he might pass one up.

Jennie let Dandy set the pace for home. She was too sore to care about speed. Once she worked out a plausible explanation for her borrowed dress and injury, she began to breathe a little easier. The real details of her trip to Fillmore could remain a secret.

She would ride up, hug her brother and grandmother, talk with Caleb, and everything would stay the same. *Nothing has to change.*

## Chapter Fourteen

Caleb pitched the last bits of hay into the corral troughs before taking his pitchfork and lantern to the barn to feed the horses. His gaze shot to the road in front of the ranch, though he knew Jennie wouldn't be home for another day. He'd started missing her about an hour after she'd left three days earlier. Things weren't the same at the ranch without her around to talk to or tease.

Was she safe and well? Ladies typically had no trouble traveling alone on a stagecoach. Or so he'd thought before Liza's accident.

He closed his mind to the memories by concentrating his thoughts on his next task. He lit into the horses' hay with a vengeance, tossing it faster than he ever had. He had one last horse to feed, minus Dandy, when he heard a noise at the barn doors.

Jennie walked inside, leading Dandy by the reins. Caleb's heart quickened with relief and happiness.

"You're home early. We didn't expect you until tomorrow night."

"It's a long story." In the lamplight her pretty face was etched with weariness.

"I'm glad you're safe," he said with practiced nonchalance, embarrassed by his earlier worry. "I'll take care of Dandy. You sit down and rest."

For once Jennie didn't protest. Instead she handed him the reins and sank down on a nearby bale of hay. "Feels good to be on something that isn't moving," she muttered, setting her hat beside her.

Caleb led Dandy into his stall and removed the saddle and blanket. "If you don't mind my asking, how'd your financial meeting go?"

"It went fine." Her exhausted tone made the words less convincing, but Caleb refrained from saying so. "I can't borrow any more money, but I hope to pay the loan off soon. Once the bank isn't breathing down our necks, we can turn this place around."

"How are you gonna pay off the debt?" he asked as he put the tack away.

Jennie didn't answer right away. Caleb lifted his head to see a look of trepidation on her face. Had he said something wrong?

"We'll be fine."

He grabbed a currycomb and returned to Dandy's stall. He gave the horse a few strokes with the brush before stopping. "I know I've said it before, Jennie, but I meant it. You don't have to pay me my wages just yet."

"It'll all work out," she said, her chin lifted in her determined stance. She released a deep yawn.

"Why don't you go on up to the house? Will and Grandma Jones will be excited to see you."

"Yes, but first I need to hear how things went with me gone."

Caleb chuckled. "Is that the reason you're home a day

early? You wanted to make sure we hadn't run the place into the ground yet?"

"Very funny," she murmured. "Did you get the garden finished?"

"Yes, and the cattle are all fine. I thought I'd start on the hay fields tomorrow."

When she remained silent, he twisted around. Her eyes were closed and her head rested against one of the stall posts. Nervousness churned his stomach, but he forced himself to walk to her side. He'd decided the night before to tell her how he felt when she returned. He was still anxious about starting a courtship, but he was willing to try—on the condition that they would take it slow, see where things went.

Crouching down beside the bale of hay, Caleb took hold of one of her hands. Jennie's eyes flew open and her gaze jumped from his face to his hand and back again.

"Wh-what is it? Are you headed into the house?"

"Not yet." Caleb stared down at her hand, caressing the lines of it with his thumb. Her skin felt warm and soft beneath his touch. "There's something I need to tell you."

"Oh?" The word came out a squeak. He quickly choked back a laugh. She was clearly as nervous as him.

"I need to admit I was wrong about something."

"What is that?"

"I should've kissed you all those weeks ago, out on the range." He forced his gaze upward, but only for a moment. "I...I...care about you, Jennie. A lot. When I think about you, my heart just wants to jump right out of my chest. I haven't felt that in a long, long time. I know I work for you and that's a bit awkward, but if you think—"

Her lips silenced the rest of his words. He drank in

their warmth, and his heart ricocheted with emotion like one of Will's bullets. He hadn't felt so alive and wonderful since courting Liza. He deepened the kiss, his hands rising to her shoulders to pull her closer, but she suddenly cried out.

Caleb jerked away. "Are you all right? Did I hurt you?"

"No, no." Jennie shook her head, but the muscles in her jaw tightened. "It's nothing—really. I hurt my arm, that's all."

"How hurt are you?"

"I'll be fine, honest."

"What happened to your arm?"

Jennie's lips pressed together in a tight line. "I cut my arm on the window casing when the stagecoach broke a wheel near Cove Fort. That's why I'm back early. I didn't want to wait around for the stage to be fixed, so I borrowed a horse and rode home today. The fort owner's wife patched me up before I left and gave me this dress since my other had a rip on the sleeve." Her face softened a little as she added, "There's nothing to be concerned about."

Caleb nodded, though he couldn't help wondering how bad the wound was if she'd needed a new dress. He decided not to press her, though, since she was so tired. Rest was probably what she needed most. Another kiss would have to wait.

Swallowing his disappointment, he carefully swept her up into his arms. "Let's get you off to bed then, young lady."

"Caleb, put me down. I can walk."

"Nope. You're going to let someone else help you for a change. Which means no work for you tomorrow."

She gave a soft laugh and wound her arms around his neck. "Fine. I promise to rest, if you promise to finish that kiss soon."

"Aha. So you admit you do like me back?"

"Who kissed you first?"

"Good point." He smiled down at her, enjoying the feel of holding her against his chest. "Let's get you fixed up."

He carried her out of the barn and toward the house, but he wasn't sure his boots actually hit the ground. He didn't know how this new relationship with Jennie would change things, but he refused to dwell on it. Tonight he simply wanted to revel in the knowledge that the spunky woman with her head on his shoulder was his to love.

Jennie lifted her arms and stretched, careful of her healing wound. She had to admit her whole body felt better after a day of resting. But if she didn't get up and do something productive today she might go mad from inactivity.

In the early-morning light, she put on a blouse and trousers and moved to the door. Only silence sounded outside on the landing.

*Good. They must all be at breakfast.* If she could show her grandmother and Caleb she was well enough to join them in the kitchen, then perhaps they'd let her do more than mending or drying dishes.

Caleb had been right, though. The time in bed yesterday had made her wound heal much faster than if she'd gotten her way and started right back into the work.

The memory of his admission in the barn two nights earlier brought a smile to her lips as she crept out her door.

"Good morning, Jennie. And where do you think you're going?"

Jennie squealed with fright as Caleb stepped out from the shadows by the stairs.

"I knew you couldn't rest for more than a day."

"I'm only coming down for breakfast," she said, tilting her chin with all the haughtiness she could muster.

"How's the arm?"

"Much better." She carefully rotated her shoulder as proof. "I can work today, honest."

"You're easier to boss when you're injured."

Jennie rolled her eyes. "I can't stand another day of confinement to the house or the porch. Besides, who is working for who on this ranch?"

He ignored her. "I'll strike a deal with you. You go back to bed after breakfast and then you can come into town with me this afternoon."

"You're no fun," she said with a pout.

Chuckling, Caleb leaned forward and pressed a kiss to her forehead. Though not as exciting as kissing him on the mouth, his touch still released flurries in her stomach. "May I escort you downstairs?"

"Yes." She linked her arm through his and they moved down the stairs.

*He's so good to me.* Her cheeks warmed as Caleb glanced at her, his blue eyes bright with tenderness. *I want to be the same to him.*

From the back of her mind, a thought marched forward: *Then give up taking money from stage bandits.* Jennie frowned.

"Something wrong?"

She shook her head, forcing a smile. "Perhaps I'm a little more tired than I thought."

After breakfast, Jennie returned upstairs. She lay down on her bed and shut her eyes, but she couldn't sleep. There were too many things to think about. She still needed one, maybe two more jobs from Nathan to eliminate her debt to the bank. And she only had two weeks to do it.

With a sigh, she sat up and stared at the walls. Fretting about the money wouldn't accomplish anything. What would she do until lunch? She reached out to finger her brown and cream dress, rubbing the fine material over her fingertips. What a lovely wedding dress it would make. Her cheeks warmed at the thought—Caleb had only confessed his feelings for her, not proposed—but she would've accepted him without hesitation if he had asked for her hand in marriage the other night. She imagined herself in the gown, her hair done up fancy, standing next to Caleb who would look so dashing in a suit.

It was just an idle fantasy for now. She needed to finish with the mortgage, and leave her shameful actions in the past. Only then would she truly be ready to be the wife that Caleb deserved. But surely that day would come soon—the day when she'd be clear of the debt and could leave the whole messy business behind her. She could hardly wait. Once that day came, if Caleb didn't propose soon, she might just ask him herself!

The dream of her own wedding made her think of her parents. Had they truly been in love when they had married? Did her mother regret the promises she'd broken by leaving? A fierce longing to speak with her mother about love and marriage brought the sting of tears to Jennie's eyes.

A knock sounded at the door, jerking Jennie back to the present.

"Just a minute," she croaked over the lump in her throat. She straightened her blouse and opened the door. Her grandmother stood there, frowning.

"You have a visitor."

"Who?" Jennie peered past her toward the stairs.

"A Mr. Blaine. He's in the parlor."

*Nathan?* That could only mean one thing; he'd found a job. Jennie rushed out the door and started down the stairs, but her grandmother called after her.

"I've never said a word about that man coming around or the fact that you've never introduced him." Grandma Jones gave her a stern look that made Jennie squirm. "Whatever your past relationship, I think he needs to know where your feelings now lie."

Jennie's cheeks burned with embarrassment. She wasn't trying to string Nathan along. After today, she hoped she wouldn't have to worry about him coming around anymore. "I'll tell him," she answered quietly.

Before her grandmother could chastise her further, Jennie hurried downstairs to the parlor. She pushed through the partially opened door, hoping Nathan hadn't overheard her grandmother's warning. He stood, hat in hand, appearing out of place even in the humble parlor.

"Did you find me a job?" she blurted out.

"Good morning to you, too."

"Have you found something?" She sat down in a nearby chair.

Nathan tossed his hat onto the sofa and took a seat for himself. "You are one lucky lady, Jennie Jones." He grinned. "Some fellow talked to me in the saloon yesterday, tipped me off to a big job tomorrow. Four men will be robbing the stage heading east from Nevada to Beaver."

"How much?"

Nathan leaned forward, his dark eyes sparkling. "How's five thousand dollars sound to you?"

Jennie's mouth dropped open. She'd never taken so much money before. Even after giving Nathan his half, she'd still have more than enough left over to pay off her loan and buy herself more cattle. The idea of being so close to freedom made her light-headed. "You're certain that's the amount?"

"I asked the man three times. Some mining company is transferring funds to a bank up north." He leaned back, stretching his arm along the top of the sofa. "It's gonna be a bit dicey for those robbers, though. The mining company's sending the cash with an armed guard and a seasoned stage driver. That means those four men aren't likely to be partial to you waltzing in and taking that cash away from 'em."

"I'll do just fine."

"*We'll* do just fine."

She lifted her eyebrows. "What do you mean?"

"If these gentlemen suspect you're coming, like those other ones did, you might do better with some help."

She could see his point, and his assistance would come in handy with her injured arm. She didn't need to get herself shot again. "All right."

"Now here's my idea of how we're goin' pull this off...."

Half an hour later, she and Nathan had devised a detailed plan to steal back the bank money. *A rather good plan,* Jennie thought, crossing her arms loosely. Only one thing troubled her, nibbling at the edges of her excitement—having to lie to Caleb and her family, again.

"I'm off, love." Nathan put on his hat and stood. "I'll meet you west of Beaver tomorrow."

He crossed to her chair and held out his hand to help her up. She ignored him and stood on her own, but Nathan stepped closer. Jennie wanted to move back, but the chair stood directly behind her.

"My offers still stands, Jennie," he said, his voice low. "We could finish this job and slip away. Leave enough money for your granny and brother to get on just fine, then we'd set our sights for bigger and better things."

Jennie bit her lip, afraid how to respond. If she told him how she felt about Caleb, would he refuse to help her? Or worse, would he work against her? She couldn't very well carry out their plan alone, but she had to be forthright. She loved Caleb, and once this job was through, she hoped to bury any connection to this part of her life, including her association with Nathan Blaine.

"I'm indebted to you, Nathan, for all you've done." She forced herself to look him straight in the eye. "But as I've said before, I can't accept your offer, for many reasons."

"Would it have something to do with that hired hand of yours?"

She blushed. "Yes."

"That explains the ugly scowl he gave me when I rode up." He took a step backward, giving her room to breathe again. "Choosing the settled life, huh?"

"We haven't talked about all that." She studied her hands.

"Well, since I probably won't be around to give you my congratulations then…" He grabbed her good arm, yanked her close and roughly kissed her mouth. Jennie shoved hard against his chest, pushing him away. What would Caleb think if he saw them?

Chuckling, Nathan let her go. "I've wanted to do that for a long time."

"Get out of here, you scoundrel." Jennie darted a quick glance at the open door.

"No one saw, if that's what you're worried about." He walked out of the room before turning back. "But you should tell him about it yourself. It'll remind that fellow of yours what a lucky man he is."

Jennie's anger softened a little at the compliment. "Good day, Nathan."

"Goodbye, Jennie." Tipping his hat, he headed out the front door, whistling to himself.

Jennie followed, pausing on the porch. She watched Nathan stride arrogantly down the front steps to his waiting horse and shook her head. Even if Nathan's kiss was meant to inspire grateful jealousy in Caleb, Jennie still didn't plan to tell him. She had enough explaining to do about Nathan's visit in general, and then, more lies regarding her plans for tomorrow. Things were looking up, though. Surely her luck would hold out one more time—it had to.

# Chapter Fifteen

Caleb finished hitching the horses to the wagon and headed to the house to collect Jennie. He paused in the kitchen doorway to observe her unnoticed. She sat at the table, a bit of pencil motionless in one hand, her chin resting on the other. She was supposed to be making a list of the things they needed to pick up in town, but she appeared deep in thought instead. She'd been that way since that stranger came by earlier.

Caleb's jaw tightened at the memory of the man strutting onto the porch as if he had a right to be there. Taking a deep breath, he calmed his jealous irritation. Jennie's description of their visit had sounded harmless enough.

"We met for the last time," she'd told Caleb, "about our plan to pull the ranch out of debt."

He hoped she succeeded in keeping the ranch going, though secretly he was relieved to hear that man wouldn't be coming around anymore.

Jennie lifted her head and a smile broke across her face. "You ready?"

He nodded.

"I'm just about finished with my list."

"Go ahead. I can just stand here and stare." He leaned his shoulder against the door frame, taking in the sight of her. He grinned when she rolled her eyes.

"How am I supposed to concentrate with you doing that?" She ducked her head and scrawled something onto her scrap of paper.

"Maybe you're not supposed to."

Her cheeks flamed red, and he chuckled.

"I'm finished," she said a minute later, pushing back her chair. She started past him, but Caleb caught her elbow and pulled her close.

"Did I tell you good morning today?"

"Hmm." She scrunched her face in mock contemplation. "Yes, I believe you told me good morning."

"Have I told you today how pretty you are?"

"In not so many words."

"You're beautiful, Jennie."

She lowered her chin, but not before Caleb saw the love and adoration she hadn't yet voiced shining in her eyes.

"Have I told you how happy this tenderfooted cowhand is to be with you?"

She laughed softly and stepped closer to him. "I don't see any tenderfoot here."

He bent down to kiss her, but Grandma Jones stepped into the hallway. Caleb's face and neck went warm.

"Sorry to interrupt," she said, smiling openly at them, "but I wanted to remind you to get me some dark blue thread, Jennie."

Her cheeks pink as well, Jennie nodded. "We're leaving now."

Caleb followed Jennie outside. He helped her onto the wagon seat and climbed up beside her. Lifting the reins, he gently slapped the backs of the team and guided the wagon toward Beaver.

The sky shone bright blue above them, not a cloud to be seen. The day hadn't been too hot either, and a pleasant breeze blew across Caleb's face. He liked working down here, but starting his business in the north, close to the railroad, made the most sense. Maybe he could convince Jennie and her family to come with him in a few months.

"You ever thought of selling the ranch? Starting over up north?"

"Sell the ranch?" Her eyes went dark with anger. "You think I ought to sell the ranch?"

"It's an idea…"

She angled away from him, her shoulders hunched as if to ward off a blow. "I don't want to sell the ranch, even if things are bad. This is all Will and I have from our parents. I haven't worked so hard for so long to hand it over to someone else."

Caleb reached for her hand. She flinched at his touch, but she didn't pull away. "Jennie?" He waited until she shot him a glance before he went on. "I thought it might help things if you sold the place to the bank. Then you'd be free from your debt, free to do what you want. That's all."

"The ranch is what I want."

Her chin lifted stubbornly, and Caleb decided to drop the subject. He'd pushed his suggestion far enough. He gave her hand a gentle squeeze to let her know he hadn't meant to upset her. Though she kept her face pointed forward, she squeezed his hand back. He understood the silent acceptance of his apology.

Once they reached town, Caleb tied the horses to

the post in front of the general store and helped Jennie down. Inside, he relinquished the lead to her, following her around the full barrels and shelves while she placed needed objects into his outstretched arms.

"Is that everything we need?" She studied her list. "We can ask for the hayseed and then—" Jennie sucked in a sharp breath.

"What is it?" Caleb leaned forward as best he could with his arms full. Was she sick?

Without answering, Jennie bolted toward the back of the store. Caleb strode after her, trying to keep from dropping the goods he held. He peered at her in concern. She looked more angry than ill, her mouth set into a tight line. "What's wrong?"

"We have to leave—now."

"But we didn't get the thread yet that your grandmother asked for."

"It doesn't matter." She gave a frantic shake of her head. "Marshall King is here, in the store."

"Really?" Caleb glanced surreptitiously over his shoulder. He didn't have to guess which customer was King. A man in a worn leather vest with dark hair falling over his collar stood watching the two of them from his place in line. A rascally smile graced his weatherbeaten face.

"Please, Caleb, let's just leave. If I so much as go near him, I'll start shouting."

"You won't need to, and we don't have to leave, either. I'll stand in line. You wait here." He nodded at one of the wooden chairs arranged around the cold stove.

"Caleb, I don't think—"

"It'll be fine. I can handle him."

She released a heavy sigh. "All right. Thank you."

She slipped several bills into his hand so he could pay the clerk.

He gave her a grim smile. "I might have to put a fist in the man's stomach myself." He slowly spun around and started for the short line.

If King had been smiling before, his face lit up even more as Caleb approached. His lack of contrition for stealing Jennie's cattle sent flashes of hot anger through Caleb, and he had to force himself to breathe deeply.

Unfortunately, King stood at the back of the line, so Caleb had no choice except to take his place behind him. He didn't have to give the man the pleasure of his company, though. Caleb stared in the direction of the front door and tried to think of other things than smashing the man's ample jaw.

"You must be Miss Jones's hired help."

Caleb eyed King, annoyed and surprised at the man's attempt to make casual conversation. "I am."

"I've been meaning to ride over and make you an offer."

"An offer for what?"

"I'd like to give you a job. My sources say you're a good, hard worker." Mr. King folded his arms across his meaty chest. "You come work for me, and I'll pay you a lot more money than you're earning now."

For a moment, Caleb was too stunned to reply. After allowing his cowhands to rustle Jennie's cattle, did King honestly think Caleb would join up with him? *Don't give him the satisfaction of seeing your anger,* he told himself as he lifted his head and looked the man square in the eye. *He's only trying to goad you.*

"If you were the last employer on earth, Mr. King,

I wouldn't accept a job with you." In a low, hard voice, he added, "I don't work for thieves."

The rancher grinned in a dangerous way. "Oh, I wouldn't be too sure about that."

"What're you talking about?"

"Why don't you ask Miss Jones?" King scoffed, his gaze flicking toward the back of the store.

Caleb turned and regarded Jennie. Even from a distance, he could see her pale face and troubled expression. "I don't know what you're getting at, old man."

"Why don't you ask her how she's managed to keep her ranch going for so long?" His words hissed like water hitting hot flames. "Why don't you ask her the real reason she takes off for town or Fillmore all alone? Or why she meets with that fellow from the saloon?"

How could King know any of those things unless he'd been spying on Jennie? His hands clenched into fists as Caleb considered dropping his load to the floor and pounding the conceit out of this man. "How dare—"

"She's robbin' stage thieves, you fool." King brought his sneering face within inches of Caleb's. "She waits 'til the bandits steal the money, then steals it back. She's using it to keep that sorry ranch of hers alive."

Something deep inside Caleb went cold at King's words. Jennie—robbing stage thieves? The same type of criminals he'd hunted down as a bounty hunter? *Impossible.*

He surveyed her beautiful face and tried desperately to erase the suggestion of her carrying out such a deceitful deed. His heart rebelled at the thought, but his head argued that King's story made some sense. It would explain the thugs chasing after Jennie when Caleb had helped her on the trail, the "financial" meetings with the rough-looking stranger, the excuses to leave the ranch unaccompanied.

"Changes things a bit, don't it?" King said, his affable manner returning. "My offer still stands—whenever you decide to quit the place."

Caleb shook his head, forcing his mind to concentrate on the present and nothing beyond that, for the moment. "Whether I leave or stay, I'd never work for you."

"A pleasure meetin' you all the same." Tipping his hat, King took his place at the cash register to purchase some feed.

Caleb's jaw and neck muscles tensed as he glared at the man's back. Maybe he should have punched King straight away—then he wouldn't have heard the man's accusations about Jennie, accusations that brought too many unanswered questions. Finally, King left and it was Caleb's turn to step up to the counter.

Numbly, he set down the load of goods and paid the clerk. As he started for the back of the store, he felt an almost tangible weight pulling at his feet, slowing each step. How could he face Jennie with King's words still ringing in his ears, especially when a part of him wondered if they held any truth?

"Caleb, are you all right?" Jennie leaped up and grabbed his arm. "What did King say?"

Swallowing hard, Caleb made himself meet her gaze. "He offered me a job."

"He didn't!"

"I refused, of course." He shifted his pile carefully into the crook of one arm, so he could hold her hand. Just the feel of her fingers intertwined with his helped alleviate some of his growing fear.

"Is that all he said? You looked more upset than I've

ever seen you before." She peered intently at him as they headed for the door.

"He's a scoundrel," Caleb said, avoiding her question. He hid his conflicting emotions with ease, another skill he'd learned as a bounty hunter. "Let's go home."

*We'll talk about it sometime this evening,* he told himself. *I'm sure there's a logical explanation for King's wild assertions.*

A voice inside Caleb, growing more insistent by the minute, claimed otherwise, warning him that his conversation with Jennie might very well rob him of the happiness he'd felt the past few days and steal his second chance at love.

Jennie volunteered to care for the horses when they returned from the trip to town. To her surprise, Caleb didn't offer to help. Instead he told her that he'd take over watching the cattle for Will and left the barn.

Why had Caleb been so quiet on the way home? she wondered as she brushed the horses until they gleamed. Was there something more to his conversation with King? She didn't believe a job offer would provoke the kind of shock she'd seen on Caleb's face.

*Could he know my secret?*

King might have learned the truth from his cowhand, the one she'd seen at the saloon in Fillmore and who'd trailed her in town a few weeks earlier. The rancher might have told Caleb what the cowboy had observed.

"But Caleb would've mentioned it," she said, trying to reassure herself. "Wouldn't he?"

She didn't see him again the rest of the afternoon. She and Will continued the work on the spring planting that Caleb had already started, and by suppertime,

Jennie was so tired she'd almost forgotten the encounter with King in town. Almost.

She told Will to go help Caleb bring the cattle into the corral while she fed and watered the horses. For some reason she felt reluctant to face Caleb. When she finished with the horses, she surveyed the barn, desperate for something else to do. The place was immaculate. It had been ever since Caleb had come to the ranch.

The memory of seeing him come through the brush, handsome and confident, after helping her against Bart and his thugs made her heart swell with pride. She loved him and couldn't stand the thought of losing him. Why couldn't things be simpler? No financial burdens, no stage bandits. Just her and Caleb and her family, living happily.

Blowing out a deep sigh, she left the barn and secured the doors behind her. A hand on her arm made her cry out in surprise.

"Caleb. You scared me."

"Maybe you need scaring," he muttered so softly she wasn't sure she'd heard him correctly. To her disappointment, he released her arm, his hand dropping to his side. "We need to go somewhere and talk."

"I think Grandma Jones is expecting us for supper," she hedged. The anxiety in his blue eyes set off warning bells inside her head.

"She'll understand if we don't come in for a while."

If she went with him, something told her things would never be the same. But she didn't usually back down from hard things and she wouldn't now.

"All right."

Jennie licked her lips and followed him past the house. She tried to breathe evenly as she forced her steps to keep up with his. Maybe he wanted to talk about his wages or his earlier suggestion for her to sell the ranch. And yet, if it were either of those wouldn't he hold her hand? Fear knotted her stomach and the distance between them felt much wider than a few feet.

Caleb stopped at the far end of the corral. Jennie swallowed hard and waited for him to speak, feeling lost and unsure. At any other time, she would have had the comfort of his warm smile or his shoulder resting against hers to calm her nerves and give her strength. Now he stood away from her, his brow furrowed, his shoulders stiff.

"I need to ask you something."

The tightness in his voice frightened her almost as much as his words. She gave a silent nod and clasped her trembling hands together.

"However strange or absurd it might sound, I want you to answer the question."

"What is it?" she forced herself to ask, wishing she could run to the house and hide.

"Why were those bandits chasing you that day on the trail?"

Jennie stumbled backward, his question knocking the breath from her as if she'd been punched in the stomach. She reached out and grabbed the fence to steady herself. "I…" She bit her lip and tasted blood. "I…told you already. They were after my money."

"Was it your money?"

"What do you mean?" She twisted around to look at the fence, the milling cattle, the distant mountains—anything but Caleb.

"Just answer the question, Jennie. Was the money they were after rightfully yours?"

"W-why are you asking me this?" A spark of anger ignited inside her and she stoked it with defensive thoughts—afraid if she wasn't angry, she might drown in his displeasure. Did he have to go and ruin everything when she was so close to winning the ranch back? Couldn't he leave well enough alone? "I wouldn't do anything I didn't feel was best for my family."

Caleb slammed his fist against the fence, making her jump. "You're avoiding the question. Was that your money or not?"

"No, it wasn't." She folded her arms and pressed them together, trying to hold in the ache beginning in her chest. "I took it from them, all right? But the money was already taken from its original owners, and the men who had it would have spent the money on drinks or worse. I used it for something good and decent."

"Decent?" He blew out his breath. "The money was stolen. It doesn't matter what they would've spent it on. It belonged to someone else."

"Why are you asking me this?" she repeated, her voice rising in pitch as anger and fear battled inside her. "Why now? Why today?"

"Because Mr. King," Caleb said, his jaw clenching, "was kind enough to share your exploits with me during our conversation at the store."

"Now who's being dishonest?" she lashed out in defense. "You said he only talked to you about working for him."

"I said he offered me a job and that he is a scoundrel. All of that is true. I wasn't trying to keep the rest of our conversation from you, but I needed time to…to think."

"And what have you decided?" Her voiced sounded as small as she felt.

Instead of answering, Caleb countered with a question of his own. "That wasn't the first robbery was it?"

She hazarded a glance at him and regretted it at once. The hurt and betrayal on his face nearly stopped her heart altogether.

"How many stage robberies have you committed, Jennie?"

"None," she whispered to the ground. "I never robbed a stage. I only robbed stage thieves."

Caleb's harsh laugh brought up her head. "My mistake. How many times have you taken money from thieves like the ones shooting at us that day on the trail? Like the ones I spent more than a year of my life tracking down?"

She swallowed, trying to bring moisture to her dry mouth. "Four."

"Four?" Caleb echoed before sweeping off his hat and whacking it against his leg. "Only four, huh? Well, that's good to know, I suppose. 'Cause I was worried it might've been more." She glanced away, stung by his sarcasm. "Do you know why I became a bounty hunter?"

His question caught her off guard but she welcomed the change in subject. "No. You didn't say the other day."

"It's because of Liza." When he paused, Jennie peered up at him. Fresh pain etched his face. "The stage she'd taken was robbed by four men. When they shot the driver, the stage flipped and she was killed."

Fresh guilt washed over her. She knew she wasn't responsible for those hurt by the stage thugs she took from. Still, she'd never thought about those people's lives.

"I spent over a year tracking down three of those men. The fourth got away…after I killed his partner. But to think those are the type of people you've been dealing with…" He shook his head, his voice strangled. "I'm not sure I can stay here any longer."

Did he mean a few days or forever? Jennie hadn't fooled herself into thinking he wouldn't be mad. But leaving? She didn't want to think about him going away for good. She had to make him see, make him understand. "I'll tell you the whole story, just please…" She sniffed back the threatening tears, her chin wobbling with the effort. "Don't leave—not until I've explained."

He frowned, but stood still.

"The day we met in the store when you helped me with the spilled candy, I…" She exhaled, forcing out the words with her next breath. "I'd just come from the bank. The bank president told me that if I didn't pay five hundred dollars of my loan before the end of the month—and the other thirteen hundred by this August—he'd foreclose. I was on the stagecoach back home, desperately trying to think of a way to get the money, when I met my first bandits. They got drunk during the ride and it loosened their tongues. From what they had said, and from what I'd overheard about the robbery in the mercantile earlier, I realized they were the ones responsible, and that they had two thousand dollars with them."

"Wait a minute," Caleb interjected with a shake of his head. "I heard about that robbery. The sheriff got his hands on the thieves and the stolen money."

"Not all of the money. I took the five hundred I needed. Then I got rid of the men's guns and alerted the stage driver by firing my pistol. We tied up the thieves and turned back for Fillmore. I made it onto another stage before the sheriff arrived."

"So that's how it's been with all of them?" His bitter

tone made her cringe inwardly. "You pit yourself against dangerous men and walk away without a scratch?"

"No." She gave a helpless shrug but didn't say anything more, afraid to tell him about the bullet graze to her arm.

He ran a hand through his hair as he angrily paced away from her and then returned. "What were you thinking? Why would you put your life at risk to do something so morally wrong?"

His words seeped like poison into her heart, igniting fresh resentment. "That's not how I see it. This place is my life, Caleb. It's all we have. I couldn't bear the thought of losing what my father had worked so hard to keep. I had to fight for it, in whatever way I could. That's why I've only taken money from criminals— money that's already been stolen."

"Is that what these meetings with that ruffian were all about? The robberies? Or whatever you want to call them?"

"You still think it's some kind of affair, don't you?" Jennie didn't wait for his reply. "Nathan Blaine is a business partner, nothing more. He spends enough time in the saloons to learn who'll be robbing what stage and when. I pay him for his help with half the money I take."

Caleb's face went pale and he grabbed her arm, hard. "Did you say that man's name is *Nathan Blaine*? Is his first name Otis?"

His reaction made her pulse race with new fear, though she wasn't sure why. "I don't know. He only told me he was called Nathan Blaine."

"Did he used to rob stages?"

"I—I don't know for sure."

He let go of her arm and marched past her, then

seemed to change his mind. He spun back, his eyes dark blue with barely controlled anger. "You said the other day that you wouldn't be meeting with him again. Does that mean you're done robbing stage thieves?"

The roar of her heartbeat in her ears nearly drowned out his question. How could she tell him no? "Caleb…" She lifted her thumbnail to her mouth and then dropped her hand. "The bank called my loan due in twelve days. I still owe five hundred and fifty dollars. There's another stage robbery planned for tomorrow—"

"What? No." The muscles in his jaw tightened again. "No." He stalked toward the house.

Jennie raced after him. "Caleb, wait."

She gripped his sleeve, but released it when he spun around. The pain in his eyes eerily matched the pain in another pair of eyes, ones Jennie hadn't seen in eight years. Her mother had looked as troubled and hollow the day she'd left as Caleb did now.

"Where are you going?" she asked, her voice rising with alarm.

"I'm not going to stay here and watch you ride off to do something illegal—something dangerous. If you were caught, you'd go to *jail,* Jennie. Jail. For a long time. What would happen to your family then? What would Will and Grandma Jones do?"

"What I am supposed to do? Say goodbye to all of this?" She swept her arm in an arc, taking in the house and barn with the motion. "I've worked for years to make this place beautiful and profitable like my father wanted. But I can't…" She stifled the sob rising in her throat with a fist to her mouth. "How can I do that if I lose the place? Are we just supposed to start over with nothing?"

Caleb reached to hold her hand for the first time all evening. His touch sent a jolt of hope through her until he spoke. "You could walk away from it. Start over, like I suggested this morning."

*Abandon the ranch?* "I can't—not yet." That couldn't be the only answer. "Maybe we could sell the cattle to hold the bank off a little longer. I could go see Mr. Dixon and beg him to reconsider." She realized her mistake the moment the words were out.

"Isn't that who you went to see in Fillmore?"

Jennie flushed.

"You didn't go, did you? It was just another ruse for a robbery, wasn't it?"

"I could talk to him, for real this time. Maybe he'd extend the loan." She squeezed his hand, hoping he'd understand. "Please, Caleb. I can't give up—not like my mother."

"Is that what this is really all about?" He yanked his hand from her grasp. "Not giving up like your mother?"

"You don't know anything about it." She wrapped her arms around herself to ward off the sudden cold inside her.

His answering gaze seemed to pierce into the hidden corners of her soul. "Maybe not. But I know this. Your mother was too scared or stubborn to ask for help when she needed it most, and that's your problem, too. You judged all those people at church, while you sat out here with your nose in the air, not willing to ask anything from anybody."

"They wouldn't have helped us anyway." She no longer cared about keeping the tears back; they slid hot down her face, creating the only warmth in her body.

"How do you know? There are a lot of decent people

in this world who would've gladly lent a hand until you could get back on your feet. And what about God? Did you ask Him what to do?" Caleb rubbed a tired hand over his face. "No. You just went ahead and solved the problem your own way—by robbing bandits."

Before she could reply, he took another step toward the house.

"I'm falling in love with you, Jennie," he said, his back to her. "Even knowing all of this, my feelings haven't changed. But I think it's best if I leave."

"Wh-what are you saying?" His words resurrected the painful thumping of her heart. Why did everyone have to leave? First her mother, then her father and now Caleb.

"How can I stay?" Caleb turned slowly to face her, his expression full of grief. "I can't live here. Not when I know my wages and the ranch are paid for with stolen money."

Jennie jabbed at the tears on her cheeks with the back of her hand. "There's nothing that'll change your mind?"

He hesitated, causing Jennie to hope again, then he lowered his head. "You've made your choice clear. I'll leave in the morning. Don't worry about my pay." With that, he walked away, not looking back.

Jennie hurried to the bunkhouse, grateful for once that they didn't have any other ranch hands. She slumped to the floor, her chin resting on her knees. Her unrestrained sobs echoed off the walls.

When her shoulders stopped shaking, she twisted her head to study the loose board that concealed most of the stolen money. For the first time in eight months, she questioned the course she'd taken that day in the stage with Horace and Clyde. She hadn't meant to do anything wrong or hurt the people she loved.

Was it too late to make things right? Or was she in too deep to turn back now? The stillness of the room held no answers.

# Chapter Sixteen

Grandma Jones served Caleb's favorite dish for supper—flapjacks and fried potatoes. But despite the delicious smells and the sweet taste of the molasses he drizzled over everything, he could barely choke down the meal.

"You haven't touched much of your food, Caleb," Grandma Jones said, giving him a long look.

Caleb ate another bite and swallowed. "Not because it isn't excellent. I guess I'm just a bit tuckered out."

"You aren't the only one." She nodded at Will who'd fallen asleep in his chair, his head resting beside his plate on the table.

Caleb didn't want to say goodbye to Will or Grandma Jones tomorrow. They'd become like family the past six weeks and he hated the idea of them being hurt by Jennie's foolish choices.

Should he turn Jennie in to the law? No, he couldn't do that. But he did know someone who deserved to be brought in. He stood abruptly and took his half-full plate to the sideboard.

"I think Saul and I are gonna go for a ride. Will you

tell Jennie?" he asked Grandma Jones. "I'm not sure where she went."

Grandma Jones lifted an eyebrow. "I'll tell her when she comes in. You going to be gone long?"

"We'll be back in a few hours."

He left the kitchen and went to his room. Inside, he loaded his revolvers and placed them in the holster he buckled around his waist. He slipped outside and headed to the barn. He hadn't seen Jennie since before supper. Thankfully she wasn't in the barn. He needed to complete his plan before he saw her again.

After saddling Saul, Caleb led the horse toward town. With sunset coming later in the evening, he would have plenty of time to do what he had to and be back at the ranch before too late.

His earlier anger and hurt at Jennie's confession rolled through him again as he rode. How could she have lied to him and her family? How could she have participated in something so wrong? And then to throw in lots with the likes of Black-Eyed Blaine.

Thoughts of Nathan led to thoughts of Liza and her unfair death. This man had never paid for robbing Caleb of his fiancée and his dreams of marriage and family; he had escaped any consequence. *Well, that ends tonight.* Caleb clenched the reins tight as seeds of hate and revenge sprouted anew inside him.

This time Caleb wouldn't let him go. This time Nathan would see justice served for all his misdeeds, starting with robbing Liza's stage. Vengeance burned hot through his veins and he urged Saul into a gallop. He would finally bring in his last man.

Caleb rode straight to the saloon, certain from Jennie's story that Nathan would be there. He pulled his hat low and entered the crowded establishment. Raucous laughter and the smell of booze filled the air. Taking a seat at an empty table at the back, Caleb searched the room for Nathan. He didn't see him.

Tasting bitter disappointment, he started to stand when a couple coming down the stairs caught his eye. He sat back down when he realized it was Nathan and a saloon girl. Fresh loathing for this man washed over Caleb, and he grit his teeth to keep from leaping up and shooting him at once. Instead he slipped one of his guns from his holster and concealed it beneath his jacket as he waited for Nathan and the girl to find a table.

Once they were seated, Caleb rose to his feet and ambled in their direction. He paused at a table where a poker game was in full swing, feigning interest so he would appear to be just one of the crowd. He didn't want Nathan to see him coming until too late.

Caleb angled his way across the room to come in at Nathan's back. The stage robber had obviously gone soft in the three years since robbing Liza's stage to sit in the open with his back to most of the room. Bringing him in would be easier than Caleb had thought.

He approached the two who were whispering, keeping his footsteps light. Someone on the other side of the room shouted something and Nathan turned in that direction. Caleb quickly dropped into a seat at the table next to theirs. He held still as Nathan returned to his conversation with the saloon girl.

Scooting his chair out from the table, Caleb twisted in his seat and brought the gun from beneath his jacket. His heart lurched with familiar anticipation, just as it had when he'd brought in Nathan's three partners—two alive, one dead.

*One dead,* his mind repeated.

Caleb froze, his fingers gripped so tight around his gun that they started to ache. He wasn't wrong to bring this criminal to justice—was he? *No, but you made a promise.*

Remorse every bit as sharp as his hatred cut through him and he had to gulp in several deep breaths. He might have killed Nathan's partner in self-defense, but Caleb's dreams of revenge had brought him to that fateful situation. After that, he'd promised God he would give up bounty hunting, he would give up his thirst for retribution. Neither one would bring back Liza or restore peace to his life.

*So how can I go through with this?* he asked himself, glancing over his shoulder at Nathan's bent head. *Help me do right, Lord.*

A new idea emerged from his troubled thoughts—a way to keep his promise, but also keep the man from implicating Jennie if Caleb turned him over to the sheriff. As much as Caleb disliked Jennie's choices, he hated even more the thought of her being put away behind bars and leaving her grandmother and Will to fend for themselves. Standing, he stuck his gun against Nathan's back and leaned forward over the man's shoulder.

"Howdy, Mr. Blaine."

Nathan lifted his chin slowly and shot a glance up at Caleb. "Howdy. You're Jennie's hired hand." He turned to the girl beside him whose face had gone white. Even if she couldn't see the gun in Caleb's hand, she clearly sensed he wasn't being friendly. "Is this some jealous rampage?"

"No." Caleb allowed a mirthless laugh. "This is actually your lucky day…" He bent toward Nathan's ear and whispered, "Black-Eyed Blaine."

The color drained from Nathan's face and he frowned. "Will you excuse us, Bette? No need to look so alarmed, love. This here's a business meeting."

The girl eyed them both before climbing to her feet. She walked away, throwing them one last glance over her shoulder. When she was out of earshot, Nathan demanded, "What do you want?"

Caleb shifted the gun barrel to the man's side and slid into the seat next to him. "The way I see it is I've got enough information on you to see you jailed for life. Not just for robbing my fiancée's stage three years ago and indirectly killing her." Caleb paused as Nathan visibly swallowed hard. "But also working with Miss Jones to rob a lot of good people of their money."

"How's this my lucky day then?"

"Because I'm gonna let you go."

Nathan's brow furrowed. "I don't understand."

"Then I'll make it real clear, Mr. Blaine." Caleb pressed the gun farther into Nathan's side to show he meant business. "You are going to leave this saloon in sixty seconds or less and then you are going to hightail it out of town. I don't care where you go or what you do. But if I ever hear the name Nathan Blaine around here again or learn you've been mixing with stage thugs, I'll have you arrested so fast you won't have time to grab your boots. Is that clear enough?"

Nathan gave a slow nod.

Caleb rose to his feet and slipped his gun beneath his jacket again. "Now get up and walk out that door."

Nathan stood, his eyes meeting Caleb's. "You were the one in that cabin, weren't you?"

"Yes."

"Why'd you let me go twice?"

Caleb frowned, fighting the urge to change his mind. "I guess you could say it has to do with redemption."

"Then I suppose you'd offer some to another?"

Caleb didn't know what he meant.

"Miss Jones," Nathan said, his voice thoughtful. "She's not a criminal—not like me. Just desperate to hold on to the only thing she's got left."

Caleb frowned. He didn't care to discuss the matter with Nathan Blaine.

"Much obliged." Nathan gathered up his hat from off the table and put it on. With another nod to Caleb, he headed for the door.

Blowing out his breath, Caleb sank back down in his chair. He'd come so close to breaking his vow, to giving in to the hate again. His limbs felt shaky. He allowed himself a few minutes to gather his strength again before he left the saloon. Nathan was nowhere to be seen, but his last words stayed with Caleb. Did Jennie really think the ranch was the only thing she had left? When he let himself think about it, he realized that she probably did. The ranch was her home, her legacy from her father and her opportunity to give her brother and grandmother a safe haven.

Had he ever had anything in his life that mattered that much? Not until recently, Caleb realized. In fact, he'd spent the past three years running from everything that he used to consider valuable and important—his home, his family, the places that reminded him of the life he'd wanted to have. It was as if he'd thought by cutting all ties to the people and places that mattered to him, he could keep from getting hurt again.

He'd been wrong—and so had Jennie. Running from any type of connection the way he had wasn't the answer, and neither was clinging to the past, like Jennie. Maybe the best choice was to hold on to the things that really mattered—the *people* who really mattered. And for him, that was Jennie. But could he truly see past what she'd done—what she planned to do *again?*

Caleb climbed onto Saul and started back for the ranch. Nathan's words echoed in his mind about redemption for Jennie. Did she deserve it? *Did I deserve it after letting vengeance rule my life?*

The question made him hang his head with sudden shame. If he had obtained forgiveness for his mistakes, then surely Jennie could, too. Somehow there had to be a way out of the mess things had become, for both of them.

The house stood dark, except for a light in the kitchen. Had Grandma Jones left a lamp on for him or was someone still up? He slipped inside and down the hallway to the kitchen. He froze when he saw Jennie seated at the table, a plate of untouched food before her. Should he talk with her or go to bed?

Something prodded him forward and he stepped into the room. Jennie looked up, her eyes red-rimmed. "I thought you'd gone to sleep."

"Same." He considered telling her about Nathan, but decided against it. She might be angry at him for sending Nathan away. "I went on a ride."

"Oh." She pushed the food around her plate with her fork. "Are you still leaving in the morning?"

"I guess that depends—on what you choose to do."

The hope in her countenance added to his own. Maybe they could set things right after all.

"I'm sorry, Caleb. I still…I mean…I don't expect you to understand. You probably don't know what it's like lying there at night, wondering how your family's going to eat…" She stopped and took a deep breath as if to steady her voice. "How you're going to survive the winter."

"I didn't exactly grow up with great wealth, Jennie. My parents came here from Nebraska with only the few things they could cram into a wagon. They worked hard to make our farm what it is, and we worked right along beside them."

"I know. But I don't have my parents to help or all those siblings like you. It's just…me." The sight of her lovely face etched with concern still made his heart pound, made him want to protect her—especially from herself.

"It doesn't have to be that way. You have your brother and your grandmother. And me." He crossed to the table and took a seat. "I'll always be your friend, Jennie. Always."

"Just a friend, huh?" Tears swam in her deep brown eyes.

"You don't have to go through with this robbery tomorrow. There has to be another way. We can still make a life together."

"I told you before. I can't leave this ranch behind— not yet. Mr. Dixon will have to drag me off the property before I'll abandon everything I've sacrificed for."

"Is that what this is about? Making sacrifices?" He leaned forward. "A sacrifice is only worth something if it's right. Sacrificing your integrity, your happiness, your freedom—that won't bring you anything but misery. I know, because I tried."

She rubbed at her temples. "Maybe you're right. But haven't you ever loved something so much you thought you might die if it was taken away?"

"Yes," he said. He stopped to swallow the lump in his throat. "You."

A soft cry escaped her lips before her face crumpled and she covered it with her hands. Caleb watched, helpless, for a minute as she cried, then he reached out and placed his hand on her shoulder. He could feel the quiet sobs shaking through her.

In that moment of shared grief, Caleb knew with certainty that he loved her and he always would. His future would be bleak indeed without this redhead by his side.

"Jennie, please look at me."

Slowly she lifted her head, agony burning in every feature.

"I love you, despite everything you've told me." He brushed a piece of hair from her damp cheek, her skin warm and soft beneath his touch. "Your friendship is dearer to me than anything I possess right now or hope to one day have. To show you I mean it, I have something to give you. Wait here."

Caleb hurried out of the kitchen and up the stairs. The wound from Jennie's betrayal would take time to fully heal, but he was confident it would.

He entered his room and pulled the leather pouch from underneath his mattress. Three hundred dollars wouldn't be everything Jennie needed, but it would be a start. A start toward a future together.

# Chapter Seventeen

A thud of footsteps brought up Jennie's head. Grandma Jones pulled a shawl around her long nightgown and entered the kitchen.

"I wanted to make sure you'd come in and gotten supper. Is Caleb back from his ride?"

"Yes." Jennie brushed at the tears on her face. "Thank you for saving me some flapjacks."

"You two have a fight?"

Blushing, Jennie stuffed some food into her mouth and swallowed before answering, "I'm not sure what you mean."

Grandma Jones gave an amused snort. "Come on, Jennie girl, I know a lovers' quarrel when I see one. First off, you two didn't come into supper together like you usually do, and Caleb didn't know where you were earlier. Second, your eyes are red from crying, no matter how hard you try to hide it." She folded her arms over her nightgown. "You want to talk about it?"

"No…maybe."

Her grandmother took the seat beside her, but Jennie was unsure where to start. Caleb's tender words still rang in her ears—*I love you. Your friendship is dearer to me than anything I possess right now or hope to one day have.* Did she believe him? After all she'd confessed, would he really stay?

Caleb reentered the kitchen before she could voice any of her confusing thoughts to Grandma Jones. His blue eyes appeared especially bright and he held something in one hand.

"This is for you, Jennie." He lifted a leather pouch.

"What is it?"

"Two hundred and ninety seven dollars."

"What?" Jennie choked out. Grandma Jones gave a soft gasp.

Caleb pulled a thick wad of bills from the pouch. "I want you to use this to pay some of your debt against the ranch." He set the cash on the table. "It won't be enough to cover everything, but I'm sure we can come up with a way to earn the rest."

"But…" She brought her hands to her mouth as she stared in shock at the money. The money meant to fund Caleb's freight business. She remembered the way his face had lit up when he talked about his plans. "But this is for your business. So you can have a fresh start."

"Not anymore." He knelt in front of her. "Think about what you want, but remember we can do this—together."

She couldn't form a reply. Red-hot shame burned her throat at his selfless offer.

He stood, regarding her with a level look. "I'll see you in the morning." His words were full of confidence that she'd make the right decision. "Good night, ladies."

"Good night, Caleb," Grandma Jones called after him.

Jennie watched Caleb leave and felt a piece of her

going with him. She stared down at the stack of money before her.

*Almost three hundred dollars.*

She couldn't quite believe the answer to most of her troubles sat in front of her. She imagined walking into the bank, head held high as she plunked the cash onto Mr. Dixon's desk. Where would they get the rest to pay off her loan in time, though?

There was more cash in the bunkhouse that she could combine with Caleb's money, but Jennie quickly pushed the idea from her mind. She had to do things right this time if she wanted Caleb to stay, which meant giving back the stolen money to the rightful owners. She would have to find some other way to make up the difference.

For the first time in months, Jennie allowed herself to imagine being free of her debt. No more robberies, no more lies, no more being alone. Yet her freedom wouldn't come without a price. Her ranch, for Caleb's dream.

Happy memories from the past six weeks flitted through her mind: Caleb helping her on the trail, watching him learn to be a cowboy, making him laugh, kissing him for the first time, talking of their lives and their feelings for each other.

"You ready to talk?" Grandma Jones asked.

Jennie had almost forgotten her grandmother sitting there. She pushed aside her plate, her stomach too wound in knots to eat. She fingered one of the bills. "I think I've made a terrible mistake, Grandma."

"Oh, honey." Grandma Jones tipped up Jennie's chin, her eyes warm and caring. "That's what life's about. You start down one path and realize you should have taken another. The important thing is recognizing when you need to switch."

Jennie set down the bills and took a steadying breath.

"Did you ever make any big mistakes?" she asked as she stood and took her plate to the sink.

Grandma Jones laughed. "I've made hundreds and hundreds of little ones—like we all do. Made my share of big ones, too—like leaving home so young and writing only sporadically. I didn't even make it back to Illinois after my mother's death. I don't know if my father and sisters ever quite forgave me that." She clasped her hands together and rested them on the table. "But there's one decision I still shudder to think I almost got wrong."

"What was it?"

"I almost didn't marry your grandfather."

Jennie whirled around. "What happened?"

"That's a long story." Her grandmother smiled and nodded at Jennie's vacant chair. Jennie returned to her seat. Anticipation tingled through her, nearly erasing her worries—this wasn't a story she'd heard before. "I met your grandpa when I was finishing up my third year of teaching. We courted some, and I liked him very much. But I decided to accept my aunt's offer to spend the summer traveling with her.

"I'd always wanted to go to Europe and New York City. Then your grandfather started talking marriage and settling down. I didn't know what to do. I wanted to marry him, but I also felt this was my one and only chance to see the world. So I told him he'd have to wait until I came home to marry me."

"Did you go and see all those places?" Jennie tried to picture seeing the ocean or a castle, things she'd only read about in her grandmother's collection of books.

Grandma Jones shook her head, her gaze distant. "I never went. When I climbed aboard the steamboat to leave, I had the strongest feeling I needed to get right back off, find Matthew Jones and accept his hand in marriage." She shrugged her thin shoulders. "That's what I did. We were married a week later. He was such a faith-filled man—always sharing his love of the Lord with others. I don't know if I would have grown as close to God as I have if I hadn't married your grandfather." She traced a grain in the tabletop. When she spoke again, her voice sounded full of unshed tears, "Not a day goes by that I don't thank God for nudging me hard enough to get off that boat."

"Didn't you regret not seeing all those lovely places, though?"

Her grandmother lifted her chin. "Sometimes. The only places I've seen since then have been mostly wilderness." She chuckled. "But usually the hardest thing to do is the right one. I know now that the people and the God I love are far more important to me than seeing Paris or London."

Jennie rested her chin on her hands. She hadn't put God and the people in her life ahead of material things, like the ranch. A new wave of remorse ran through her.

"I'm sorry, Grandma."

"Whatever for?" Grandma Jones reached over and gave Jennie's arm a gentle squeeze.

"You must have missed going to church all these years."

"Yes, but I knew it'd be hard for you to return—at least until you were ready."

"It's not that I stopped believing in God. I just didn't want to hear the rumors about my mother. I didn't want to face seeing the possible truth in the eyes of all those people whispering about her." Jennie lowered her hands to the table. "I couldn't face feeling responsible for her leaving."

"Now, Jennie girl. Nothing they said is true. And you certainly weren't at fault for your mama leaving." She rubbed Jennie's arm. "Your mother left because she couldn't handle life out here anymore. She loved your father, but she didn't share his dream of building a home out here in the West. She went along with it, moved from one place to another, starting over again and again without complaining, but she couldn't be truly happy that way." Grandma Jones released a sigh. "She wasn't used to that kind of life, not after growing up in a wealthy house with everything she needed in easy reach. She still loved you and Will and your father, though. She told me so the night before she left. She just had to figure out what she truly needed to be happy. I think if she hadn't taken ill, she might have come back and done just fine."

Jennie sniffed back fresh tears. "I'd like to think so."

Grandma Jones pulled Jennie onto her knees and gave her a fierce hug. Jennie embraced her and then rested her head in her grandmother's lap. "Your mother did have a backbone on her. Don't think she didn't. To start over like that, you have to have something in you. You've gotten that from both your parents." She stroked Jennie's hair. "You're strong, Jennie. But don't make the mistake of being so strong you forget to let others help you. We all need that."

Jennie swiped at her runny nose with her hand and nodded. She'd tried to be strong for so long, but she'd done it alone. Now she needed help, and surely she could be humble enough to ask.

Lifting her head, Jennie forced herself to meet her grandmother's eyes. "This is one of those times I need help, Grandma. But first, I have to tell you something. Something I'm ashamed to admit..."

Jennie slipped into her room and softly shut the door behind her. She guessed it must be after midnight, but strangely, she felt more awake than she had this morning.

After changing into her nightdress, she started to climb into bed. The trunk beneath the windowsill drew her notice. A longing to bridge the gap of misunderstanding between her and her mother pushed Jennie to her feet.

Kneeling before the trunk, she opened the lid and drew out the unopened letter. She stared at the wrinkled surface, imagining her mother's hands—those soft, delicate hands—sealing her words inside.

Jennie swallowed the anxiety pulsing through her as she tore open the envelope and removed two sheets of paper, filled with the faded but familiar handwriting of her mother.

Using the trunk as a seat, she pulled back the curtains and read her letter by moonlight.

August 10, 1863
Dearest Jennie,
I hope this finds you well and happy. Your father wrote and told me what a great help you've been to him, and I thank you for it. He also says you've grown taller this past year. I can hardly imagine my little girl a grown woman now.

Your hair has probably darkened, though I imagine it will always stay that rich red color that you inherited from my side of the family. With your pretty brown eyes, I cannot help but think what a beauty you must be. I wish so badly I could see and hold you. Are you too old, daughter, to sit again on your mother's lap, resting your head against my shoulder as you used to?

How are Will and Grandma Jones? Be certain to listen to your grandmother; she is a wise woman. Are the cattle faring well? And your father? He seems content enough, but I often wonder what heartache I have inflicted on him and you children.

Every day I live with the guilt of running away, but I no longer felt capable of being a good mother. I thought returning to my home would heal my heart, but now I've found I left it out West with you.

Never be ashamed, my dear girl, to stumble about sometimes, but also find the courage to ask for help when you need it most. I pray to God each day for forgiveness. I know now I cannot move through life without His help. Remember that, Jennie.

I have often packed my things with plans to return before I unpack them again. Perhaps it is cowardice of me, but I fear your rejection. Maybe one day I will be able to forgive myself and come home at last. Until then, know I love you. You will be an extraordinary woman, stronger and more capable in that wilderness than I ever was. But leave room in your heart for love and softness too, Jennie. Without both strength and tenderness, you may find life much more difficult.

Please write, if you wish to. I long for any word

from my family. I shall write again soon if I am
able. I seem to have left my good health at the
ranch, but do not worry. I am to see the doctor here
soon, and everything shall be fine.
All my love,
Your mother, Olivia Wilson Jones.

Jennie could hardly make out her mother's signature
through the tears spilling down her face. She'd never
wept so much in her life.

Leaning her head against the cool windowpane, she
allowed her anguish to flow uninhibited. She cried for
her mother's pain and for her own, for her selfishness in
not reading the letter years earlier, when she could have
written back. For so long, she had concentrated only on
the hurt she felt, never thinking of the shame and suf-
fering her mother might have experienced.

"I'm sorry, Mama," she whispered into the dark, hoping and praying her mother could somehow hear her
words, even in heaven. "I should have written. I should
have tried to see you, at least once before you died. I'm
so very sorry."

Jennie covered her mouth with her hand to muffle the
sound of her sobs. She didn't want to wake the rest of
the family. When she could breathe normally again, she
read the letter through once more, then tucked it again
inside the envelope. Instead of putting it in the trunk,
she returned to her bed and slipped the precious pages
beneath her pillow. *To read often.*

She climbed beneath the covers, but a thought made
her sit up. Her mother had told her to remember God.
That meant voicing to Him the truth she'd told her grandmother and Caleb tonight. His help was the real one she

needed in the days ahead. Feeling a bit awkward, she knelt beside her bed, unable to remember the last time she'd gotten down on her knees to pray.

*Perhaps if I'd prayed earlier I wouldn't be in such a mess.* The realization both surprised and humbled her. Bowing her head, she silently reviewed everything she'd done the past eight months, starting with the day she had left the bank, overwhelmed with despair at possibly losing the ranch. When she finished cataloging all her wrongdoings, she tentatively pled for forgiveness.

Once she ran out of things to say, Jennie ended her prayer and sat on the bed. She felt nothing at first, then slowly a feeling of peace began to spread throughout her body. A feeling similar to the one she'd felt during the singing at church. A feeling almost like an embrace.

She kept still for a few minutes, hugging her knees to her chest, as she relished the emotion. When it faded, she got into bed, feeling hope for the first time in months.

## Chapter Eighteen

Caleb woke the next morning feeling like he hadn't slept much at all. He hadn't been able to find a comfortable position, and when he had finally drifted to sleep, he had a disturbing dream. It wasn't his usual nightmare. This time when he burst into the cabin, he found Jennie there with Nathan, wearing a bandanna over her face and carting her pistol.

*She's given all that up,* he reassured himself as he climbed out of bed and got dressed. No matter how troubling his dreams, he'd seen the remorse in Jennie's eyes last night and felt confident she'd accept his money to help the ranch. Besides, without Nathan around to help her, she'd be forced to give up robbing stage thieves.

Relieved he wouldn't have to say goodbye to the family, Caleb hurried down the stairs, eager to see Jennie. He planned to take her into his arms and give her a good, long kiss, even in the company of her brother and grandmother.

Caleb skidded to a stop inside the kitchen doorway. Grandma Jones and Will were moving about the kitchen getting breakfast onto the table, but Jennie wasn't there. Alarm began to worm its way up his throat.

*Maybe she's in the barn, getting an early start on chores.*

"Morning," he said, relieving the stack of plates from Grandma Jones. As he placed them around the table, he noted there were only three, not four. "Did Jennie eat already?" He kept his voice as casual as he could, despite the sudden pounding of his heart.

"She left about half an hour ago." Grandma Jones took a seat and motioned for Will and Caleb to join her. "Said she had some business to take care of in town this morning."

Caleb gripped the plate in his hand so hard he thought it might snap. She didn't still plan to go through with the robbery, did she? No, she wouldn't. Not after their talk last night, not after he'd given her his hard-earned money. "Will she be long?"

"Probably most of the day, but she said not to worry."

Something in the woman's green eyes told Caleb that Grandma Jones knew more than she was saying. But she wouldn't know about Jennie robbing stage thieves, so it didn't matter what lie her granddaughter had told in order to go to town alone.

"Sit down, Caleb. Have some biscuits." It sounded more like a command than a suggestion.

He shook his head. "I'm not hungry this morning. I think I'll go out to the barn." Turning away, he prayed they hadn't seen the pain seeping into his face.

Instead of heading outside, Caleb stepped quietly up the stairs to his room. He removed his pack from beside the bureau and opened the top drawer.

All the betrayal and frustration he'd felt the day before rushed back full force and he had to stop and take several deep breaths to calm himself. He had forgiven Jennie's past deeds, but that was when he'd thought she was willing to change her ways. He refused to be a witness to her deceitful and dangerous actions—no matter how much he still cared for her.

Distance and time would eventually heal his heart—again—though he vowed to be done with love. Too much pain, not to mention the loss of all the money he'd saved. Bitter disappointment cut through him at the thought of having to find another job and putting off his dream of a freight business another year, maybe two.

Once packed, Caleb shouldered his bag and grabbed his guns. He managed to slip outdoors without Will and Grandma Jones noticing. He planned to saddle up Saul and come back to the house to say goodbye. The waiting horse would show the family he meant to leave—now. He needed to be long gone before Jennie came back. Seeing her again would be too painful.

He strode with heavy steps to the barn and entered the building. Inside, he set his pack on the ground and grabbed the horse's tack. Saul pawed at the straw as if sensing Caleb's eagerness to leave.

The sound of pounding horse hooves brought up Caleb's head in time to see a horse and rider rush past. Caleb hurried out of the barn. *Who would come to the house this early unless something's happened?* Anxiety for Jennie's safety filled him.

"Hello there," he called to the rider, who'd dismounted near the porch. "Can I help you?"

The man came around the side of the horse. He didn't even reach the top of the saddle. Grabbing the lead rope, he led his horse toward Caleb.

"Do I know you?" Caleb asked. The man didn't answer, but as he drew closer, Caleb recognized him as one of King's cowboys—the one called Gunner. "Hold up there a minute. I told Mr. King I wasn't working for him, and that hasn't changed. You can hop right back on that horse and leave." Turning his back to him, Caleb started for the barn.

"Wait. You're Miss Jones's hired hand. There's somethin' I need to tell ya."

*I was more than that to her, at least until yesterday,* Caleb thought. "What do you want?"

Gunner stepped closer as he spoke. "The thieves she's planning to rob today aren't really thieves."

Caleb's eyes narrowed with suspicion. "How'd you know about that?"

"Because Mr. King and three of his men are gonna rob that stage. It's a trap for Miss Jones."

Caleb scowled at the cowhand. How he'd like to maim that arrogant rancher. "What does King have against Jennie?"

Gunner licked his lips and studied the ground. "He wants her land. That's why he paid off the bank president to call her loan due, why he's rustled her cattle and why he had me follow her all over town and up to Fillmore." He threw a guilty glance at Caleb. "When he found out she's kept her ranch going by robbing stage thieves, King set a trap for her. He knew she couldn't resist five thousand dollars. He's gonna rob the stage first and wait for Jennie to come rob him."

"Then what?" Caleb's pulse thundered in his ears as the weight of the cowboy's confession hit him.

"He'll likely shoot her and claim self-defense."

Mistrust and worry battled inside Caleb. "Why should I believe you? You're a cattle thief and a spy."

"Even so, I don't condone murder." Gunner remounted his horse with surprising ease despite his lack of height. "I gotta go before someone at King's ranch notices I'm gone."

"What stage are they robbing?" Caleb asked. His lingering doubts had disappeared. The cowhand wouldn't risk his job—and possibly his life—to ride over and tell anything less than the truth.

"It's the stage coming east from Pioche, Nevada. King'll overtake it in Milford Valley before the stage reaches the Mineral Mountains. Good luck to you, cowboy." With that, he thrust his spurs into his mount's side and took off at a gallop.

Caleb sprinted to the house, but he slowed his steps before he entered the kitchen where Will and Grandma Jones lingered at the table.

"I realized I've got some things I need to do in town today myself," Caleb said, keeping his voice light, despite the urgency pulsing through him.

"Can I come?" Will's face lit up with excitement.

"Not today, Will. With Jennie and I both gone, someone needs to watch the cattle this morning."

Will blew out his breath in obvious disappointment, but he nodded acceptance.

"I shouldn't be too long." Caleb moved to the door. "I'll try to find Jennie, and we can ride back together."

Grandma Jones gave him a questioning look, but Caleb simply forced a smile. "Save some supper for us," he said as walked out the front door.

Once outside, he let the smile drop from his face as he ran to the barn. Having his horse already saddled saved him time. However much he didn't agree with Jennie's actions, he wouldn't stand back and let her walk into mortal danger.

*I only hope I'm not too late,* he thought as he urged Saul toward the distant mountains.

Jennie tied Dandy to the hitching post outside the sheriff's office. She brushed away the dust sticking to her brown and cream dress and made sure the breeches she had on underneath didn't show. Her work pants would give her more mobility for the hard ride ahead, but for now, she needed to look the part of a proper young lady.

Resolved she'd made the right decision, Jennie inhaled a deep breath, tugged her kid gloves into place, and forced her feet in the direction of the door. Anticipation and worry pulled equally at her heart as she turned the handle and stepped into the building.

A young deputy sat with his boots resting on top of an empty table, one hand drawing his revolver and spinning it back into its holster. When he saw her, he immediately put his gun away, jerked his feet to the floor and sat up straight.

"Can I help you, miss?"

Jennie nodded. "I need to speak to the sheriff."

The deputy arched an eyebrow in open curiosity as he studied Jennie. "One moment."

He rose from his seat and knocked on the inner door situated at his right. After a moment a muffled response came from the other side. The deputy opened the door and stuck his head inside. Jennie could easily hear his words, however quiet.

"A lady to see you, sir... No, she didn't say what it's

about… All right. I'll send her in." He stepped back into the main office and motioned Jennie forward. "He'll see you."

Jennie thanked him and strode purposefully into the tiny room. A man with a drooping, sandy-colored mustache and a silver star attached to his waistcoat stood up from his desk.

"Come in, miss. Let me get you a seat."

The sheriff plucked a hardback chair from the corner and positioned it in front of his desk. He motioned for Jennie to sit down while he shut the door.

"Now what can I do for you?" he asked, taking his seat behind the desk again.

Jennie swallowed hard—there was no going back now that she was here.

"I've come to inform you about a stage robbery taking place today."

The lines on the man's forehead bunched together in consternation as he eased back into his chair. "A stage robbery? Today?"

"That's correct." Jennie kept her gaze steady on his blue-gray eyes.

He studied her, the corners of his mouth lifting in hidden amusement. "You mind sharing a few more details with me, Miss…"

"Jones," she finished. "I'm afraid that's all the information I can give you at the moment, sheriff, unless you agree to help me with something."

"Is that right?" He joined his hands to form a steeple and tapped his index fingers against his chin.

Bestowing a ladylike smile, she leaned forward. "I am more than happy to share everything you need to apprehend the bandits and keep a very large sum of money safe if…" She paused long enough to secure his full attention. "If you'll agree not to press charges against me."

This time the sheriff did laugh, but it trailed off when she didn't join in. "You're serious, aren't you?"

"Very serious."

He shook his head, a smile still peeking out beneath his mustache. "And what sort of fiendish behavior are we talking about, Miss Jones? Selling whiskey to the Indians? Sneaking milk from a neighbor's cow?"

Jennie tried not to appear offended. He certainly underestimated what she was capable of, but he also held the key—or the lock—to her freedom.

"No, sir." She lowered her head, staring hard at a particularly large knot in the wood of the desk. *You can do this,* she told herself. *It's the right thing to do, no matter what he chooses to do afterward.* She thought of Caleb and the admiration on his face once she told him about coming to the sheriff, even if it was from behind bars. The thought of his reaction gave her the courage to lift her chin.

"I've been robbing stage thieves."

When she'd finished telling the sheriff the particulars of her financial troubles and the different robberies, purposely leaving off mention of Nathan, Jennie slumped back into her chair and waited for the man to cast his judgment. He sat quiet for almost a minute. Jennie fiddled with her gloves as she waited, her heart thumping louder in the ensuing silence.

"Very interesting account, Miss Jones." The sheriff bent forward and plucked at the end of his mustache. "We don't take stealing lightly around here. I could throw you in one of our jail cells right now."

Jennie swallowed hard, pushing the words out of her throat with effort, "Yes, sir."

"But I understand you're in a hard way and I don't want to see your kid brother and grandmother suffer any more." His face relaxed. "I also admire your gumption for wantin' to make things right."

A tiny puff of air escaped Jennie's lips, and she realized she'd been holding her breath.

"My concern now," he said, drumming his fingers on the desk, "is that you repay all that cash you stole. It needs to be to the rightful owners in a month's time. If you can do that, then I see nothin' wrong with keeping a lady like yourself from spending time behind bars."

"Really?" A month wasn't much time, but Jennie had entertained only a glimmer of hope that he'd go along with her plan.

"Now I'd like you to tell me everything I need to know to keep that stage safe and you a free woman."

Jennie lifted her mouth in a genuine smile. "The stage from Pioche, Nevada, has five thousand dollars on it for a bank up north. It will be attacked by bandits as it crosses Milford Valley in about two hours. Once they steal the money, the thieves will seek refuge in an abandoned shack north of the trail."

"Incredible," the sheriff murmured.

Jennie didn't know if he meant the bandits' scheme or her knowledge of it, but she nodded anyway, hoping it was enough to buy her freedom. He paused, long enough to make her squirm again with worry.

"If you're right, Miss Jones," he said at last, "and we're able to keep that stage and the money safe, I'll agree not to press charges against you. However, in light of your past actions, if something goes wrong and that money gets away, I'm going to assume it ended up in your pockets. Is that clear?"

"Yes, sir. You can trust me on this."

"Good. I'll round up the rest of my deputies and we'll head out there." As he pushed away from the desk and stood, Jennie rushed to her feet.

"I'd like to go, too, sheriff." When the man started to shake his head, Jennie hurried to finish. "I know you'll say it's too dangerous, but I've been living with that sort of danger for eight months. Besides, you need someone along who knows how these bandits operate."

The sheriff frowned hard at her before giving a curt nod of his head. "Perhaps you're—"

The door to the office flew open, and the deputy burst in. "I'm sorry, sir. Amos just rode up and said Old Man Lackerdey is causing a big fuss over at the saloon. He's breakin' chairs and threatenin' to shoot anybody that comes near him."

"Most likely inebriated." The sheriff cursed softly. "Miss Jones, you wait here. I'll quickly take care of Lackerdey and gather up the rest of my men. They're not gonna like having a woman with us, but I think your skills might come in handy."

Jennie graciously inclined her head. "Thank you, sir."

Nodding in return, the sheriff left his office. "See that she's comfortable, Daniels," he barked to the deputy as he headed out the door.

"Can I get you anything, miss?" Daniels grinned, making Jennie glad she had something else to do besides wait in the cramped space with the overly attentive deputy.

"Actually, I have an errand to run first." She moved past him toward the door. "I'll be back."

She escaped the building, making her way down the street to the boardinghouse where Nathan stayed. Inside, she inquired after him. A rotund housekeeper with a tight bun told her that he hadn't come in last night. *Probably too drunk, no doubt.*

Jennie asked for a pencil and paper and scrawled a quick note, telling him she couldn't meet him today and apologizing for changing her mind. She felt certain Nathan would understand the cryptic message and the housekeeper would not.

Satisfied, she left the boardinghouse and turned in the direction of the sheriff's office. She walked slowly, reluctant to face the deputy again. What was Caleb doing at the moment? *Feeding the animals most likely,* she concluded, squinting up at the sun. She hoped the sheriff hurried, so they could warn the stage in time.

Daniels jumped up as she entered the office again and offered her a chair by the window. After thanking him, Jennie sat down and turned her shoulder to him. Undaunted by her coolness, he tried making small talk with her.

When he finally fell silent, Jennie gratefully stared out the window at the comings and goings of the townspeople on the other side of the glass. What were the towns like farther north? Could she and her family be happy there? Knowing she couldn't keep the ranch from being foreclosed on, she had to consider the possibility of moving somewhere. If she could just stay near Caleb.

A sense of loss filled her at leaving Beaver. She'd miss the town and its people, despite her choice to live so isolated on the ranch these past few years. Still, there were likely to be kind neighbors wherever they went, and if they headed north, she would finally be able to see Salt Lake City, something she'd always wanted.

*But right now, we need to get to that stage.*

Jennie spun away from the window and released an impatient sigh. Any longer, and the sheriff and his men would be too late to save the money and catch the bandits. Then she'd have to forfeit her freedom.

"Do you know the time?" she asked Daniels.

His face lit up at her sudden attention, and he made a show of removing a fancy pocket watch from his waistcoat. "About half past nine, miss. Are you hungry? Can I buy you something to eat from the hotel?"

She gave an emphatic shake of her head, mentally calculating the distance to Milford Valley. If the sheriff came now, they would have just over an hour to meet the stage before the bandits did. Jennie stood up. That might be too late. If she didn't ensure the safety of that stage and its valuable freight, she would lose her bargaining chip.

"Listen," she said, stepping to the table. "A stage coming here from Nevada is going to be robbed very soon. I need you to go get the sheriff—now. Or we'll be too late."

Daniels climbed to his feet. "I'll go down there, miss. But sometimes Lackerdey takes time to calm down."

"I don't have time." She whirled around to face the door, calling over her shoulder, "Tell the sheriff I'll meet him and his men in Milford Valley."

"B-but, miss. He told you to wait—"

"I can't. It'll be easier to protect that money than steal it back." Jennie hurried out the door, not bothering to close it.

"Miss?" he called, coming outside.

Ignoring him, Jennie untied Dandy, made certain her gun was still inside the holster on her saddle and swung onto her horse. She had a stage to catch.

# Chapter Nineteen

By the time she broke free from the mountains and descended onto the sagebrush plain of Milford Valley, Jennie was glad she'd eaten very little for breakfast that morning. She'd never been so nervous to deal with stage robbers—but then, she'd always been fairly certain of the outcome. Shifting the reins from one hand to the other, Jennie wiped her sweaty palms against her dress and took a long, shaky breath.

She urged Dandy into a faster gait as she cautiously searched the valley for any sign of the bandits. Without knowing where the robbers would ambush the stage, she focused her attention on reaching the western chain of mountains and the stagecoach before they did.

A flash of movement caught Jennie's eye, and she turned northward to determine the source. A quarter of a mile away a lone rider raced in the same westerly direction as she was moving. It couldn't be one of the bandits—there were supposed to be four of them.

Twisting in the saddle, she scrutinized the landscape again, but the rider appeared to be the only other person on the prairie besides herself.

Jennie urged Dandy a little faster and focused on the mountains ahead. From the corner of her eye, she saw the rider change directions, riding straight toward her now. She immediately reached for her pistol, keeping the weapon out of sight at her left side. She reined in her horse and searched the area for some place to hide. The nearest juniper trees weren't thick or tall enough to hide behind.

Panic pulsed through her. What should she do? Whipping around to look at the rider again, she frowned in confusion. The horse could almost be Saul. But that was impossible. Caleb and his horse were at the ranch.

Lifting her pistol, she aimed to miss, wanting only to warn the man she wasn't defenseless. Before she could squeeze the trigger, a familiar voice shouted, "Jennie!"

Jennie wheeled her horse around and charged toward Caleb, her heart racing with surprise and anticipation. How had he found her? She hadn't even told her grandmother the details of her plan, afraid of worrying her.

"Caleb," she yelled as she waved her hat in the air. She couldn't wait to tell him her plan for staying out of jail.

She jerked Dandy to a stop and dismounted at the same time Caleb dropped to the ground beside Saul. Spinning around, Jennie rushed forward to hug Caleb, but she froze when she saw his stiff stance and pain-filled gaze. His disappointment washed over her, scorching her happiness.

*He thinks I'm going through with the robbery.*

The horrid realization made her stomach sink to her shoes. "No. It's not what you think, Caleb. You don't under—"

"I'm here to warn you," he said, his voice tight.

"About what?"

"King's going to rob the stage. It's a setup. He plans to steal the money, and then when you come get it, he'll shoot you."

She sucked in her breath. "But why?"

"One of his cowhands rode over this morning and confessed the whole story." He wouldn't quite look at her. "King wants your land. He bought off the bank president in Fillmore to call your loan due, so he could claim the ranch sooner. When that didn't go like he'd planned, he tried stealing your cattle and then decided to lure you in with this stage robbery."

"You rode all this way to tell me?" Her voice quavered as unshed tears filled her throat. Even betrayed and upset, he'd still come to her aid—again.

A tortured expression contorted his handsome features. "I couldn't leave without warning you that your life is in danger. And now I need to go."

"Wait." She grabbed his sleeve before he could mount his horse.

"There's nothing more to say, Jennie. I hold no malice toward you, but I think it's better if I—"

"I'm not here to rob the bandits, Caleb."

The look on his face slowly changed from anguish to surprise. "You're not?"

Jennie shook her head.

"Then what are you doing?"

"I have to warn the stage about the attack." She forced her fingers to release his shirt, though she feared if she let go he might leave. "I've got to keep that money safe, so the sheriff won't bring charges against me."

Confusion furrowed his brow. "I don't understand."

"I struck a deal with the sheriff. I gave him the information about today's stage robbery, and if I help keep the money safe, he agreed not to press charges for the other robberies. I have to figure out a way to pay back all that money in a mon—"

He robbed her of her words when he pulled her close and pressed his lips firmly to hers. It was the first time he'd initiated a kiss between them. Jennie's heart leaped at his strong but tender touch and she threw her arms around his neck. She never wanted to let go. The thought that he might have said goodbye for good without hearing her explanation made her cling to him even tighter. He was largely the reason she was attempting to set things right today.

After a long minute, he released her, one hand cradling the side of her face. "Why didn't you wait to tell me what you were doing or leave a note? You could've got yourself killed."

"I'm sorry I didn't tell you before I left, but I wanted to be sure everything worked out with the sheriff first."

"I'm sorry I doubted you."

Jennie blushed and stared at the weeds by her boots. "I haven't given you much reason to trust me."

"I still love and believe in you," he said, tipping up her chin with his finger. "Especially now."

The rumble of distant horse hooves and wheels filled her ears and she turned toward the sound. "The stage. I have to go."

"Not by yourself, you're not." Caleb helped her into the saddle.

"The sheriff and his men are coming," she said, throwing a hopeless glance over her shoulder. "He was held up at the saloon by some drunk. I can't wait, Caleb. I have to keep that money away from King or I'll go to jail."

Caleb grasped her hand where it held the reins. "That's exactly why I'm coming with you."

Jennie smiled down at him. "Then mount up, cowboy. It's time to ride."

"What is it?" Caleb asked moments later, jerking back on the reins when he realized Jennie had come to a stop beside him.

"Something's wrong with the stage."

He studied the stagecoach moving fast over the sagebrush less than a quarter of a mile away. Instead of traveling in an easterly course toward Beaver, the stage appeared to be racing south.

As Caleb watched, the coach dropped sharply to the left, a wheel slipping into some unseen crevice, before the whole thing bounced wildly back out. Screams carried through the morning air and Caleb cringed at the frightened sound.

He couldn't see anyone sitting on the high seat. "Something's happened to the driver."

"Then we're too late," Jennie said, bitterness coating her voice. "King must have beaten us to the stage. He probably shot the driver and took the money." She threw a glance in the direction of the stage, then northward where she'd told him the bandits would be, and finally back at Caleb. "I can't lose that cash, Caleb, or the sheriff isn't going to help me. You go save the stage, and I'll go—"

"No," he interrupted. "I'm not letting you go against King alone."

"I'll just scout things out. I won't do anything rash." She threw him a pleading look. "If they decide to leave, I can follow them and then come back for help."

He scowled at her, hating the idea of being separated, but he could see her point. "All right. But you'd better be in one piece when I find you. Promise?"

Jennie nodded, a hint of a smile on her lips. "Ride straight north, about three miles. There should be an abandoned cabin there. That's where they'll be hiding out." With that, she and Dandy took off, heading north.

Caleb didn't waste time staring after her. He raced west toward the careening coach. He had a job to do, too, and the sooner he finished, the sooner he could reunite with Jennie.

The thundering of horse hooves and the cries of the panicked passengers grew louder as he drew closer to the stage. Caleb's mouth went dry with nerves. Could he really save these people?

For one horrid moment he felt as though he were chasing down Liza's stage, before it flipped. He'd done that in his dreams right after her death. He imagined her black hair flapping through the open window, her dark eyes wide with fear as she stared at him.

*This isn't Liza's stage,* Caleb told himself, shaking his head to clear the image. He hadn't been able to save Liza, hadn't even been there. If he had, he might have been killed himself instead of being the hero. *But I can save these people.*

He scanned the terrain ahead and noticed a slight ravine in the direct path of the runaway stage. Gauging the distance between the stage and the ravine, Caleb knew he'd have to hurry to keep the coach from smashing apart in the gully and killing the horses and passengers.

"Let's go," he said, urging Saul even faster. As they came even with the back of the stage, one of the leather curtains over the windows swooshed back and a feminine boot poked out. A moment later it was joined by a dark curly head.

"What are you doing?" Caleb hollered above the racket. The crazy woman was going to climb out. "You're going to kill yourself. Get back inside! I'm going to try and stop the stage."

The girl retreated most of the way back through the window. She pointed toward the front of the stagecoach and shouted, "I think our driver's been shot."

Just as Jennie had predicted. Caleb hoped the man hadn't been killed. "You stay put. I'm going to slow the horses."

He nudged Saul as close to the runaway stage as the horse could get and stretched out his hands. Finally his fingers clasped the side of the luggage rack. He wished for a better position to jump, but there wasn't time. Too many lives depended on his speed.

Making certain he had a good grip, Caleb lunged toward the stage. His stomach lurched as he flew through the air, then he crashed into the side of the coach. He groaned with the momentary pain, but he couldn't stop now.

Dust and dirt plowed into his face and gritted teeth as he clung tightly to the bouncing stage. Slowly he slid his hands down the luggage rack. The driver's seat was in sight. He worked one arm as far down the rack as he dared stretch.

A sudden drop in the wheels brought Caleb's head against the side of the stagecoach with a horrible crack. His left hand slipped off the rack as his vision blurred. He hung on with his right hand, his arm straining, pulsing with pain. His body smacked against the stage as it hit another bump. Would it end here? he wondered. Before he could save the stage, before he and Jennie could finally be together?

Thoughts of Jennie, alone with King, fueled his body with new energy. Ignoring his burning muscles, Caleb lifted his left arm and gripped the rack again with both hands. He inched toward the seat again, and at last, his fingers touched the side. He swung himself upward and onto the seat, only to be greeted by the barrel of a shotgun. A haggard face stared at him from the other end.

"Don't shoot," Caleb said in between gulps of air. He attempted to raise his aching arms to show he meant no harm, but he couldn't. "Hold on, I'm just tryin' to get you stopped."

"Please, help. The reins are caught on my boot." The stranger lowered his gun and collapsed against the seat.

Caleb hurried to untangle the reins from the man's foot. He noticed a dark patch of blood on the man's thigh, but they'd have to deal with the injury later.

He pulled back on the reins, using all his weight, and shouted at the two horse teams, "Whoa, whoa!"

The taut leather burned against his palms as he tested his strength against the frightened horses. Instead of slowing, they ran faster, leaning into the bits in their mouths. Fighting panic, Caleb gripped the reins even harder. His heart pounded loud in his ears. The gully loomed closer. Perhaps his fate was to be the same as Liza's. He had no other solutions. Except…

A memory propelled itself forward in his mind— something his father had said to him once. "If you've lost control of your horse, turn him in a nice, tight circle. Horses can't bolt when they're turning."

With no other choice, Caleb all but dropped the left rein and pulled the right with every last ounce of strength. *Please, God, let this work. Let me see Jennie again. Let these people be safe.*

"Come on, horses," he muttered, sweat forming beneath his hat.

The coach swung around sharply, one wheel teetering on the brink of the gully before righting itself. Then the stage shuddered to an abrupt stop.

Caleb pried open his hands and released the reins. He collapsed onto the seat behind him. *We did it, You and me, Lord.* He released a huge rush of air from his lungs. "That was for you, Liza," he whispered to the blue sky above him.

A groan from the injured man brought Caleb's attention back to the task at hand. "How badly are you hurt?"

"I was shot...in the leg." The man's face turned a shade whiter. "We were...ambushed... Ol' Phil was shot, too...he fell off."

Caleb figured Ol' Phil must be the stage driver and this wounded fellow was the shotgun messenger, sent to guard the money.

He assessed the man's wound and removed the bandanna from around his own neck. "I'm no doctor, but it looks like the bullet went straight through. I'll tie it up for you until you can get to town." Caleb secured the cloth around the bloodied leg. "There you are. Now I'd better go check on the others."

The shotgun rider nodded as Caleb lowered himself to the ground, a much simpler task now that the stage wasn't moving.

"So glad you came along, stranger," the dark-haired girl said as she exited the stage. She could almost be Liza, minus the curly hair and saloon gown. "You ma-

neuvered that climb easier than I would've in this dress."
She lifted the ruffled bottom and laughed.

"Is everyone all right?" Caleb tried to see inside the
stage.

A blond girl hopped down the steps. "Thanks to
you, we're right as rain. Don't know about Mr. Fulman
though." She gave an indignant sniff. "He sat there the
whole time, screamin' and shakin' like a leaf. Apparently he's got no stomach for adventure or danger, not
like Ellen and me."

As if on cue, a tall, bony man bent his way out of the
stage, his face pale. "Are they gone?"

Caleb whistled for his horse. A minute passed before
Saul trotted up, appearing no worse for their adventure.
"How many bandits were there?"

"Four," Mr. Fulman said, sinking to the ground next
to the stage. "They stole the cash box. All five thousand
dollars." He covered his face with his hands and moaned.

"The sheriff should be along soon to help you," Caleb
said, mounting his horse. Now that his head and arms
were no longer throbbing, he was impatient to get going.
A nagging worry at the back of his mind was growing
more insistent by the minute. If he knew Jennie, she
might not wait for the sheriff. "I'm sorry I can't stay."

"Where you off to in such a hurry?" Ellen asked.

"I'm going to help my…girl. She already followed
after the bandits to see about getting the money back."

The blonde laughed. "No offense, but every one of
them men were armed. How are you and your girl gonna
take them all?"

Before Caleb could answer, the shotgun messenger
called down, "Name's Amos. With this busted-up leg, I
can't do much, but I'd like to help just the same."

"Thanks, Amos," Caleb said, admiring the man's determination to be of assistance despite his injury, "but—"

"Clara and I want to help, too," Ellen interjected. "We both know how to throw a hard punch."

Caleb frowned at the motley group. He didn't think the shotgun messenger would be of much help, but the girls might prove to be useful. "All right. Load back up then." He turned to the depressed bank man. "What about you, Mr. Fulman? You comin' with us or waitin' here for the sheriff?"

Mr. Fulman peered nervously around the prairie, then his face hardened. "I want my money back."

"You know how to drive a team?"

The bank man nodded.

"Then get up there and follow me."

Mr. Fulman scrambled up next to Amos on the seat and maneuvered the stage around. Caleb pointed Saul north and nudged the horse's flanks with his heels. The stage had better keep up. He and Jennie had been apart long enough. It was time to beat Mr. King at his own game.

# Chapter Twenty

Jennie tied Dandy to a tree, a safe distance from the ramshackle cabin. Four horses were tethered out front, but she saw no sign of King or his men. Licking her lips, Jennie drew in several deep breaths.

*I'm only going to check out the situation,* she reassured herself as she removed her pistol from the holster on her saddle. *Nothing foolish.* Keeping low to the ground, she sneaked across the yard toward the back of the cabin, diving to the ground at any little noise from inside.

When she drew alongside the back wall, she crouched near the window and listened. She could hear the scuffling of boots and a labored sigh from someone inside. Scooting onto her knees, she tried to peek over the window ledge.

"She should've come by now," King bellowed.

Startled, Jennie dropped flat to the ground. Her nose filled with the acrid smell of rotting wood as she lay facing the cabin's lowest logs.

"She'll be here, boss," someone said. Jennie heard a disgusted snort and guessed this came from King. "Gunner said that Nathan fellow was real excited about the robbery. Asked him lots of questions."

"Excitement and questions don't mean she's coming for certain," King replied. The sound of a fist pounding the wall carried on the air. "She'd better take the bait."

A moment of quiet followed King's words before another voice said, "I thought you were just gonna claim the place after she lost it."

"I am. But I need to make certain Jones and her family don't try to stop me."

Jennie felt the color drain from her face. What did he mean? Would he shoot her like Caleb had said and then go after her family?

*I won't let that happen.* Her jaw clenched with anger. *We'll stop them somehow.*

Turning to look at the log closest to her, Jennie discovered a chink in the wood. Several more littered the back of the cabin. She crawled to one and then another, but both were too small to get a good view of the room. At last she found a hole smaller than her fist, but not so big she'd be seen by those inside.

Positioning herself in front of the hole, Jennie peered into the cabin's interior. A chair leg and a box obscured most of her view, but by craning her head, she was able to locate three of the men. Two sat against the far wall, their guns held close. Jennie thought she recognized them as the rustlers who'd stolen her cattle, though she'd only had a brief look at them that night. The third man appeared to be standing by the door. She couldn't see King, but she guessed he had to be sitting on the chair, judging by the nearness of his voice when he talked.

*If I could just see him...* She considered moving far-

ther down the wall to find another chink until she realized what had been blocking her view. *The cash box.*

The five thousand dollars, the ticket to her freedom,
sat beneath Mr. King's chair, less than six inches from
her face. She tried to reach through the hole to touch the
box, but her hand wouldn't fit. She swapped her pistol for
the knife she'd hidden in her boot and silently whittled
away at the soft wood. When she could maneuver her
hand through the hole, ignoring the scrape of splinters,
Jennie let her fingers explore the metal surface of the
cash box. Thankfully the lock had been broken.

She couldn't leave now—not when the money was lit-
erally within reach. It was her ticket out of jail, and she
had to try to get it, even without Caleb's help.

Sliding her hand back out of the hole, Jennie stuck
her knife into her boot and pressed her forehead against
her fist to think. If she could open the box, the lid would
help hide her movements as she removed the money.
Then no matter what happened, the cash would be safe
and she'd have her freedom payment.

Gritting her teeth in determination, she pushed her
hand through the hole and grasped the lid of the cash
box. When she lifted it, one of the hinges creaked. Jennie froze.

"Did you hear something, boss?" one of the cowhands said.

Jennie's heart jumped into her throat, beating so loud
she feared they'd hear it, too. She bit her lip, trying not
to breathe.

After a long pause, King laughed. "I don't hear a
thing, Haws. How you ever became a cowhand, I still
don't know. You're the jumpiest son-of-a-gun I ever
met."

Haws grumbled in response, his words inaudible.

Exhaling, Jennie slipped her hand inside the box and touched the bundles of money, feeling their size. She'd have to be extra careful to keep the lid from slamming and giving away her position. She grasped one of the bundles and slid it slowly up and out of the box. Sweat beaded on her upper lip as she pulled the cash through the hole. A rush of euphoria swept through her as she reached in for the second wad of cash.

She emptied the cashbox of all five bundles, stopping once more when she heard King shifting his weight on the chair above her. Once all five thousand dollars sat outside the cabin wall, she softly pushed the box's lid into place, withdrew her hand and rolled onto her back in the grass.

Making certain to keep out of sight, Jennie climbed to her knees and placed the bundles and her gun onto her lap. She lifted the hem of her skirt, cradling the cash and weapon inside, and crept away from the cabin. By the time she reached Dandy, her whole body was damp with sweat.

She stuffed the money into her saddlebag. How she'd love to see the look on King's face when he realized she'd fooled him. She smiled, ready to climb onto her horse, but the other mounts tethered in front of the cabin caught her eye. If she let the animals go, King and his cowhand thugs wouldn't be able to make their escape— or worse, ride to the ranch and hurt her family—before the sheriff arrived.

She spun around and struck out for the cabin again. She inched along, keeping behind the taller brush when possible. As she drew parallel to the building, she went down on hands and knees and crawled along the ground.

*Wish I hadn't worn my best dress now.* She could only imagine what condition the brown silk would be in after today.

To keep from scaring the horses and alerting King, Jennie gave the animals a wide berth before approaching slowly from the north. She walked half-crouched over, her free hand extended toward the nearest horse until she touched its velvety nose.

After rubbing the horse's muzzle, she untied him from the tree where he'd been tethered. She looped the reins around her hand and guided him toward the next horse. After she'd freed all four animals, she led them a little ways from the cabin. She released all four sets of reins and slapped the rump of the horse next to her. "Go on."

The horse loped through the brush, snapping branches, while the others followed. A shout came from inside the cabin. "Someone's out there, boss. I really heard somethin' this time."

Whirling around, Jennie sprinted south toward her own horse. If she could reach Dandy before the men reached her, she'd be fine. She kept her eyes on the ground as she ran, but she could plainly hear the commotion behind her as the men exited the cabin.

"The horses. They're gone," someone shouted.

King swore loudly. "It's Jennie Jones's doing, I know it."

"Look there, boss," another cowhand yelled. "There she is. Running toward those trees."

Jennie pushed her legs faster, her lungs burning. *Just a little farther.* She ran down a slight incline, but instead of finding her feet back on flat ground, her boot caught on the hem of her dress. She crashed to the ground, her pistol slipping from her grasp. For one horrible moment, she couldn't breathe. Gulping air, she scrambled to her knees and frantically searched the dirt for her gun. Two sets of ironlike hands stopped her.

"You're comin' with us," a cowhand said, his tobacco-stained teeth showing through his cocky smile. The other, one of the two she recognized, picked up her pistol from off the ground and nodded.

"No." Jennie fought their hold, kicking at their legs with her boots and pulling back as hard as she could against their hands. But she wasn't much of a match for men used to wrestling thousand-pound cattle.

As they half dragged, half carried her toward the cabin, she glanced up to see King standing out front, grinning. *At least he won't have his money,* she told herself as she stared at the Colt revolver in his hand.

Tears of regret stung her eyes, and she willed herself to hold them back. She wouldn't give these men the satisfaction of seeing her cry. If only she'd left after taking back the money or waited for Caleb in the first place, she wouldn't be facing the possibility of her own death. Why did she insist on doing everything on her own? Even she—strong and independent as she liked to think of herself—needed help now and then.

"Surprised to see us, Miss Jones?" King asked as she and her captors came closer to the cabin. "We've been waitin' for you." Even at a distance, she saw the cold triumph blazing in his dark eyes.

She craned her neck to see past the man holding her left arm, hoping Caleb or the sheriff would ride up at that moment. The sagebrush plain stood empty, but there was still One she could petition for help. Not caring what

King thought, she dropped her chin to her chest and silently prayed.

*God, I'm trying to make things right. But I need Thy help. Please give me strength and let me live to see Caleb and my family again....*

Jennie fought back the panic that threatened to overwhelm her as the men dragged her toward the cabin door where King waited.

"Do come in." He grabbed her roughly from his cowhands and shoved her inside. The others filed in behind them. "I knew you couldn't resist the lure of five thousand dollars to save your little ranch."

King pushed her down onto the floor in a corner of the room. Jennie hit the hard-packed dirt with a muffled groan. She watched helpless as the cowboy with her pistol stuck it in his holster.

"I've heard all about your robberies," King bragged, "so I planned this little get-together myself. Had my man Gunner drop hints about today's robbery to your partner, Nathan. Then we rode out here first thing this morning and robbed that stage." He waved his revolver in the direction of the cash box before pointing it at her.

Jennie wanted to smile, pleased she'd stolen the five thousand dollars right out from under his nose, but she could hardly swallow, and her head had begun to pound with fear.

She kept a steady eye on his gun as he went on talking. "As soon as I can get to Fillmore, I'll claim your ranch and join it with mine. I reckon you won't object—seeing how you ain't got a cent for that bank president."

Jennie feigned surprise at the mention of Mr. Dixon,

deciding to play along. She even managed a soft gasp from her dry throat.

King grinned, pushing his face so close to hers that Jennie could smell the bacon he'd eaten for breakfast.

"That's right, missy. Mr. Dixon and I are good friends. We worked out a nice little arrangement for speeding things up for me to get what I want." He drew back and ran a finger over the barrel of his revolver. "'Course, in the end, he still moved too slowly for me."

"Did you kill him, too?" she asked, not bothering to hide the bitterness from her voice.

With a laugh, King cocked his gun. "No, Miss Jones. He ain't standing in my way of having the largest cattle operation in the territory. You are." He pressed the cold metal against her throbbing temple. "You understand, don't you? I can't have you tryin' to win the place back again."

"Boss…" one of the cowhands interjected.

"What is it, Smith?" King shot a glance at his men while keeping the gun against Jennie's head.

The man didn't respond right away, and in the long pause, Jennie managed a quick sideways glance in his direction. With a pained expression on his face, the cowboy stared at the dirt floor. Jennie noticed the other two were also looking everywhere but at her and King.

"Well, boss," Smith answered, "I—I know you said you might have to shoot her, but can't we just rough her up a bit instead?" Murmurs of agreement sounded from the other cowboys, apparently giving Smith the courage to continue. "I don't mind wounding stage drivers," he said, his voice stronger, "but killin' women?"

Jennie hardly dared believe his words. Hope beat sharply in her chest. Could she somehow turn these men against King and escape? They could easily gain the upper hand in number and weapons.

Turning slowly, King brandished his gun at his men. "You wanna repeat your pretty little speech, Smith?" The venom in his tone made even Jennie shiver, blotting out all hope.

Smith lowered his head. They were clearly too afraid to go against their boss.

"Good," King snarled. "'Cause if any of you liver-bellied boys think you can bail out now, you're wrong. If you try, I'll keep the small fortunes I promised ya, and you'll be lucky if I don't plant a bullet in your backsides, too. Is that understood?" All three men nodded.

"All right, then." King turned to Jennie. "Now we can get on—"

The cabin door flung open, banging against the opposite wall and sending a tremor through the old building. King whirled around, his eyes wide with surprise. His men scrambled to draw their guns. A man with a dirty bandanna over his mouth and nose appeared in the doorway, a shotgun in his hand.

Jennie recognized his dusty clothes and blue eyes at once. *Caleb.* Relief flooded through her, calming the frantic beating of her heart. Two young women Jennie didn't know, one blonde and one dark-haired, cowered behind him, their hands tied. Who were they and what was Caleb doing with them?

She leveled a gaze on his partially covered face, trying to communicate that she recognized him. But he ignored her. Something in his rigid stance told her to keep quiet, let things play out without her interference.

"Who in tarnation are you?" King demanded, aiming

his revolver at Caleb's head. Jennie swallowed hard. She hoped Caleb's plan—whatever it might be—would work.

Caleb lowered his shotgun, but only a little. "I'd ask you the same question. This here's my hideout and I don't take kindly to strangers using it for their hostages." The girls' crying rose in volume. "Silence," he barked at them before turning back to King. "Seeing how you've got me outnumbered, though, I'd be willing to share it with you gentlemen."

"We're conductin' a little business meeting." King trained his gun on Jennie again. "So if you don't mind steppin' outside, I'd like to finish up."

Caleb lifted a hand in surrender. "Fine by me." Pushing the girls ahead of him, he headed out of the cabin. Jennie watched numbly as the door swung shut. She rushed to her feet, but King pushed her back to her knees.

"Sit down, Miss Jones."

*Caleb,* she wanted to scream. *Come back.*

As if he'd heard her thoughts, the door opened again and Caleb stuck his head inside. "Could you show me the spot where you hid your horses? I need to get mine out of sight, too."

King exhaled loudly. "They ain't hidden—this young lady let 'em go." He pressed the gun harder against Jennie's temple. She swallowed, trying to ignore the ache behind her eyes and praying Caleb had a good plan.

"That little slip of a thing released your horses?" Caleb chuckled. Jennie scowled at him. This was no time for jokes.

"Is that funny to you, boy?" King growled, swinging his gun from Jennie to Caleb.

"Nope." Caleb sobered immediately. "If you do need

some horses, I've got a few extras." He straightened up, his tall frame filling the doorway. "I'll sell 'em to you cheap. Send one or two of your men out here to pick what you want."

His gun still pointed at Caleb, King narrowed his eyes. Was he really considering Caleb's proposal? Jennie held her breath. She had no idea how Caleb meant to rescue her.

"All right." King motioned with his gun at Smith and the cowhand with Jennie's pistol. "Haws and Smith, you go check out the horses. Make sure they ain't old or feeble."

The two men followed Caleb outside and the door closed behind them. Jennie released her breath in a soft rush and contemplated her chances of escape. Two men would be easier to handle than four, but she still didn't have a weapon.

King frowned. "Let's get this over with."

Jennie eyed the window. Perhaps she could make it before King shot her. Just as she tensed to move, a loud cry followed by a heavy thud sounded outside the cabin. All three of them turned in the direction of the door.

*Please, come back, Caleb,* Jennie silently cried to the walls. Had King's men done something to him?

"What was that, boss?" the remaining cowboy asked.

"Don't know," King snapped, his face turning red with irritation. "Go find out what's goin' on. I'll tie her up." Glaring down at Jennie, he gripped her wrist hard and added in a low hiss, "I don't need no more interruptions."

The cowhand hurried through the door. Before it swung shut again, Jennie strained to see outside as King pulled a rope from his belt. She hesitated too long in her decision to stay put or run, and the rancher had her wrists tied before she could move.

Another shout floated in through the gaps in the logs. King cursed and slammed his fist against the nearest wall.

"Time to end this." He aimed the revolver at Jennie again. His jaw tightened in deadly resolve, and his lips lifted in a sneer. "Who's got the upper hand now, Miss Jones? You got no friends or guns to help you this time. It's just you and me."

Jennie licked her lips, keeping her chin held high even as she prepared for the inevitable shot.

"Any last words before I pull the trigger?"

"Yeah. Step away from my girl!"

Sucking in a sharp breath, Jennie felt her whole body sag at Caleb's words. She'd been so focused on the gun barrel trained at her head, she hadn't heard him enter. Now he stood in the doorway, appearing every bit as strong and capable and handsome as the day they'd met on the trail. The bandanna around his face had been removed, and he pointed his shotgun straight at King.

Still facing Jennie, King didn't move a muscle. But Jennie detected the glint in his eye just before he swung around toward Caleb.

"Caleb, look out," she shouted.

Jumping to her feet, she plowed her shoulder into the lower back of the giant rancher. King's gun blasted above their heads, bringing bits of wood and dirt from the ceiling raining down on them. Jennie hit the floor hard enough to crush the breath from her lungs a second time and cause the room to spin around her. When her vision cleared, she scrambled to sit up in time to see King kick Caleb's shotgun away. Caleb lunged toward him and drove a fist into King's gut. The man grunted, but connected a punch to Caleb's lower jaw, sending Caleb backward.

As the two wrestled each other, Jennie brought her boot to her bound hands and managed to pull out her knife. She twisted her hand and sawed at the rope. A loud groan brought her head up. In horror, she watched Caleb curl into a ball and roll away from King.

"Caleb!" she screamed.

Spinning on his heel, King lumbered toward her, his eyes wild and dangerous. Jennie dropped the knife and tried to crawl away, but she couldn't move fast enough with her bound hands. King grabbed her foot and yanked her back. She shut her eyes, fear turning her blood to ice in her veins. A grunt made her open her eyes. Caleb had pulled King back to the floor, but she could see the weariness on Caleb's face. She had to help.

With renewed energy, Jennie found the knife again and cut at the rope until it slipped off. Finally free, she searched the floor for King's revolver. She located his gun on the floor and picked it up. Standing, she crossed to King and Caleb, still locked in a battle of strength.

She offered a rushed prayer for help and lifted the gun in the air. She waited until King rocked back on his heels, breaking from the flurry of swinging fists and feet. Seeing her chance, she brought the revolver down as hard as she could against the man's head. The rancher roared with pain. Caleb seized the pause in momentum and plowed a fist into King's jaw. This time the rancher crumpled to the ground and lay unmoving.

Jennie sank to the floor with a cry and set down the gun. Her hands were shaking too badly to hold it anymore. She bit her lip, hard enough to taste blood, to keep from crying.

Caleb crawled over to her. His nose and lip were bleeding and one arm cradled his stomach. He pulled her to him with his free hand. "Thanks for the help." He released her to pick up the rope near her feet. "We need to tie him up."

"I'll do it," she said, knowing he was in pain. She looped the rope around King's wrists and attempted to tie a knot, but she had to pause until she stopped trembling. Finally she secured his hands. "How long do you think he'll be unconscious?" she whispered, peering into the man's battered face.

"It might be a while," Caleb said. "The sheriff can deal with him—if he and his men ever show up."

He sat on the ground beside her and wrapped her protectively in his arms again. Jennie pressed her ear to his chest, more grateful than she could ever say to hear his heart beating beneath his dusty, blood-stained shirt.

Releasing her, Caleb pushed her sweaty hair off her face. "I thought you weren't going to do anything foolish."

Jennie managed a laugh. "I didn't plan to, until I found the money. I got it out of the cash box without King knowing." She pointed in the direction of the box, still sitting underneath the chair. "I meant to leave after that, but I thought I should get rid of their horses first..." She let her voice trail off; he could guess the rest.

Caleb pulled her close again and rested his chin against her hair. "You crazy girl. I'm glad you're safe."

"Mr. Johnson?" A feminine voice hollered.

Jennie eased back. "Who's that?"

Caleb managed half a smile. "Come meet your other rescuers."

They emerged from the cabin, and the two young women Jennie had seen earlier hurried over. They didn't appear helpless now. From their lavish dresses and dark rouge, Jennie suspected they'd worked in a saloon.

"You all right, Miss Jones?" the dark-haired one asked.

"This is Ellen," Caleb said, motioning to the girl who'd spoken. "And this is Clara." He pointed to the blonde. "They were passengers on the stage. After today's performance, I think they ought to join an acting troupe."

Before Jennie could respond, a thin gentleman rushed up to them. "Did you find the cash box?" he asked.

"Mr. Fulman is the bank man from Nevada," Caleb explained.

Jennie smiled, grateful for both her sake and the bank man's that she had the cash. "Your money is safe, Mr. Fulman—all of it. I'll get it for you just as soon as someone tells me how all of you managed to get rid of King's men."

"It was Amos's idea to have them come out to see the horses," Caleb said. He pointed north to where the stagecoach sat behind some trees. "That's him on the driver's seat. He's the shotgun messenger. Took a bullet in the thigh, so he's acting as guard."

"When those thugs left the cabin," Clara interjected, "we knocked 'em out and tied 'em up. We just finished putting them all inside the stage."

"Best time of my life." Mr. Fulman brushed at the front of his dirty suit and chuckled. "Beats sittin' behind a desk all day. Maybe I should become a deputy."

Jennie joined his laughter. "Thank you, each of you, for your help. I'll get your money, Mr. Fulman."

She headed for the tree where she'd tied Dandy, but she hadn't gone far when a hand gripped hers. Turning, she found Caleb beside her, his face somber despite the twinkle in his blue eyes.

"You coming, too?" she teased.

He nodded and squeezed her hand. "I plan on stickin' extra close from now on, Jennie Jones. I don't need any more bandits or lawmen or cattle spiriting you away. Deal?"

Laughing, Jennie gently kissed the corner of his mouth that wasn't bleeding. "It's a deal, cowboy."

# Chapter Twenty-One

Jennie collected the money from her saddlebag and untied Dandy, recounting for Caleb how she'd managed to pilfer the cash out of the box. Only then did she notice the state of her brown dress. It was dirty, sweaty and torn at the hem. She felt bad for ruining the dress Caleb had paid for, but she consoled herself with the possibility that Grandma Jones might be able to salvage it.

She and Dandy followed Caleb back to the cabin and she gave Mr. Fulman the money. The bank man sat right down on the ground to thumb through it. He placed the bills inside the cash box he'd removed from the cabin.

"We ought to check on King again," Jennie said, not wanting to give the man a chance to escape.

"He was starting to moan when I crept in there," Mr. Fulman said. He shut the lid to the cash box and stood. "The money appears to be all there—thank you."

"Better load King into the stage while he's fairly unconscious," Caleb said. "Will you help us, Mr. Fulman?"

Jennie tied Dandy near the stage before trailing Caleb and Mr. Fulman into the cabin. Sure enough audible groans came from King's split mouth, but his eyes remained shut. Caleb hefted his shoulders while Jennie and the bank man each took hold of a leg. They lifted King and started slowly from the cabin.

Halfway to the stagecoach, Jennie heard the sound of approaching horses. She glanced toward the east and saw four men riding at a gallop toward them. "I think the sheriff has finally arrived."

"Miss Jones?" someone shouted as the riders drew closer. Jennie recognized the sheriff's voice.

Shifting the weight of King's leg, she gave a quick wave. "I'm here, sheriff."

The sheriff and his deputies came to an abrupt halt beside her. "Miss Jones." The man's eyebrows rose sharply as he took in the scene before him and the nearby stage filled with groaning captives. "What in the world happened?" he asked as he dismounted.

Jennie met Caleb's amused look over her shoulder. "It's a rather long story, sheriff."

"I'm anxious to hear it." He waved a hand to include the rest of the stage passengers who had gathered around. "All of you will need to come to my office for questioning."

He barked orders for his men to carry King to the stagecoach. Jennie relinquished her post gladly—her head and muscles had begun to ache again from all the drama. Once the rancher had been placed inside the stage, the sheriff walked up to her, his face somber. For one dreadful moment, Jennie worried he'd changed his mind about not pressing charges. Then his face broke into a smile.

"My apologies, Miss Jones, for my delay. I hadn't the foggiest idea what you were going to do when I heard you'd come out here alone. I wondered at first if you were taking the money for yourself. But I couldn't quite believe that. So I figured you had to be either crazy or extremely stubborn." The sheriff shook his head and chuckled. "Now I see it's a bit of both."

"I couldn't agree more, sir." Caleb took her hand in his. She pretended offense at his words, but inside she felt only deep gratitude and love for him.

The sheriff sized up Caleb. "Who might you be?"

"The man I love," Jennie answered with a smile at Caleb. "Mr. Johnson's also our hired hand and the finest cowboy around."

The sheriff's gaze sparked with pleasure at her confession before he turned and swung onto his horse. "I want to get these men to the jail, so let's load up."

Jennie climbed onto Dandy, grateful to be heading closer to home, and waited as Caleb mounted Saul. Mr. Fulman volunteered to drive the stage again, and Ellen and Clara piled on the back of two of the deputies' horses.

With everyone situated, the sheriff waved the stagecoach forward. He and his deputies took up positions on either side while Jennie and Caleb rode at the back. They hadn't gone far when Caleb yelled for the sheriff to stop.

"What's wrong?" Jennie asked.

"We forgot Ol' Phil, the stage driver."

Caleb rode ahead to tell the sheriff. The entourage headed southwest under Amos's directions until someone spied the stage driver near a patch of sagebrush.

The sheriff and his men, along with Caleb, went to assess the body while Jennie sat in the saddle, chewing on her thumbnail and praying the man wasn't dead. Somehow she felt it would be her fault if he was, since she hadn't intercepted the stage sooner.

Was this the sort of weighty guilt Caleb had carried after Liza's death? The knowledge he'd tried to fix things—even if he believed it was the wrong way—struck her as ironic. Perhaps his past had made it easier for him to forgive hers. That thought brought a measure of peace to her troubled mind.

When two of the deputies hoisted the man, Jennie saw his lined face contort into a grimace. Gratitude coursed through her. The sheriff made one of the cowhands ride on top of the stage so the driver could be placed inside.

Jennie nudged Dandy next to Caleb and Saul as the whole group started their trek eastward again. "Will the driver be all right?"

"I think so. He got a bullet in the hip and one to the shoulder, but they think the doctor can fix him up. He ought to be driving again before too long, though he may end up with a limp."

Jennie gave a quick nod and turned away from him. Now that the whole ordeal was almost over, she couldn't restrain her tears anymore.

"What's wrong?"

"I've been a fool." Her voice cracked on a sob, and she had to clear her throat to continue. "I realized that as King's men were dragging me back to the cabin and I saw him standing there with his gun. I jeopardized my life, your life and the lives of all these people…" She waved her hand to include those on the stage and those riding beside it. "All because of my stubborn insistence on doing everything myself."

"Jennie, look at me."

She regarded his kind face, now furrowed with concern.

"Everything's going to be fine. Amos is going to heal,

the stage driver will, too, and you got the bank's money back. You're free to live your life, to do and be whatever you want now."

Jennie sniffled and rubbed her nose with the back of her hand. "I'm still going to lose the ranch." She hated how the words tasted on her tongue—full of defeat and pain.

"I love you, Jennie," he said, prodding his horse closer to hers. "I'm proud of you for doing the right thing."

She smiled at him through her tears. "Now I just have to find a way to pay back the money I stole by the end of the month."

"You can start with the money I gave you. Then we'll just do the best we can to come up with the rest until all of it's paid back."

Jennie murmured agreement, grateful he wanted to help, but she didn't want to use Caleb's hard-earned money to pay for her mistakes. She hated to think he wouldn't be able to have his freight business because of her.

"King told me he planned to lay claim to the property once I lost it. I suppose he still can." Jennie frowned at the thought of such a horrid man taking over her beloved home.

Caleb shook his head. "I think he's going to be locked up for quite a while."

"One of his men could still do it for him." She studied the prairie and the green-flecked mountains on both sides. "Maybe Grandma Jones, Will and I should go up north with you."

"You mean that?" The hope was unmistakable in his voice.

The events of the past twenty-four hours made the

idea of starting over in a new place very appealing. Especially if it meant being close to Caleb. "Do you think you could stand to have us nearby, after today?"

He chuckled. The tenderness in his eyes set her heart racing. "Life would be mighty dull without you around, Jennie. I've sort of gotten used to it."

Jennie held her breath, hoping he'd say more. Maybe ask for her hand in marriage, even though they weren't alone. Caleb glanced away, but not before Jennie caught a mischievous smile on his lips. *He's thinking the very same thing.* The possibility of being engaged to Caleb soon tempered her impatience and increased her excitement at the prospect of heading north.

Would she and Caleb start another ranch? Jennie didn't think so. It would take more capital than she'd have at the end of the month and Caleb was looking forward to owning his freight business. She tried to picture a life without cattle and branding and doing more around her home than caring for farm animals and tending a garden, but she couldn't.

Despite her enthusiasm to follow Caleb north, hopefully as his fiancée, she couldn't ignore the misgivings whispering at the back of her mind. Worries about the cash she had to pay back, about leaving the ranch. Acquiring the stage money today had been harder than she'd thought, and she suspected the sacrifices in her future would be every bit as difficult.

But when she looked over to see Caleb riding at her side, she knew that any struggle would all be worth it to have his love and respect. Grandma Jones had said that the hardest things to do were usually the right ones. And as Caleb caught her eye and grinned, she knew that nothing could ever be more right than this.

* * *

When the group reached town, the sheriff directed his men to unload the prisoners and lock them up in the jail. Jennie and the others were directed into the sheriff's office next door for questioning. King had woken up on the ride to Beaver, and as two of the deputies dragged him inside, Jennie plainly heard his cursing—most of which he directed at her.

"All right, Miss Jones," the sheriff said, taking a seat at the table where Daniels had been practicing his gun work earlier. "Why don't we start with you? Would you kindly explain what happened from the time you left my office to the time we found you at the old cabin?"

Jennie stood straight; she had nothing to hide this time. "I would be glad to, sir."

With Caleb's hand resting reassuringly on the small of her back, Jennie recounted all that had gone on after she met Caleb in the valley, and how he and the others had rescued her. When she finished, Caleb and the stage passengers added their stories to hers.

"Thank you for your help," the sheriff said, rising from his chair. "Those of you from the stage are free to go. Miss Jones, if you and Mr. Johnson would remain behind, please."

Before Jennie could step toward him, she and Caleb were surrounded by Amos, Mr. Fulman and the two girls. They talked over each other, repeating their thanks for the help and wishing her and Caleb good luck. Jennie hugged each one and offered her own thanks. If they hadn't come to her aid, she might not be standing here alive. With a mixture of gratitude and sadness, she watched them file out of the jail.

"Now, Miss Jones." The sheriff resumed his seat and

folded his arms. She and Caleb stepped closer to the table. "Since you met the terms of our arrangement, I'm happy to inform you that I will not be pressing charges of theft." Leaning forward, he wagged a finger at her. "But you'd better have that money paid back by the end of the month or our agreement is null and void. Is that clear?"

"You have my word, sir." Jennie wanted to laugh and cry and shout all at the same time. She didn't know yet how she'd pay back all that money, but she was almost free.

The sheriff nodded. "Based on your accounts, I am going to hold Mr. King and his men here until their trial, on charges of theft and attempted murder. Is that all?"

Jennie exchanged a long look with Caleb. She knew what he was thinking. "There has been at least once incidence of him and his men cattle rustling, sir. I don't want to see the man hung, especially since we took my cows back this last time, but I thought you should know."

"Cattle rustling?" The sheriff pounded his fist against the table, his eyes blazing. "Why that no-account…" He shook his head. "Are you sure you don't wish to add that charge to the list, Miss Jones? We don't take cattle rustling lightly around here."

"I only wanted you to know, so you could be on the lookout once Mr. King and his men are allowed to go."

The sheriff stared at her, his face thoughtful. "I've got a better idea. Would you come with me please, Miss Jones?" He stood and went to the door.

"Where are we going?" Jennie asked.

"To visit Mr. King."

Caleb wrapped a protective arm around her waist. "Is that wise, sheriff?"

"She'll be perfectly fine in my company, Mr. John-

son. We'll be back in a few moments. Please wait here."
He held open the door for Jennie.

"It'll be fine," she murmured to Caleb before stepping outside. Still, apprehension twisted her stomach as
she followed the sheriff next door to the jail.

The two deputies seated at the room's only table stood
up, their faces registering their surprise at seeing her and
the sheriff. The animated conversation between King's
cowhands stopped and they peered suspiciously at them
from their shared cell.

"I need to see Mr. King," the sheriff announced. Taking Jennie gently by the elbow, he led her past the deputies to the last of the three cells.

"Mr. King?" the sheriff called out to the dozing figure on the cot.

King lifted his head and blinked. When his saw the
sheriff, his face turned a shade pale. "What do you
want?"

"I have a proposition for you, Mr. King." The sheriff
threw Jennie a conspiratorial grin. Baffled at what his
plan could be, she didn't return the gesture.

King's eyes narrowed with suspicion as he stood and
crossed to the cell door. "What is it?"

Turning to Jennie, the sheriff asked in her a low voice,
"How much money do you need to repay, Miss Jones?"

Jennie shot King a quick look before whispering,
"Thirty-eight-hundred dollars."

If the amount shocked him, the sheriff didn't show
it. Instead he spoke to Mr. King in a firm voice. "I want
you to buy Miss Jones's ranch—for thirty-eight-hundred
dollars."

Jennie wasn't sure who looked the most surprised at
the request—her or Mr. King.

"Buy it?" the rancher said with a smirk. "Why would I do that? It ain't worth that."

"From what Miss Jones has told me, you're probably right." The sheriff appeared thoughtful, but with his next words, his face hardened. "But that's the asking price for your life."

King frowned. "Whatdaya mean? The bank man on that stage got his money back and she ain't dead. I won't be in here long."

The sheriff leaned forward as if imparting a great secret. "Yes, but the penalty for cattle rustling is hanging. Isn't that true, Miss Jones?"

Jennie bit back a smile herself. "Yes, yes it is, sheriff."

"Cattle rustling," King repeated in a strained voice. He rubbed a hand over his stubbled jaw, the fight visibly draining from him. He glanced at Jennie and then back at the sheriff. "If I buy her ranch, you won't press that...uh...other charge?"

"You have my word, but Miss Jones will need the money before the end of the month."

"If I don't have it?"

Unable to resist, Jennie stepped forward. "I know an excellent banker in Fillmore who might make you a loan."

King glowered at her. "Fine. I'll have my man Gunner ride over with it next week."

"I thought you said you didn't have it," Jennie said, folding her arms.

"Guess we all have our secrets, don't we?" King sneered.

The sheriff touched Jennie's arm. "You now have a buyer for your ranch, Miss Jones. Shall we go?"

Almost dizzy with excitement, Jennie trailed him

down the line of cells and past the deputies. "Thank you," she said, pausing in front of the door.

The sheriff tipped his hat to her. "My pleasure."

Though she'd still lose the ranch, she would be able to repay the money she'd stolen. She'd be free, and Caleb would be able to keep his hard-earned cash.

"Thank You," she murmured again, this time with a meaningful glance toward the ceiling as she and the sheriff stepped outside. She couldn't wait to give Caleb back his money.

# Chapter Twenty-Two

Caleb stared into the orange flames flickering in the fireplace, his arm around Jennie as they sat on the sofa. He couldn't recall ever feeling so exhausted. *But then again,* he thought with a smirk, *I've never stopped a runaway stage, rescued the girl I love from being shot and told the same story a dozen times, all in one day.*

"What's so funny?" Jennie said, poking him in the side. She'd been lost in thought, too, ever since her grandmother had shooed them off to the parlor to rest after supper.

"I was thinking I definitely earned my keep today." He smiled when she rolled her eyes. "In fact, I think I've earned my keep for a lifetime, which means you're heavily in my debt."

"In that case, how can I repay you?" she asked, warming up to his game.

Caleb rubbed his chin in mock contemplation. "You could start with a kiss." Jennie pushed up from the couch and kissed him. He loved the way her lips fit against his. He was so grateful she was here beside him, alive.

"Next," he said, easing back, "I think you could take over some of my cattle watching times."

"I think I can manage that. Anything else?"

Caleb peered down at her pretty face. His pulse skipped faster. He knew what he wanted to ask—had known ever since this morning when he learned Jennie's plan for setting things straight. But would she say yes?

Taking a deep breath, he reached for her hand. "How about marrying me?"

Her eyes widened and her free hand rose to her mouth. "You mean that?"

With a nod, he slid off the couch and knelt in front of her. "Jennie Aurelia Jones, will you agree to be my wife?"

"Yes, cowboy," she half whispered before throwing her arms around him. He nearly toppled over but managed to keep them both upright.

He loosened her arms from around his neck so he could kiss her, but she squirmed out of his embrace and stood up.

"Did I miss something?" he protested. "Doesn't a man deserve another kiss after proposing?"

"Yes, but I just remembered something I wanted to give you." She gave him an impish smile. "I'll be right back."

Caleb returned to his seat on the sofa. In the kitchen, Grandma Jones was washing dishes and singing to herself. The front door creaked open, and Caleb guessed Will had finished tending to the animals.

"Good night, Grandma," the young man called out before he appeared in the parlor doorway. "Where's Jennie?" he asked Caleb.

"Getting something upstairs, I think."

"I still can't believe what you two did today." Will leaned against the door frame. "The only things I did were watch those boring cows and muck stalls. Saving runaway stages sounds a lot more exciting."

Caleb chuckled. "I used to think so, too, but after today, I think I'll stick with tending animals."

"Did Jennie really rob all those bandits like she said?"

"Crazy, isn't it?" Caleb couldn't describe the relief he felt to have Jennie done with robbing thieves. "But remember what she said if she ever finds out you've done something like that."

"I know, I know." Will held up his hands as if in surrender. "She'd tan my hide within an inch of my life. I got it." He ducked out the door. "Good night."

"'Night, Will."

"Thanks," he said, pausing in the hallway.

"For what?"

His shoulders lifted in his characteristic shrug. "For helping Jennie…and our family."

A strange lump formed in Caleb's throat, and he had to swallow hard to loosen it. "You're my family, too. Your sister just agreed to marry me."

"About time," Will said with a grin before he turned and bounded up the stairs.

Caleb glanced at the fire again, realizing how much he meant what he'd said to Will. Jennie's family had become as dear to him as his own. And now that he'd decided to stop running from his past, he was ready to reconnect with his family again. He couldn't wait to show Jennie the Salt Lake Valley. God had blessed him so much in the past six weeks, in ways he'd never imagined. He offered a prayer of thanks, finishing just as Jennie entered the room, her hands hidden behind her back.

"Are you ready?" she asked.

When he nodded, she lifted a small bundle of cash for him to see.

"What's this?"

Jennie's eyes glistened in the firelight with unshed tears. "It's yours, Caleb. It's the money you gave me."

"But…" He shook his head, not understanding. "I thought you were going to use it to pay back the money you still owe from the robberies."

"I was." She handed him the money and sat down. "Then the sheriff forced King to buy the ranch for thirty-eight-hundred dollars. More than enough to pay back the robberies and the bank."

Caleb stared at the cash in his hands, then back up at Jennie. "Are you crazy?"

"Crazy in love with you."

"I meant crazy to let someone like Marshall King buy your ranch."

Jennie wiped at her wet eyes. "Maybe. But I didn't feel right about using your money to pay for my wrong-doings. It would take us months, or even longer, to earn it back."

"You're sure King will pay up?"

"Yes." She wriggled under his arm and rested her head against his shoulder again. He liked holding her this way. "The sheriff told King if he didn't buy the ranch he'd be charged with cattle rustling. King agreed to buy the place and said he'd have one of his men bring the money over next week."

"Is that what happened when you and the sheriff went to the jail? You did seem rather pleased when you came back." He playfully tapped the end of her nose with his finger.

They fell into comfortable silence until Caleb remembered he hadn't yet told her about Nathan Blaine. If they were to marry, he didn't want any more secrets between them.

"Remember how I asked you yesterday about Nathan— being a stage robber or not?"

Jennie's brow furrowed. "Yes, why?"

Caleb cleared his throat, expecting the old anger and urge for revenge to fill him as he recalled the events of the past. This time he felt only peace, which gave him the courage to continue. He twisted around on the sofa so he could face Jennie. "Nathan Blaine was the fourth man involved in the robbery of Liza's stage."

"Oh, Caleb." Her face went pale. "I—I had no idea."

He pressed his finger to her mouth to silence her worry. "I know you didn't. But you need to know that part of my story before I tell you where I went last night."

"I didn't know you'd gone anywhere."

"I went to town, to the saloon, actually. I found Nathan there, but…" He interlocked his hand with hers. "I'd planned on the ride over to haul him into the sheriff. When I went to arrest him, though, I couldn't do it. I realized I was letting my old hate and need for vengeance drive me again. So I persuaded him to leave town."

"How?"

"I detailed the charges against him and said if he didn't leave town right then, that I'd turn him over to the law. I also let him know I didn't ever want to hear his name associated with stage robbing again." Caleb let out the breath he'd been holding. "I knew it was the right thing to do, but I also hoped it would prevent you from dealing with anymore stage thieves yourself or winding up in jail, if Nathan implicated you."

Jennie squeezed his hand. When he looked at her,

she reached up to touch his cheek. "Thank you. For telling me and for being merciful to Nathan. No wonder he wasn't around this morning when I went to the boardinghouse to tell him not to help me." She snuggled back under Caleb's arm.

Relieved to have this last confession off his chest, he stroked her hair, liking the softness slipping through his fingers.

Jennie yawned. "Aren't you sleepy?"

"Not after a day like this one." He smiled down at her. "How do Will and Grandma Jones feel about you selling the ranch?"

"I haven't told them yet. I figured they've heard an earful already today. They knew we were going to lose the ranch anyway." She shut her eyes. "I'll tell them tomorrow. Along with the news that we're engaged. Maybe that will make things easier."

"I already told Will."

"What did he say about it?"

"His exact words were 'about time.'"

Jennie released a soft laugh. "I imagine Grandma Jones will say something similar. Should I tell them we'll be heading north with you after the sale of the ranch?"

Caleb pulled her closer to his side. "I'm not going anywhere, Jennie, not without you."

"What will your parents say when you show up with three extra mouths to feed?"

"They'll love you, just like I do."

She cracked open her eyes, tenderness shining in their brown depths. "When do you think we should marry?"

"Yesterday," he said, grinning. "But since that didn't work out, how about in a month?"

"Sounds good, cowboy," she murmured as she shut her eyes again.

Caleb pressed a kiss to her forehead, soliciting a murmur of contentment from Jennie. He understood the feeling. Despite the events of the day, he felt joy and hope for the future. Soon he'd be returning home, with more than he could've hoped for when he'd left three years before.

Another lump formed in his throat as he gazed down at his sleeping bride-to-be. *That's the second time I've almost cried in less than an hour.* To cover his own embarrassment, he let his mind fill with plans.

Tomorrow he'd write his parents and tell them about Jennie and her family. He was glad she would be living near them during his absences with his freight business. Eventually he could have others do the traveling for him, but to begin, he would have to make the treks southward himself. The thought of being away from Jennie so much brought a tangible ache.

Would she adapt to life up north without her ranch? Caleb couldn't picture her wearing a dress and apron every day like his mother or sisters. She needed her men's breeches and old hat, a rope in one hand.

He stared down at her sleeping form again, her beautiful features soft and relaxed. Out of love for him, Jennie would become a freighter's wife, with some land to farm to get them by. But he knew instinctively how much she'd miss this place. The ranch had been her lifeblood.

Tears formed in his eyes, and Caleb let them leak out as he tightened his arm around her shoulders. He couldn't give Jennie back her ranch, but he had an idea of what he could do to keep that vibrant light in her eyes.

# Chapter Twenty-Three

*Four weeks later*

Jennie woke to semidarkness outside her window. Sitting up in bed, she stretched and wondered what her grandmother was making for breakfast. Then she remembered. She wasn't at the ranch; she and Will and Grandma Jones were now living with Caleb's family. And today she would become Mrs. Caleb Johnson.

*The one day I was told I should sleep in,* she thought, shaking her head with amusement, *and I'm up at dawn as usual.*

Hugging her knees to her chest, Jennie smiled as a tremor of excitement ran up her spine. Her life had changed so much in the past four weeks that her memories of the ranch felt as hazy as if months had gone by instead of days.

Of course she'd been too busy to dwell for long on saying goodbye to her home. Gunner had come with the money as promised, and Jennie managed to keep her tears in check as she relinquished the key to the house. By then, she'd learned of the man's daring visit to warn

Caleb about Mr. King's plot. In gratitude, she told him to take two of her best heifers to start his own herd before she sold the rest.

The trip northward had been long, but thankfully, uneventful. The morning after they stopped in Fillmore—the very day her loan was due—Jennie had insisted on going inside the bank alone to present her money to Mr. Dixon. The man's balding head and clean-shaven face had paled as he'd listened to Jennie explain about the robberies and the sale of her ranch.

"There's enough money here to absolve my full debt and repay what was stolen." She slid the overstuffed bag of money across the tidy desk. "I have a note here outlining the dates of the various robberies and amounts. I also have a letter from the sheriff in Beaver, requesting your help in seeing that this money is returned to its rightful owners." She handed him both papers. "The sheriff and I agreed this would be a suitable way to redeem yourself, Mr. Dixon, for becoming involved with Mr. King."

Mr. Dixon wiped away the sweat glistening on his head with a handkerchief, his face turning from white to red. "I…uh…don't know what to say, Miss Jones. Other than I appreciate your willingness to work with me." He swallowed, and Jennie couldn't help a smile.

"It's all right, Mr. Dixon." She rose and tugged her hat more securely on her head. She hadn't bothered to change out of her breeches. "As someone recently informed me, we all have our secrets."

The bank president was still sputtering for a response as Jennie left the bank, chin held high with real victory this time.

They'd pulled into the Salt Lake Valley a week later, sore and tired. Jennie, Will and Grandma Jones were immediately taken in by the Johnson family with as much warmth and kindness as if they'd known each other for years.

They all attended church together that first Sunday in the valley, with Jennie clutching tightly to Caleb's hand. After a while she relaxed and even spoke with a few of the neighbors when the services ended. She still feared being accepted into the church community, but she wouldn't quit going. She knew the price she and her family had paid during their years of absence, and she was determined never to repeat that mistake again. She needed God, and as Caleb kept reminding her, He needed her, too.

A knock on the door scattered Jennie's thoughts. "Come in." She pulled the covers up to her chin, though no one could see much of her in the unlit room.

Caleb stuck his head around the door, a lamp in his hand. "I thought you might be up."

Jennie pretended to scowl at him. "Isn't it bad luck to see the bride before the wedding?"

He lifted the lamp and scrutinized her. "I think that only applies to seeing your wedding dress. How fast can you get ready?"

She blinked at him. The most important day of their lives and he wanted her to rush? "I didn't think we had to go for another couple hours. I still need to iron my new dress, and your sisters are coming over to do my hair…" She let her voice fade out when he shook his head.

"No. I meant how quickly can you dress for an outing?"

"An outing? Where are we going?"

He wouldn't answer her question, and Jennie imagined the playful glint in his eyes. "Ma put together some breakfast for us to take along. Get dressed, and I'll go hitch up the wagon."

"All right. Give me five minutes."

He set the lamp on the bureau and shut the door behind him. Throwing off the covers, Jennie jumped out of bed. She quickly scrubbed her face with the ice-cold water in the washbasin, put on one of her old dresses and pulled a brush through her hair. Though it was now June, the mornings could be cool, so she threw a shawl over her shoulders and blew out the lamp. The house stood quiet around her as she hurried down the stairs.

As she made her way down the hall, she heard Caleb and his mother, Rachel, in conversation. She didn't mean to eavesdrop, but their words floated easily through the quiet house.

"You think she'll like it?" Rachel asked. *What could she mean?* Jennie wondered, pausing just outside the door in hopes of unearthing the secret behind Caleb's outing.

"I know she will."

Jennie heard the rustle of a skirt. "I'm so proud of you, Caleb. Your decisions these last two months have made us so happy. We worried about you when you left here three years ago. We still loved you then and understood your grief, but it pleases me so much to see you finally at peace."

"You really are proud?" Jennie heard the hope and relief in Caleb's voice.

"Very much so. Jennie is so good for you and I think you'll be good for her."

"I couldn't agree more." Footsteps headed for the back door. "I'm gonna hitch up the wagon."

Jennie remained where she stood a moment more, resisting the urge to run after him and kiss him soundly in front of his mother. The knowledge that she could be a help to him as he had so many times to her made her heart nearly burst with love.

She smoothed the front of her dress and stepped into the kitchen. Warm air wrapped itself around her.

Rachel glanced up and smiled before returning to her task of kneading dough in the light of another lamp. "Your breakfast is in that basket by the door."

Jennie thanked her as she crossed the room and picked up the basket. With her hand on the doorknob, she turned back to Rachel. "Is this improper, an outing with the bride before the wedding?"

The older woman laughed, reminding Jennie so much of Caleb. "For other grooms perhaps, but not for my Caleb."

Jennie slipped out the door. She waited as Caleb hooked up the team of horses to the wagon. When he finished, he helped her onto the seat and placed a blanket over her lap. He stowed the breakfast basket beneath their seat.

"Ready?" he asked.

"I suppose," she said with a laugh.

They drove away from the rising sun, toward the dark sky in the west. Jennie could see a few stars still twinkling above them. Caleb put his arm around her, and she snuggled into his warmth, completely content. They spoke quietly of their plans for the day, and Jennie successfully thwarted Caleb's attempts to wiggle information out of her about her dress or how she planned to do her hair.

"I have to maintain some surprise," she teased.

Before long, the sky began to lighten, and soon the

chain of western mountains stood out more clearly. Fewer farms occupied this side of the valley.

"Where are we going?"

"This is it," Caleb said, pulling on the reins. "We're here."

Jennie glanced more closely at the landscape. Sagebrush and wild grass swayed in the breeze, and from a stand of nearby trees, some birds chirped their morning calls. "What is this place?"

Instead of answering, Caleb jumped to the ground and hurried around the wagon to help her down. He kept her hand in his and led her a few yards from the horses. "This," he said, sweeping his arm in an arc in front of them, "will be our new home."

"Oh, Caleb, it's perfect." *This is where we will live and raise our family.* She went up on tiptoe and kissed his cheek.

"I bought it two days ago, but I wanted you to see it before the wedding."

Jennie smiled, the love she felt for him washing over her anew. "We'll still need to purchase a place in town for your freighting office."

Caleb led her around, pointing in different directions as they walked. "Here is where I thought we'd build the house, so we'd have a nice view of the mountains to the east and a place for a vegetable garden."

Jennie found herself growing more excited as he voiced his plans.

"Over there, we can build the barn and an icehouse one day." Caleb drew her farther away from the wagon. "The property goes all the way to the foothills, so we can plant a few crops and then the rest of the land will be for the cattle."

She'd been nodding as he inventoried the possibilities, but when she heard him say "cattle," she stopped bobbing her head. "We won't need so much space for a milk cow or two."

"I didn't say they'd be milk cows."

"But what kind—"

"I figure if we're going to have a ranch we better have a lot of range for our cattle."

"You mean…" She grasped his arm, afraid she hadn't heard him right. "You mean, you're not going to be a freighter? We're going to have a ranch instead?"

At his nod, a lump formed in Jennie's throat, making any more words impossible. Caleb pulled her into his embrace, and she rested her head against his shirt.

"What is it they say?" he whispered into her ear. "You can take the woman from the ranch, but you can't take the ranch from the woman?"

Jennie sniffled. "Is that what they say?"

"Whether they do or not, it's true. You need a ranch, Jennie Jones, and I need you. So I guess my cattle days aren't numbered."

Reaching up, Jennie placed a hand against his cheek, loving the smoothness of his freshly shaved jaw. "Thank you, Caleb. Thank you today, and tomorrow and forever. Next to having you as my husband, I can't think of a better gift."

"Seeing your smile every day will be thanks enough," he said as he pressed his forehead to hers.

A new round of tears temporarily blurred her vision. "Are you sure you knew what you were doing that day you accepted my job offer?"

"No, but God did."

Jennie smiled, then easing back, she gave him a serious look. "You don't wish you were marrying someone else? Another girl might cause you a lot less trouble."

Caleb shook his head, his blue eyes devoid of teasing. "I've known for a while that you're the girl for me. Even with your men's clothes and your stubborn ways, I love you, Jennie. And I always will."

Jennie threw her arms around his neck. "Does that mean you won't mind sleeping next to me and my pistol?"

"As long as you aren't pointin' it at me."

Her heart thudded wildly in her chest as Caleb bent down and kissed her. She felt breathless and filled to bursting with joy. Whatever lay ahead, she and Caleb would face it together.

"You ready to head back?" he asked as they ended their kiss.

Nodding, Jennie reached for his hand and gave it a squeeze. "Let's go get married, cowboy."

\* \* \* \* \*

Dear Reader,

I've always had a great fascination for the pioneers who settled the West. As a kid, I loved exploring abandoned mining towns with my dad and sisters, hoping to uncover an antique artifact. I never tired of hearing pioneer stories and imagining what life was like back then. This captivation spilled over into my writing. If I couldn't wear a fancy bustle dress or ride in a stagecoach in everyday life, then my characters could.

From this story's beginning, I wanted a romantic, high-adventure tale. And what's more romantic in the Old West than a young lady who, in desperation, turns to outlawing to save her ranch?

Western outlaws have long been the stuff of romantic legend, including Utah's most famous, Butch Cassidy. As I prepared to write this book, I read about his life and those of other outlaws, male and female. Many of these, like Jennie, came from religious homes and were good people at the core, but a desperate need drove them to a life of crime. Unlike most, Jennie eventually chooses the difficult road back to a life of honesty.

While outlaws existed in many parts of the West, I chose to set this story in my home state of Utah. The pioneers who settled here were no strangers to hard work and deprivation. Working together, they turned the desert land into thriving communities. This rugged setting with its civilized towns and regular stage travel became the perfect backdrop for Jennie and Caleb's love story.

I enjoy hearing from readers. You can contact me through my website at www.stacyhenrie.com.

All the best,
*Stacy Henrie*

## Questions for Discussion

1. Why does Jennie insist on handling the ranch's financial troubles alone? Why does she keep her robberies a secret from her family?

2. Where is Jennie spiritually at the beginning of the novel? How does she change by the end?

3. Why does Caleb choose to let Nathan go rather than arrest him for his past crimes?

4. What ultimately prompts Caleb to forgive Jennie for her robberies?

5. When can worthy endeavors—like Jennie's desire to save her ranch or Caleb's desire to prove himself to his parents—become vices?

6. Caleb finds it challenging at first to learn the skills of ranching. What skills or occupations in your life were most difficult to master?

7. What are the different ways Jennie and Caleb deal with grief at losing loved ones?

8. Caleb and Jennie must both overcome bitterness at the effect other people's actions have had on their lives. How are their reactions similar? How are they different? How are they able to let go of bitterness and embrace peace?

9. What is the turning point in Caleb's faith before he meets Jennie? How is he able to help her along her spiritual journey?

10. What was your favorite scene in the book? Why?

11. Did the book fit your idea of life in Utah at that time? Why or why not?

12. Grandma Jones tells Jennie, "You start down one path and realize you should have taken another. The important thing is recognizing when you need to switch." What paths have you started down in life, only to realize you needed to make a change? What helped you choose to go in a different direction?

13. Jennie has a great love for the ranch—a place she works hard to keep. Is there a particular place or house from your past that holds great significance?

14. Are there ever times, like Jennie helping herself to some of Horace and Clyde's stolen loot to buy the ranch more time, when the end justifies the means? Why or why not?

15. What sacrifices did Caleb make out of love for Jennie? What sacrifices did Jennie make out of love for Caleb?

## COMING NEXT MONTH
### from Love Inspired® Historical
AVAILABLE OCTOBER 2, 2012

## THE GIFT OF FAMILY
*Cowboys of Eden Valley*
**Linda Ford and Karen Kirst**

Surprise visitors and warm welcomes bring holiday hearts together in these two stories that show that home and family are the greatest Christmas gift of all.

## A GROOM FOR GRETA
*Amish Brides of Celery Fields*
**Anna Schmidt**

When Greta Goodloe is jilted by her longtime sweetheart, love starts to seem like an impossible dream...until Luke Starns comes calling.

## THE PREACHER'S BRIDE
*Brides of Simpson Creek*
**Laurie Kingery**

The new preacher in town is certainly handsome and kind—and he seems quite interested in Faith Bennett. But will his feelings for her fade when he learns her secret?

## MARRIAGE OF INCONVENIENCE
**Cheryl Bolen**

Marriage to the Earl of Aynsley seems so sensible to Miss Rebecca Peabody that she does the proposing herself! It's up to the earl to convince her that true marriage is based on love.

LIHCNM0912

# REQUEST YOUR FREE BOOKS!

## 2 FREE INSPIRATIONAL NOVELS
## PLUS 2
## FREE
## MYSTERY GIFTS

*Love Inspired.*
### HISTORICAL
INSPIRATIONAL HISTORICAL ROMANCE

---

**YES!** Please send me 2 FREE Love Inspired® Historical novels and my 2 FREE mystery gifts (gifts are worth about $10). After receiving them, if I don't wish to receive any more books, I can return the shipping statement marked "cancel". If I don't cancel, I will receive 4 brand-new novels every month and be billed just $4.49 per book in the U.S. or $4.99 per book in Canada. That's a saving of at least 22% off the cover price. It's quite a bargain! Shipping and handling is just 50¢ per book in the U.S. and 75¢ per book in Canada.* I understand that accepting the 2 free books and gifts places me under no obligation to buy anything. I can always return a shipment and cancel at any time. Even if I never buy another book, the two free books and gifts are mine to keep forever.

102/302 IDN FEHF

| | |
|---|---|
| Name | (PLEASE PRINT) |

| | |
|---|---|
| Address | Apt. # |

| | | |
|---|---|---|
| City | State/Prov. | Zip/Postal Code |

Signature (if under 18, a parent or guardian must sign)

### Mail to the **Reader Service:**
**IN U.S.A.:** P.O. Box 1867, Buffalo, NY 14240-1867
**IN CANADA:** P.O. Box 609, Fort Erie, Ontario L2A 5X3

Not valid for current subscribers to Love Inspired Historical books.

**Want to try two free books from another series?**
**Call 1-800-873-8635 or visit www.ReaderService.com.**

* Terms and prices subject to change without notice. Prices do not include applicable taxes. Sales tax applicable in N.Y. Canadian residents will be charged applicable taxes. Offer not valid in Quebec. This offer is limited to one order per household. All orders subject to credit approval. Credit or debit balances in a customer's account(s) may be offset by any other outstanding balance owed by or to the customer. Please allow 4 to 6 weeks for delivery. Offer available while quantities last.

**Your Privacy**—The Reader Service is committed to protecting your privacy. Our Privacy Policy is available online at www.ReaderService.com or upon request from the Reader Service.

We make a portion of our mailing list available to reputable third parties that offer products we believe may interest you. If you prefer that we not exchange your name with third parties, or if you wish to clarify or modify your communication preferences, please visit us at www.ReaderService.com/consumerschoice or write to us at Reader Service Preference Service, P.O. Box 9062, Buffalo, NY 14269. Include your complete name and address.

---

LIH11B

*When Greta Goodloe is jilted by her longtime sweetheart,
she takes comfort in matchmaking between newcomer
Luke Starns and her schoolmarm sister. Yet the more Greta
tries to throw them together, the more Luke fascinates her.*

*Read on for a sneak peek of A GROOM FOR GRETA
by Anna Schmidt, available October 2012
from Love Inspired® Historical.*

\*\*\*

"So what do you intend to do about this turn of events,
Luke?"

"Do? Your sister made her feelings plain last evening.
She does not wish to spend her time with me."

Greta sighed heavily. "She does not know what she
wants. The question is, are you serious about finding a wife
for yourself or not?"

"I am quite serious."

"Then—"

"What I will not do," Luke interrupted, "is go after a
woman who has declared openly that she has no interest in
making a home with me."

"And what of her idea that you and I should…" She let
the sentence trail off.

"That depends," he said slowly.

"On what?"

"On whether or not you are able to put aside your feelings for Josef Bontrager. Your sister believes that your feelings for him were not as strong as they should be for two
people planning a life together. Do you agree?"

"Lydia is…I mean…oh, I don't know," Greta replied.

"How can either of you expect me to know what it is that I'm feeling these days? It's too soon."

"If Josef came to you and asked for your forgiveness and pleaded with you to reconsider, would you?"

"No," she finally whispered. "I would not."

Luke felt his heart pounding, and he realized that over the months he had been in Celery Fields, he had taken more notice of the beautiful Greta Goodloe than he had allowed himself to admit. He had learned a hard lesson back in Ontario and he had been determined not to make the same mistake twice.

But if Greta had come to realize that Josef was not for her...

On the other hand, surely the idea that she might be firm in her decision to be rid of Josef did not mean that she was ready for someone new.

\*\*\*

*Don't miss A GROOM FOR GRETA by Anna Schmidt,*
*the next heartwarming book*
*in the* AMISH BRIDES OF CELERY FIELDS *series,*
*on sale October 2012 wherever Love Inspired® Historical*
*books are sold!*